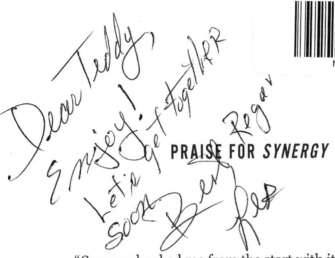

PRAISE FOR *SYNERGY*

"*Synergy* hooked me from the start with its complex and interesting main character and plot. I escaped into the mysterious and exciting world of big money, espionage, corporate greed, and terror that surrounds the main character as he struggles to protect his family, serve those to whom he owes a fiduciary duty, and preserve his moral values. For me it was like brain candy and pure mental exhilaration. I binge-read it from the first page to the conclusion, like a mental bullet train. I highly recommend it to anyone who loves, or could use, the thrill of a mental adventure. Read it."

—Russel Stewart Marriott III, Entrepreneur and CEO of Antigua Veritas Productions

Synergy

by Leslie Lo Baugh Jr.

© Copyright 2023 Leslie Lo Baugh Jr.

ISBN 978-1-64663-976-2

Published by

 **köehlerbooks**™

3705 Shore Drive
Virginia Beach, VA 23455
800-435-4811
www.koehlerbooks.com

SYNERGY

A THRILLER

LES LO BAUGH JR.

VIRGINIA BEACH
CAPE CHARLES

This work of pure fiction is dedicated to Joe, Ava, Louis, Annelise, Ryan, Joshua, Gabe, Lee, Christina, Dani, and my wife, Marnie. They make my life meaningful and bring me great joy.

The Chinese philosopher Confucius once said something like this: We all have two lives to live; when we realize we only have one life to live, that is the beginning of our second life.

PART I

PROLOGUE

Oaxaca, Mexico

In Oaxaca, Mexico, in an old church amid the colonial buildings struggling to survive the assault of the modern urban environment, candles burned in the darkness. No priest was there. Cameras recently hidden in the chandeliers took in the hard, cold, Spanish-tile floor, chipped and stained by time. Pigeons softly cooed on the beam above the massive wooden doors. A man knelt; his head bowed. At first his face was hidden in an ominous shadow. Then he lifted his face, searching the church for any sign of help. There was none. To the young man, the room was a blur.

Three people entered the front doors, all masked. The pigeons burst into startled flight, scattering into the darkness like bats.

"Where am I?" the junior analyst barely whispered.

From the shadow he heard a voice disguised by an electronic device.

"Mexico."

"I don't know anything."

The young man was still dressed as he had been when he was abducted in San Francisco, in an expensive, black label Armani suit, a Rolex on his left hand. His shoes, alligator, also Italian, were handmade to order. But the shoes sat several feet away from him. His hands were tied behind his back, and putrid vomit clung to his clothes. The smell of bile made him nauseated.

A needle entered his neck, and the plunger went down.

The speaker from the darkness laughed beneath his hood. "Just a little serum to help you speak the truth." He violently smacked the Linus analyst in the back of the head, knocking him forward. The young man cried out in pain, and the ropes cut into his wrists as he fell to the hard floor. Blood ran over his new Rolex.

The muscles in his arms had been cramped so tight for so long that it seemed as if the pain had always been there. His face had been beaten badly. One eye was swollen shut. Part of his eyelid hung limply like a dead fish. The bottoms of his bare feet had been burned by an electric taser, which lay a few inches away.

The young man tried to speak but could only gasp, "Please!"

As the three masked individuals below kept watch over their prisoner, two masked men and a woman remained in the shadows of the balcony above. The hooded man slapped the prisoner hard across the face, the sharp sound echoing throughout the church. Several teeth had already been knocked out, and the analyst spat blood. He was yanked to his feet.

"Fuck you!" he tried to shout, but the words were garbled.

Another man stepped out of the shadows in a black cloak, blue masquerade mask, and hood and circled him. His sadistic laughter crackled. The man took out the young man's testicles, put them in a rubber band, and showed him a razor blade. Then he grabbed him around the neck and threw him violently to the ground.

Looking up at his torturer, the young man pleaded, "What do you want? Please, tell me. I'll do anything you want. Anything. Please."

The hooded man laughed again. "Veritas. The truth will set you free."

The analyst looked to the crucifix over the alter and cried, praying aloud, "What did I do for you to forsake me like this? God, please help me."

His captors laughed, and the hooded man slapped him hard across the face. The man in the blue Mardi Gras mask grabbed the young man's blond hair and pulled his head up, hissing in his ear, "What do you think we want?"

"I don't know," the young man whimpered.

"Where is the file?"

"What?"

The man in the Mardi Gras mask had lost patience. He yanked the analyst around and shoved his face an inch from the wet, crumpled face of his captive. "Where is the fucking Linus file, the thumb drive you stole?"

The old brass church bells rang ten times. The young man wanted to be unconscious, for all this to disappear. He struggled to speak through his swollen lips and broken teeth. He searched for words that would end his suffering and through his mangled mouth begged, "Please. Please let me go. I did everything you asked. I do not know anything else! I don't even know who you are. What do you want from me? Please stop."

The woman on the balcony stepped forward to get a closer look. The man with her moved into the dim light, wearing a green Mardi Gras mask, and replied, "Maybe he doesn't know anything else."

The hooded man answered, "Yes. I agree." He turned to the young man and said, "Thank you. It was unfortunate that we had to persuade you. We apologize, but that was your fault for being foolish and stubborn. In our business, we need to know what is real and what's not. Truth matters."

Feeling he might have a chance of survival, the young man replied hopefully, "It's alright. Really. Just let me go. You have everything you want. I pulled the file, and I did what you asked. Like you wanted, I hid the flash drive. Look in the heel of my left shoe."

Blue Mask picked up the shoe and pulled the heel off with a

hunting knife. He put the flash drive in his pocket and pressed a .45 pistol with a silencer to the back of the young man's head. He spoke warmly and with a smile. "You are funny! Goodbye."

The pistol discharged. Blood splattered all over the Spanish tile.

A rope from the balcony was lowered with a black briefcase attached. The hooded man, the pistol still in hand, opened it. It was full of stacks of hundred-euro bills.

One of the men from the balcony shouted down, "How do we get ahold of you if we ever need your help again?"

Blue Mask replied in a friendly tone, "Anonymity is like a warm glass of hot chocolate. Go."

This whole thing had been more difficult and time consuming than the three masked people in the balcony had anticipated. They told themselves that they had given the young man an opportunity to cooperate, but he declined for too long. He had done everything they asked of him and more. But his loyalty to them meant nothing. To their thinking, it was a matter of stupidity. Not having a parachute, not having some sort of blackmail, and trying to hide the extra thumb drive on his person were great shortcomings. The young man had caused his own suffering. They could not trust someone that stupid. Best to reduce risks as soon as possible.

The three senior individuals in the balcony left the others to dispose of the remains and clean up the mess. Without looking back or speaking, they exited the church, each getting into a separate car. A woman down the road, behind the church bell tower, photographed them as they got into their vehicles and left, but she could not get a picture of their faces. The man in the green Mardi Gras mask removed his mask when he was behind the wheel, and she shot a frantic series of pictures but only captured the back of his head.

The three men who stayed behind were professionals. They did their jobs well. Two of the thugs knelt, threw out a plastic tarp, and rolled the young man up into it. They then carried the wrapped body and threw it roughly into the back of their van.

Inside the church, a man hidden in an old, wooden confessional hit reverse on the computer DVR, and the screen displayed the final minute just before the young man was shot in the head. The video stopped with a view of young man lying dead on the floor in his own blood. The man in the confessional was satisfied that he had adequately captured the execution and the dead body. He pulled the hard drive from the DVR, walked quickly out of the church, and got into the van. The van raced out of the parking lot and into the busy city traffic.

CHAPTER 1

The First Morning

It all began on an ordinary Monday in Tiburon, California. Kozlov, my white, fully grown borzoi, woke me up with two front paws to the chest while I was still asleep at 5:30 am. My reliable wake-up call. He wanted his morning run. My wife, Anne, had already left for work. She had a lengthy drive to a San Jose court to provide a psychological assessment of a convicted felon. Kozlov and I climbed into my car and headed for the waterfront by the ferry terminal.

The bright-orange sun had started to rise over the green hills of Tiburon. Its warm light lay across the blue San Francisco Bay, but fog still clung to the surface of the water. When we got to our favorite running lane by the bay and parked in the ferry lot, Kozlov smiled his big toothy smile. We ran together along the peaceful waterfront. We always ran four miles. Kozlov usually pushed me to run faster and would often peer at me with the same look of disapproval I used to see on my Navy SEAL instructor when he thought I was not pushing hard enough.

Our run ended at the foot of the steps leading from the gray gravel path to the parking lot above. Today, Kozlov started first up the stairs but then suddenly turned towards me, leaping against my chest and knocking me to the ground. At first disoriented, I heard rifle shots screaming through the morning air and lay still on the ground, my heart pounding in my chest. My first thought was a flashback to my prior life, a battlefield, when my special ops team came under fire, a betrayal and ambush. Then my mind pulled back to the present, and I thought perhaps a police action happening nearby. But those shots had been incredibly loud. Once I got my wits about me, I crawled up the stairs on my elbows and peeked through a small space between two boulders.

I saw a black SUV, the only vehicle in the parking lot other than my Corvette. Someone was standing behind the driver's side, a rifle still propped on the hood: the shooter, trying to confirm a kill. Motionless, I waited, holding my breath. The shooter jumped into the SUV and raced away. Kozlov had saved my life.

What the hell was that? This is not a combat field. Shit! People do not try to kill corporate lawyers!

I grabbed my mobile phone from my car. The police arrived in fifteen minutes. They were thorough in questioning me but seemed skeptical that I had no idea who would try to kill me. Then they were convinced it was a case of mistaken identity.

At home, after a hot shower, I made an effort to relax, accepting the conclusion of the local police. I wanted to believe their theory of mistaken identity. I decided to go into work. Going to my office, to the normalcy of my job, was confirmation that I was not the target. *It was all an accident, a mistake,* I convinced myself. But I was still shaken.

When I boarded the ferry, the police were combing the parking lot for evidence. I went into the ferry lounge and purchased a cup of hot coffee. I held it tight in my hands—not because I was cold, but because it helped keep my hands still. I scanned the area for any sign of danger, my senses on high alert as my old military training kicked in. Taking a deep breath, I tried to relax, clear my mind, and focus. It was another beautiful day on the San Francisco Bay, but I still felt as if I had escaped from a war zone.

I visited the ferry café again to wrap my hands around another steaming-hot cup of coffee and went back outside. Jack

Names was there, a fellow employee at EDGE and a good friend. Jack was openly gay and married to a Berkeley professor of astrophysics. Both were good, honest men. Jack was the assistant general counsel for Linus Corp, a military consulting think tank and one of many EDGE subsidiaries. One of my roles as general counsel of EDGE was to be general counsel of all its subsidiaries, so he reported to me.

He was a former Marine and a dropout "Virginia farm boy." In his mid-thirties, Jack had earned a master's in computer programing from MIT and a law degree from Georgetown, my alma mater. Jack was a highly respected former spook. He still had excellent worldwide intelligence connections in the arms sales business and the highest possible security clearance, which he needed to work at Linus. I was in the same security boat.

Jack was sitting on a bench at the bow this morning, intently working the crossword puzzle in the newspaper. This was his typical morning routine. He glanced up at me and motioned with his eyes for me to come over. I approached but stopped when he held up one hand. I waited, placing my hands on the cold, white steel railing bordering the deck.

From there I noticed two men in blue jeans, running shoes, white T-shirts, black leather jackets, sunglasses, ball caps, and earpieces positioned at the bow. I wondered why they had earpieces. *Certainly not to listen to the latest offering from social media*, I mused. I also noticed a bulge in their breast pockets. *They are carrying.* I judged them to be in their mid-thirties, muscular, fit, and vigilant but trying to appear calm. *Cops? Or DEA?*

One of the two guys had an eight-ball tattooed on his right hand. *Tweedledee.* He glanced at me and quickly looked away. Then he pulled out a cigarette from his jacket pocket and handed it to the other guy, Tweedledum. This guy had an Army Rangers tattoo on the inside of his wrist. These two were so obviously local or federal agents it was silly. As soon as they lit their cigarettes, they looked at me again, then quickly turned away and stared at Jack. Jack got up and came towards me.

We had ridden the ferry for three years, but he had never approached me here. He always waited until we exited the ferry in San Francisco. That was the pattern he established, not me. Now he looked deeply troubled as he stopped, turned, and looked at the two men on the deck. That worried me. We briefly stood face-to-face, separated by less than a foot. He patted my chest with his newspaper. As he did, he slipped a flash drive into my top jacket pocket and whispered, "Ryan, we need to talk."

"Okay, Jack."

"Do you know whose voice is the piano player in Charlie Brown?"

"What are you talking about?"

Jack studied me for a moment and then whispered again, "Things are not always what they seem. Look out at the Golden Gate Bridge and wait here for one minute. Then take the second newspaper from the top. Eyes only."

He walked quickly into the ferry café. I wondered what Jack was up to. I had never seen him like this, even when we had collaborated on various ops when I was working with the Navy SEALs. He provided satellite and data support. That was why I hired him. I knew I could trust him with my life.

The hair on the backs of my hands rose, always a danger signal. The two government men passed me on their way into the café. I grabbed my smartphone and pretended to take a selfie, and the photo captured Tweedledee and Tweedledum. As they walked past me, both made direct eye contact. I instinctively put my hand under my left arm, looking for my pistol, but of course it was not there. That was my former life. They passed me and entered the ferry's lounge.

Jack had told me to wait one minute. It seemed like an eternity. All my muscles tightened. My focus sharpened. I looked at my watch and tried to watch Jack in the reflection of the glass. He picked up a newspaper from the large stack for sale in the café and put his paper underneath. Then he exited the back of the café onto the stern deck as Tweedledee and Tweedledum followed. As I turned to enter the café, one of them tapped Jack firmly on his left shoulder. They all veered to the right behind the back door to the café. I had no idea what was going on.

In the café, I bought a third cup of coffee and the second newspaper in the stack. The top headline read "The Trial of the Century." Jack had drawn a circle around the headline.

I looked around but did not see Jack, Tweedledee, or Tweedledum—just a cigarette left burning on the deck. I wandered the deck, looking for my coworker. My instincts told me something was desperately wrong. I concluded that the shooting at the ferry parking lot had made me paranoid.

I finally spotted Jack. He was back in his seat at the bow, with Tweedledee and Tweedledum watching from a distance. When we got to the office, Jack had some explaining to do. I wondered what was on the flash drive and why the newspaper. I hoped this whole thing was a joke, but it felt deadly serious. I stood in the ferry lounge, drinking hot coffee and watching Jack. My attention was drawn to the news on the lounge TV.

The morning news commentator, who normally struggled to make sense out of the chaos and dysfunctionality of Washington, was presenting a retrospective on Ernst Mathews. In practiced tenor tones, he said, "Ernst Mathews was the CEO of Expanse Corp, one of the largest US energy companies. During Mathews's term as CEO, Expanse stock rose from $7.50 per share to $182. Then it collapsed from $182 a share to $5 a share when it was learned earnings were grossly overstated."

The news commentator stressed that "Mathews was a major A-list player" in society, politics, and business. During his entire term as CEO, Mathews had taken most of his salary and all bonus payments in stock and stock options, with his initial employment contract allegedly granting him an option for fifty million shares at the price of $4.50 a share.

The TV commentator sounded excited as he explained, "Mathews exercised all his stock options and then sold it when the stock was at its high of $182 per share. When the stock collapsed to $5 a share, Mathews bought the company back, sold its individual assets, and pocketed $43 billion. The DOJ claimed foul play, and a grand jury indicted him."

The passengers on the ferry were glued to the television in the café lounge. This story of corporate malfeasance had drawn added attention because Mathews had died before having to suffer the consequences. The news showed a clip of Mathews walking out of the courthouse, grabbing a microphone from a reporter, and angrily making a statement.

"The government's case is a travesty, a sham. The dark, corrupt conspirators behind this witch hunt, not the Russians, not the Chinese, not foreign terrorists, are the greatest threat to our freedom and our Constitution. Our elected officials better be listening!"

The ferry whistle blew loudly, drowning out the TV. The passengers hustled to pick up their belongings and prepare to disembark in San Francisco. Tense and apprehensive, I headed ashore to walk with Jack to our office in the Financial District off Market Street. Tweedledee and Tweedledum were in front of me on the gangplank, looking back to the ship, looking for Jack. I walked slowly, expecting Jack to catch up. Fifty feet further, I reached the end of the dock and stopped, wondering where Jack was.

Before I could turn to face the ferry, gunshots suddenly rang out behind me. People panicked, screamed, and ran off the ferry towards the street. I turned against the rushing crowd to look for Jack and watched him fall off the stern of the boat. He seemed to fall in slow motion. Even with all the people screaming, I heard the splash as his body hit the cold bay water.

Jack floated facedown. He did not move. Red blood quickly spread across the surface. Tweedledee and Tweedledum ran back up the gangplank, fighting their way through the panicked crowd, flashing badges.

Tweedledee shouted, "San Francisco PD! No one is to leave."

But people ran like wild animals from a fire, some stumbling and falling, then getting up and running as fast as they could. It was a mad stampede. I stood to the side and stared at Jack floating lifeless in the water as the two officers fished him out. There was nothing I could do for him.

Tweedledee came down the gangplank with his phone to his ear. I identified myself and handed him my business card, my hands shaking. I told him I knew Jack. He ordered me to keep moving and clear the area, saying the police would contact me at my office for a statement.

I felt angry and sickened as I stumbled towards the EDGE building. First the shooting in Tiburon and now this. Something was horribly wrong, but I did not know what. What was happening to my world?

CHAPTER 2

At the Office

I entered the grand lobby at the EDGE corporate headquarters and rushed to my office in numb shock. I called Jack's boss and gave him the tragic news. He had no idea who could have done this or why. Then I called the San Francisco Police Department, asked for Homicide, identified myself. They immediately sent over two detectives to get my statement.

Two hours later, when the detectives finally ran out of questions and finished recording the interview, they promised to keep me posted. I showed them the picture of Tweedledee and Tweedledum. The detectives told me they did not recognize either of the men.

Word spread quickly through our building. People were shocked and horrified. Jack was not only a colleague but also a good friend. I could not allow someone to kill him and get away with it. I called the FBI. After I explained that Jack was a senior employee at Linus with a top security clearance and his killing could relate to work he was doing for the federal government, their interest level skyrocketed. It took an hour to answer all their questions. As an afterthought, I told them of the attempt on my life.

The local newspaper called twice and wanted a statement. I declined. Our press department issued a statement expressing our shock and sadness at the senseless murder of one of our most valued employees. The Tiburon police called and taped a formal statement regarding my own attempted shooting over the phone. Then they asked me the obvious questions: "Why and who?" I answered honestly, "No idea." They had already heard of Jack's murder and asked me to tell them what I knew.

Given the circumstances, it had been a very, very lousy day, and it was not even noon. Coming to work had been an automated action, but as I sat at my desk, I felt lost. I decided to go home early. First, though, I called my wife, Anne. I told her about the shooting in the parking lot and that our friend Jack had been murdered on the ferry. Then came the stream of questions, not the least of which was why I had gone to work in the first place after getting shot at. I had no good explanation.

"Who would do such things? Is this about Linus?"

"Anne, I do not know. I wish I did."

"What are the police doing about it?"

"They will investigate, of course."

Anne was not satisfied with that answer. "That sounds insipid. They need to find the killer and whoever shot at you. They need to do it right away!"

"I can't tell them how to do their job."

"Why not, Ryan? You spend the entire day at the office telling folks what they can do, what they cannot do, and what they should do."

I chose my words carefully. "I promise to keep the pressure on them."

Anne was still unsatisfied. "Fine. We will talk more after I get home."

• • •

That evening after dinner and after our three sons went to bed, we called Jack's partner and spoke for over half an hour.

Anne offered to do anything to help. Later in our room, we talked about someone trying to kill me. It defied logic to think that there was no connection with Jack's murder, but I could think of no reason for either shooting.

When I undressed for bed, I found the flash drive Jack had given me on the ferry and was annoyed at myself for having forgotten about it. I told myself that lapse could be forgiven, considering the events of the day. The data on the thumb drive could be office material I needed to keep confidential, unrelated to the killing. But it might be evidence that the police needed to see.

CHAPTER 3

The Morning After

When I reached my office the next morning, three gentlemen and a woman from the FBI were waiting to see me, all in similar blue suits and matching conservative blue ties. *They must buy their clothes in the same resale shop*, I thought. Even their brown leather briefcases looked the same. They were very polite, very formal, and very brief. After they provided me with their IDs and business cards, the female FBI agent, who was in charge, provided a canned speech she had uttered many times before.

"This is an official courtesy call to inform you that one or more of your companies is now subject to a formal federal investigation. Now, we cannot tell you anything further. But we do expect your full cooperation as our investigation proceeds. It is possible we will conclude there is nothing to concern us, in which case you will not hear from us again. However, if our investigation develops items of concern, we will be contacting you to advise you of the people we will need to interview and documents we will need to access. In the meantime, we are sure you will want to keep this informal visit confidential. Have a wonderful day."

After that little speech, the four of them stood as if on cue and said goodbye. The female officer stopped at the open door of my office and lowered her voice to say, "Mr. Gorman, I am sorry to hear about the death of your colleague and friend Jack Names."

This very lousy week had only just begun.

Captain Marks of the San Francisco police called me on my mobile. He assured me that Jack's murder was "high priority" and they would be working with the FBI once it assigned a case manager. I had jumped to the conclusion that the FBI visit that morning was about Jack's murder, but that now seemed to be incorrect. I thanked him for the update. He promised to keep me informed and "in the loop." When I hung up, I remembered the flash drive Jack had given me and inserted it into the USB slot of my desktop computer. I opened the single, one-page document that appeared on it:

RYAN DO NOT BELIEVE YOUR LYING EYES.
BE VERY CAREFUL. YOU HAVE ENEMIES.
VIPERS!!!! SHAKE THE SPEAR.
"LIFE IS A STAGE AND WE ARE ONLY PLAYERS."
Also, have you read Macbeth lately?

I found no more information on the flash drive. I called Captain Marks, apologized for forgetting about the flash drive, and told him its contents. He said they would scrub it deeper. Then he asked, "Mr. Gorman, do you see a connection between the attempt to kill you and the murder of Jack?"

I hesitated. "There is no evidence of a connection, as far as I can tell."

Captain Marks replied, "Mr. Gorman, my experience is that a person directly involved in this type of thing, particularly a target, is not likely to be objective about the risks."

"I understand, Captain, but—"

"So, you do not believe there is a connection between someone trying to kill you and Jack's murder. Correct?"

"That right."

"Well, let me just speculate a bit. Mr. Names was killed on

a crowded ferry with sixty other passengers, but no one saw the shooter. Correct?"

"Yes."

"Do you agree that indicates this was a professional killing, not some jealous lover or disgruntled employee?"

"Sure."

"Earlier the same day, someone tried to kill you."

"Yes."

"Does it seem reasonable to you that the person who tried to kill you at the ferry parking lot just happened to be there the moment you finished running with your dog?"

"I guess not."

"Also, Mr. Gorman, that shooter at Tiburon was obscured from your vision behind a car and waited to confirm the kill. Then the shooter sped away in a black, unremarkable SUV that is just like thousands of others in the Bay Area and left no evidence behind. Is that right?"

"Yes."

"I know I am just a police officer, but to me this also looks like the work of a professional, not an angry neighbor or disgruntled employee who finished their morning coffee and decided it would be a nice day to kill you. Agreed?"

Feeling I had been put in my place, I replied, "Yes."

"Also, Mr. Names was a senior employee at Linus. He had a very high security clearance. In addition, Linus's primary work is top-secret US national security work. You are the general counsel of Linus and also carry a top national security clearance. Correct?"

"Yes."

"So, Mr. Gorman, do you see the connections I see?"

"Yes. But that does not prove they are related."

"With all due respect, Mr. Gorman, you are thinking like a lawyer about to present a case to the jury, using a 'beyond reasonable doubt' or 'weight of the evidence' ruler. We cops need to think outside that limited box where you operate. Connections lead to patterns. Those lead to answers."

"Thank you, Captain Marks. I appreciate the lesson. Please keep me in the loop."

I needed to brief our CEO, Bill Woodworth, but when I got to his office, his executive assistant told me he had left a note that he was taking an extended vacation.

That meant I had to brief our president, Rick Farber. I did not relish such encounters and tried hard to avoid them. Shortly after arriving at EDGE a year ago, Farber began his campaign to make my life miserable. When he first called me "our little Boy Scout" at the all-officer monthly meetings, I smiled and chuckled as if it were a joke. That was six months ago. I had never become numb to his insults. I tried to limit my contact with Farber, hoping Bill would eventually realize the mistake in hiring Farber and send him on his merry way.

CHAPTER 4

Sunday at Home

After church on Sunday morning, the family came home for breakfast. While having a cup of black coffee after the meal, I watched Anne chatting in the family room with our boys, Shawn, Matt, and Aaron. Shawn was seventeen but thought he was thirty-five. Matt, the middle son, was fourteen, and Aaron was twelve. Anne patiently listened to their viewing suggestions while Kozlov lay by her feet, watching the action. She had undone the hairpin that held her long red hair in a bun atop her head, and her hair had fallen below her shoulders. It reminded me of when we first met.

She had been a senior year at Trinity College in Washington, DC, and was also working for a senator. After a few dates, I firmly told Anne that I had my career path all planned and I could not get into a committed relationship. She laughed and asked me why I thought she would ever consider a committed relationship with me. She made it clear that her own career path did not include me.

I do love a challenge. Or she just understood me. Women have a way of doing that artfully. In some of our plain's Native tribes, it was left to the women to design a warrior's shield because it was believed that women were better judges of men than men were.

The noise in the family room subsided. The boys had resolved the channel-selection issue. Anne slid into my lap at the kitchen table, kissed me gently on the forehead, and leaned back, resting her head on my shoulder. Then she looked in the direction of the family room and smiled.

"You know, Ryan, I was just thinking. In a few years, all the boys will be at college, and the house will be quiet. We should adopt three or four boys to keep us busy. What do you think?"

"I think I would join a monastery, some place where everyone had taken a vow of silence."

"I've published several articles on adolescent males and their developmental challenges—the slow development of the frontal lobes and judgment. What am I going to use for research subjects once our boys have flown the nest and get married?"

The boys moved out to the backyard and started throwing a football.

"Well, Dr. Gorman, I am sure there's not much you don't already know about the mental and emotional development of adolescent males, including testosterone poisoning. Ah! Here is an idea. You could dedicate your time to researching the optimum ways to care for the needs of an adult male."

She put on a thoughtful look and said, "That subject isn't complicated."

I laughed. She smiled, got up from my lap, and poured me another cup of coffee. Then she pointed at the kitchen TV where the program was focusing on the alleged insider trading and stock manipulation by Ernst Mathews.

"Ryan, what do you think about all this? When he got a mistrial, why was Mathews making that speech about his support for the Constitution and all that nonsense about the deep state persecuting him?"

"It was timing. The trial started at the end of the prior administration, just before the new administration was sworn in. Mathews was a big supporter of Don Bowen before he won the presidential election. Last year, Mathews raised a hundred and fifty million for Bowen's presidential campaign and another hundred and fifty million for other like-minded candidates. The mistrial occurred two weeks after Bowen's inauguration. Maybe Mathews was using the media to speak to the new president, reminding him of his prior support, just in case he needed to ask for a presidential pardon. Now with Mathews dead, the point is moot."

Anne considered that for a moment. The news flashed an image of Mathews's wife, and Anne commented, "Everyone thought Mathew's wife was the sole heir to an incredible fortune, if the government didn't seize it after the trial. But she had a prenuptial agreement. She only received his two-hundred-million-dollar life insurance, their joint bank accounts, and their houses in Beverly Hills, Florida, the Gold Coast in New York, and Cannes. Pitiful. The poor thing must be on food stamps now."

"That's sounds about right."

We sat there silently, trying to enjoy our coffee in relative silence. I always enjoyed the herby smell of good coffee.

Anne sighed, reached over, and squeezed my hand.

"Ryan, I'm sorry I've been pestering you this week. I don't expect you to know all the answers about who shot at you and who killed Jack. I just expect you to understand your life and your family are more important than that damn job at EDGE."

"Anne, I understand."

She gazed out the window, watching the boys play ball. Then she turned to me with a mischievous smile.

"Our boys want you to drop them off at the movies. Shawn hurt his knee at practice and cannot drive. I assume the movie is an awful adventure or war movie I would not approve of because they keep avoiding telling me the name of the movie. While they're gone, would you like to help me do some laundry and polish the silver? Or would you rather I take a bath, pour us a glass of wine, and wait for you?"

"Let me think about that for a nanosecond." I looked contemplatively up at the ceiling and then replied. "I have decided. You know, there's some canon law on that point. As an officer of the court, I am obligated to do my legal duty. I'll give the boys extra cash for lunch after the movie and drop them off early with a few dollars to buy snacks. That will give us more alone time. How does that sound?"

Anne whispers to me, "Like a date."

CHAPTER 5

Monday

At 9:15 am, Monday, before the monthly all-officers' meeting, a young man walked into the conference room to deliver a stack of handouts. He placed a copy on each of the piles of documents we were to review, one pile for each officer at the meeting. After he left the room, our corporate secretary picked up the various piles, added more documents to each, and placed one in front of each of our name plaques.

Farber finally entered and sat. "I see we have our Boy Scout here, so we can begin."

Obviously, he enjoyed his sense of humor more than I did.

He opened the top folder in front of him and choked on his coffee. Jumping to his feet, he looked as if he had seen a ghost. I passed behind Farber on my way to ostensibly refill my coffee cup. On top of the papers in the open folder was a black-and-white photo of a man getting into a car in front of a church.

Farber slammed his folder closed, his hands shaking. He adjourned the meeting abruptly without explanation and stormed out of the room.

• • •

When angry or stressed, I found it useful to work it off with strenuous exercise. At noon, I picked up my gym bag and racquetball equipment and headed for the athletic club. The club was housed in a mansion built during the height of the golden years before the 1929 stock market crash. It was a short walk of four blocks to the old San Francisco landmark.

All the racquetball courts were occupied except one. I entered the empty court, took my only game ball and racket from my gym bag, and proceeded to beat the hell out of the ball. I was pretending it was Farber and whoever had killed Jack. After half an hour of nonstop wailing on the ball, I was sweaty. The ball had ruptured. I took a break, sitting on the bleachers outside the court.

"Excuse me, aren't you Mr. Ryan Gorman?"

I looked up and saw a guy in workout gear holding a racket in one hand and two balls in the other. He was about my age, maybe a few years younger. Okay, ten years younger, early thirties. He was obviously in good athletic shape—better than me. I made a mental note to increase my sit-ups and crunches.

I recognized him as the guy who had delivered files earlier at the meeting with Farber.

"Yes. Have we met?"

"No sir. I am Paul Hunter. But we spoke briefly once over the phone. I saw you in the officer meeting today when I delivered a report on a proposed project. I am an analyst. I thought I should introduce myself."

We shook hands. I remembered looking through his personnel file when he first came aboard. He had connections around the globe, including the White House, and was already an incredible source of intel for the company. Linus used him on analytical jobs. My friends in the military said he was known mostly for his off-the-books, special-op projects. The month he joined EDGE, just before one of the US incursions to nation-build, the State Department had called and asked to "borrow" Paul for two weeks.

"Paul, it is a pleasure to meet you. I expect we'll be working directly together at some point. When we diversified internationally, one of our board's conditions was that I must personally monitor all those investments. We don't want to end up with a foreign corrupt practice issue or fall victim to an embarrassing fraud. Recently I've been swamped with matters in the States, but the board recently made it clear that I need to adjust my priorities. A risk-prevention strategy."

"Yes sir. I assume we will be working together soon."

"It appears so. But, Paul, if we are going to work together, you'll have to call me by my name. It is Ryan, not sir. We are not in the military."

"Sorry. Too many years in the service. Habits are hard to break."

"I understand. I was in the Navy, occasionally assigned with SEALs."

"I was in the Marines, etc. How about a quick game?"

"Sure. I just beat a ball until I broke it, but I still need to work off some steam."

We played a hard, aggressive game. In the end, I won, but I knew that Paul had deliberately missed a couple of balls at the end of the game. However, I said nothing. He could learn later that a game of racquetball was one thing in my life that I did not mind losing.

Paul smiled at the end of my victorious finish on the court.

"Congratulations. Here are my balls."

He handed me the two racquetballs, a facetious way of telling me he was loyal.

I laughed, but then I got serious. "Paul, one of the things I learned in law school was the history of judicial procedures. When a witness testifies in court, the witness swears on a Bible to tell the truth, the whole truth, and nothing but the truth. But in ancient times, before the Bible, men swore on their testicles, what they valued most. The penalty for lying was castration. The first lesson today was my name is Ryan. The second lesson is don't ever lie to me. Your analysis always needs to be brutally honest even if you think I will not like the results. Understand?"

He drew himself to attention, saluted, and said, "Yes sir, Mr. Ryan!"

We hit the sauna. Paul wanted to talk, but not about business. He steered the conversation to sports, women, food, and more about women. I must admit, I liked him. But I took the opportunity to grill Paul about his background. I learned that he graduated from a private high school at sixteen with a 4.75 grade average. His father "arranged" for him to go to Harvard and then Yale for law school. But he refused, used a false ID, and enlisted in the Marines. He earned a BA, followed by an MBA, and had been a lieutenant colonel. Very impressive, particularly before the age of thirty. *Where the hell did he get the time?* He then worked for various government agencies. EDGE was his first job in the private sector.

"Paul, why did you decide to join our company?"

"Well, for two reasons. First, I have a strong interest in international business and energy. I view both of those as national security related matters. Secondly, the company—our company—offered me a job with a great salary. Honestly, the second was the most important."

"Paul, I do my homework, as I am sure you do yours. I know your family founded one of the major airlines and owns at least three hundred million in real estate in New York City alone. You grew up near Park Avenue in New York City. I have difficulty believing the salary EDGE offered you was the primary reason for joining our company. Remember the penalty for not testifying truthfully. Now, again, why did you take the job?"

"Bill, our CEO, is a friend of my family. He asked me. I had already decided to exit government work but not where I should

LESLIE LO BAUGH JR.

land. And like I said, energy is a national security issue. I decided I would prefer working in the private sector, and the compensation is extremely fair compared to what the Marine Corps pays. Ryan, I have made it a practice not to take any money from my family. It's a matter of personal honor. Large amounts of money always come with strings attached. Even, or especially, when it comes from family. I don't want or need that."

The question was why he was sitting in a sauna with me. He had chosen this opportunity to make contact. *Why now? Brown-nosing? Doesn't feel that way.*

"Ryan, I am very sorry to hear about Jack's murder. We worked together only once, but he was obviously brilliant and a very nice man. I understand he was a friend of yours."

"Yes. We went back to when I was in the Navy. Jack oversaw internal security at Linus and reported to me as general counsel. He will be missed."

"Any idea why he was killed?"

"The FBI and police are working in concert, but as far as I know, they don't have a suspect or theory."

"Do you think it's related to his work for Linus?"

"That is one of the angles, but I don't think they have any real evidence yet."

"There is something I would like you to consider. I am just a security freak. But I tested our new computer security system. I was told EDGE spent ten million dollars for this new, state-of-the-art security system. But frankly, it sucks. May I send you an email, give you the details and a few suggestions to upgrade the system? Will you look at it?"

"Okay."

He looked at me and cautiously said, "One more thing. I know we both have top security clearance, and I learned something from my former boss that I think you should know."

"Shoot."

"There was a lot of chatter on the internet about Linus and EDGE. Dark web chatter among some of our country's enemies. One implication was that someone had an insider in Linus who could access national security data if the price was right."

"What the hell!"

"A new young analyst was compromised. But there were no real data leaks."

"I assume the FBI is aware of all the details?"

"Yes, and the CIA."

"Why haven't I heard about this before?"

"The feds want to keep it quiet. The security threat was contained. The analyst is cooperating and at a safe house. The feds had him send his resignation letter to his boss at Linus, indicating he had taken an overseas job. My former boss said it was cleared for me to brief you."

"Anything else?"

"When Jack was murdered, that news went on the dark web. Almost immediately after that, there was an explosion of chatter about the EDGE Board of Directors and senior officers, particularly you and Bill Woodworth. Its highly unusual for those folks to have a modicum of interest in US corporate affairs."

"Any idea why all that attention?"

"No. But the chatter's gone silent. What do you think?"

"Paul, are you providing me with information, trying to prove to me you still have capital with the feds, or are you interrogating me? Because it feels a bit like the latter."

Paul looked taken aback. "Sorry if I gave you that impression. I was just trying to share intel with you."

I regarded him curiously, stared directly into his eyes for several seconds, and then said, "What do you believe is the reason for Jack's murder?"

"I have no idea."

• • •

As we walked back to the office, several questions rose in my cynical mind. My recollection was that Paul's resume had outperformed the other resumes by a thousand miles. *But why is he a messenger about national security issues? How well does Bill Woodworth really know this guy or his family?* Paul was smart, interesting, candid, but careful about what he said. Good training. Bottom line, his eagerness to meet me and then interrogate me was unnerving. I wondered if he was trying to gather information for someone else.

• • •

Back in my office, I called HR and had them resend Paul's personnel file. It was interesting. My recollections were correct. HR had confirmed that he spoke twenty-six languages fluently. Another six he understood perfectly. No wonder our CEO and our international section offered him a job.

At home that evening, I opened my computer to read office emails. After reading Paul's email, I decided to request the security upgrades ASAP.

CHAPTER 6

Breaking News!

I headed to work at 7 am Tuesday. Before I boarded the ferry, I called the Tiburon police, then Captain Mark's office in San Francisco, and finally the FBI. I knew it was too early for these government folks to be at their desks, but I left messages reminding them this was an urgent and important matter. Considering the close relationship between Linus and the feds, I was surprised the feds had not told me about the dark web chatter about Linus. Maybe the national security folks decided not to share that info with the local FBI. I continued to wonder if the visit from the FBI had a connection to Jack's murder and the attempt on my life.

Once on board the ferry, I ordered a hot, black coffee. The caffeine usually had a calming effect on me. That morning, it did not work. My thoughts kept flashing back to Jack's murder.

As was normal, I got to my office at 8. My executive assistant, Cathy Wong, was already at her desk. At 9:20, my phone rang. Unknown Caller – Blocked Number. I rarely answered a blocked-number call, but that morning I did.

"Hello."

It was Rick Farber. I recognized his East Coast, Massachusetts private-prep-boys'-school accent.

"I need to speak with you in my office. Now!"

What a way to ruin the day. Rick Farber never called me

directly. *Why on a blocked number?* I looked at the newspaper on my desk, wondering if I had missed an important headline. The top story read "Major Drought and Heat Wave Hits California—Climate Change?" Nothing unusual there.

"Yes sir. I'll be right there."

"Now!" he repeated.

"I'm on my way."

I rose and quickly exited my office. My secretary looked up at me.

"I'll be right back. I'm going to see Rick Farber."

Cathy put her hands up in the air to motion "About what?" I just shrugged.

• • •

Farber was uniquely unqualified for the job. He went to a law school but never practiced law. He had been president of two other companies, neither in the energy field and both sold to other companies after their poor performance. But apparently, he was smart enough to have negotiated lucrative "change of control" agreements at both of those companies. He had walked with more millions than I would see during my lifetime. Obscene. After the second corporate sale, he joined Expanse Corp and became Mathews's right-hand man, also for reasons that escaped me. But Farber had left Expanse six months ago to join EDGE. His timing was impeccable. He sold all his Expanse stock when he left at its all-time high, just before it collapsed.

Was he just lucky with his timing, or was something else at play? I wondered now.

In the hall I saw Kalie, the head of our tax law section. She smiled and approached me.

"Hi, Kalie. What's up?"

"Any progress on finding the guy or gal who murdered Jack?"

"Not to my knowledge. The police and feds are both working it."

"Good."

"I told the police I was also on the ferry but saw nothing. They think it might be a professional hit."

"Well, his death is a real tragedy. So very sad. Some of us wonder if his murder had something to do with his work at Linus. That is a very scary concept for his fellow Linus employees."

I didn't want to discuss this with her, no matter how well meaning she might be, and said, "Sorry, Kalie, but I need to run."

"You look tense. Where are you running to?"

"Farber."

"Ryan, is that *the* Mr. Farber?"

"Yes."

"For what?"

"I don't know, Kalie. He just enjoys my company,"

"Well, since it is *Mr.* Farber, you should look your best. Your tie is crooked."

Kalie straightened my tie and patted my chest. Her hand lingered a little too long, and I tensed up further. Then she patted me on the shoulders.

"Be careful, Ryan."

"What?"

She tapped me on the shoulder again and whispered, "Just be careful. He's a man-eating shark. We need you here."

"I am always careful and think before I speak. But sometimes that is a bit of a challenge with Farber."

"I know. That's what worries me."

What the hell is this lady talking about? Be careful? What is going on this morning?

When I arrived at Farber's office, his door was open. Sitting at his desk, he motioned for me to enter. He was reading a file in a yellow leather folder and initialing each page. A slim man, about six feet tall, he was always immaculately dressed, every hair in place. He looked as if someone had just dressed and powdered him for a TV or movie camera.

Farber barked, "Close the door!"

I did as told. But I did not sit on one of the visitor chairs in front of his desk. It was his policy that no one below his level was to sit in his office unless he directed them to sit.

"I know our previous president overprogrammed you. But I have made it clear: I would prefer to never see or hear from you unless I call you."

"Yes sir. That is understood."

"Gorman, as far as I'm concerned, you are no better than other necessary evils, like paying taxes and getting vaccinated."

"Yes sir."

I pictured him in a clown suit with colored strobe lights flashing while he did a pole dance. Then I thought I should compliment him on his choice of suits, knowing he would be driven to give it to Goodwill afterwards. Just a fun thought.

"Are you listening to me?"

"Ah, yes, Rick. You were saying—"

"I will refer to you as 'you' or 'Gorman.' I expect everyone to call me 'sir' or 'Mr. Farber.'"

I still stood at attention. *What a worm.* He had given me the same speech the first week he was here. *Why repeat it now?* "Yes sir. You made that clear to every officer your first officer meeting."

I stopped what he likely thought was my attempt to sit by removing my hand from a chair in front of his desk. My mind flashed to another daydream, of me spanking him like the spoiled, arrogant child he was.

"Obviously, I am a control freak. But that is a crucial ingredient of my success."

"If you say so, sir."

"When I first came to this company, Bill Woodworth told

me that you might someday be a candidate for president of this company. But less than one in a hundred million lawyers have that capacity. I have that capacity. You do not."

He is a pure asshole. Anne's diagnosis was that he was suffering from a bad case of hubris. Impulsively, I walked to the lavishly carved antique bar in his office and poured myself a glass of ice water. Farber gasped loudly. Maggie Cohen, his executive assistant, knocked at the door.

"Fuck off!" Farber shouted at her.

She opened the door anyway. *Guts.* That lady had a high tolerance level. She could calmly stare down a Marine drill instructor.

"Good morning, Ryan. Mr. Farber. I apologize for barging into your office, but I placed that urgent call to New York. She is on hold."

"Tell her I will call her later."

"Also, you are expecting Jim Sillus. You wanted to see him immediately."

Jim Sillus, special assistant to Farber, walked into the office without knocking and stared at me. His obvious attitude was that he belonged there, unlike me.

Maggie smiled at Sillus and said, "Mr. Sillus seems anxious to see you."

Farber grumbled, "I thought that Gorman was first and then Jim, but it doesn't matter. I need to speak to you both."

I knew that I was not the person Farber wanted to see if that could be avoided. Almost all our necessary communications were done by email, his secretary, Janice, or Maggie. The two women and my secretary were good friends, all of them Tri Delt sorority ladies from different universities.

Maggie left the office, and Sillus crossed over to Farber, putting his right hand on the back of Farber's chair.

Mr. Jim Sillus IV was a blond, twenty-four-year-old new MBA

graduate. A muscular beach-boy type. He reminded me of Tab Hunter but with bulging pec implants. He always wore shirts that were too tight for him. Farber hired him a month after arriving at EDGE. Sillus carried the title of "consulting assistant," but he was more of a personal assistant to Farber. Technically he was an independent contractor, not a company employee, paid out of Farber's personal funds. The bits of analysis I had seen from him did not convince me that he was worth whatever Farber was paying him. It was clear to me that he had devoted more of his graduate school hours working out in the gym than tackling his studies. In fact, I thought he was better equipped to be an underwear model.

Farber went back to reading some files in the yellow leather folder on his desk. Sillus leaned over Farber's shoulder to get a better look at the file, periodically pointing to places on the document, followed by Farber initialing the spot or signing his name. They seemed to be comparing the documents in the file to some documents next to the file. Obviously, they had decided to ignore me. I cleared my throat, but they did not look up or acknowledge that I was in the office waiting, standing at attention with no idea why Farber had summoned me.

For several minutes, all I heard was pages being turned and Farber's pen scratching out his initials. After initialing a page in the file, the loose-leaf page next to the file was handed to Sillus, who shredded it. I continued to stand, pursuant to Farber's protocol.

Farber's left hand started rubbing Sillus's posterior. I cleared my throat. Farber quickly pulled his hand away. After several minutes of silence, Farber finally closed the yellow folder, put it into a drawer of his desk, then locked the drawer. Finally, he and Sillus looked up at me. Both were smiling broadly.

Farber said, "Ryan Gorman, you're here because there is something special that we need to discuss, something very confidential. There will be a press release later today. You will work on it with Sillus. Obviously, you will not discuss this with anyone until after the release of the press announcement. Can you understand that?"

"Mr. Farber, I have been an attorney for eighteen years, six of those as this company's general counsel. Trust me. I have the confidentiality thing under control."

That was unnecessary—a gratuitous favor for my ego. But it was highly unlikely that I could damage our already sour relationship. Farber clenched his teeth as he straightened his yellow tie. Sillus sneered through his overly tan face, his usual expression with me. Anne always reminded our boys that it took only a few muscles to smile but a lot to frown or sneer. Sillus's workout regime extended to his face as well. Farber studied me sternly.

"Ryan, the fact is, I do not trust you. But this morning I am in a good mood. It is my pleasure to be the first to tell you that your CEO, Bill Woodworth, resigned. Here is his handwritten resignation letter."

Farber handed me a letter, grinning widely. The handwriting was clearly Bill Woodworth's, and so was the signature.

"Sir, I see he asked the board to elect you CEO," I struggled to say as my heart pounded.

"The board and I discussed that this morning," Farber said with obvious pride.

Trying to not raise my voice but angry that Farber had committed this breach of established legal protocol, the words leaped from my mouth: "Why wasn't I informed of the board meeting?"

After a short, harsh laugh, Farber replied, "I explained to the board that you were unavailable, having chosen to live in some farming town on the other side of the bay."

"Mr. Farber, I have a mobile phone always turned on. Besides, you knew I was in my office. You saw me arrive in the lobby this morning. We shared an elevator. Why didn't you call me?"

Farber jumped to his feet and shouted, "It doesn't matter! The important thing for you to know is that you now work for me! Me and only me!"

Bill Woodworth had worked his way up through the ranks at the EDGE, joining the company right out of college. I always thought Bill and I were close, personal friends. But I had no inkling of his resignation. I could not imagine he would do that at the age of fifty-seven. More than that, I was shocked he had not told me personally.

Farber sat back in his chair and with obvious pleasure said, "Now the best news. The board has elected me CEO."

As far as I was concerned, none of this was good news for the company. It certainly was not good news for me. Selling my company stock and revising my resume immediately came to mind. Well, that and kicking Farber in his balls fourteen times.

Farber snarled, "Gorman, surely you know I can't stand your guts. Right after I joined this company, I told Woodworth you had to go. But he warned me the board trusted you more than anyone else. Why do you suppose that is?"

His question was like a soft pitch I could not resist hitting, "Could it be because I always tell them the truth? Sir."

Farber laughed. But it was not because he thought my smart-ass remark was funny. In a soft voice he said, "It's only fair to let you know that the first thing I did after the board elected me CEO was to inform the board that I wanted to fire your impudent ass. But apparently you have seduced them, just as Woodworth warned me. They made it clear they want you to stay. Their mistake."

"Why do you want me fired? Sir."

Farber said, "You mean in addition to the fact that you are a smart-ass and because I can't stand your gung-ho Navy, Boy Scout bullshit?"

"You mean Eagle Scout, Navy, SEAL, and JAG. Sir." *God,*

what is it going to take for this asshole to get an uncontrollable case of scorching herpes?

But Farber was not through punishing me. Now he circled to the front of his desk, stopping two feet from me. His fists were clenched, his face drawn tight and red with anger. Spitting his words, he said, "Gorman, you're a naïve fool. You act like you work for the board or the shareholders. Woodworth could tolerate that. I will not! I want a general counsel prepared to do exactly what he is told. Loyal only to me. Can you do that, Gorman? Can you?"

"Mr. Farber, the client of a general counsel is always the company and ultimately the shareholders."

Still red faced and shaking, he shouted, "Listen, fucker! Let me put it this way. If you will not resign, I will do everything in my power to destroy you personally and professionally, no matter what or how long it takes. Do you understand that?"

"Loud and clear. Sir."

"Do I have your resignation?"

"No sir. My loyalty to our company requires me to continue to serve the company the best I can."

Sillus now stared at me with a puzzled look. Fully enraged, Farber shouted, "Both of you, get the fuck out of my office! Draft that damn press release. Sillus, you make sure it emphasizes my talents, my experience, how I'm the perfect choice. Now get out!"

"Yes sir," I said, depressing my desire to salute him sarcastically.

Sillus and I trudged down the hall to my office. Cathy saw our expressions and announced she was going to fetch coffee for us. As we settled at my conference table, I was seething from Farber's harassment and emotionally shaken by Bill's resignation, including the fact that he had not told me first. Helping Farber create a myth about his credentials and talent was of no interest to me. What I really wanted to do was throw Sillus out of my office and call Bill Woodworth for an explanation. But, frustrated, I knew we had to finish the press release.

Sillus kept staring at me with a beach-boy grin. I decided to break the ice and get this thing over with. I was not the least bit interested in anything personal about Sillus or his personal relationship with Farber if it did not negatively impact the company. But I decided to make small talk with this idiot until Cathy brought coffee.

"Sillus, last time we talked, you were looking for a new apartment, closer to San Francisco."

He looked up. "Well, yes. Now Mr. Farber kindly provides me with a room in his home near the Presidio, down by the marina. That way, I am right there whenever he needs me."

"Very convenient." *What an idiot. He couldn't think his way out of a paper bag!*

Sillus smiled, and again it was more of a sneer. But I chose to ignore it. *Enough is enough.* Without Farber by his side, he seemed unsure of himself, now playing with his tie, staring down at the table.

Cathy brought a tray with hot black coffee, cream, honey, sugar, and two cups, then closed the door to my office.

"Sillus, what do we say is the reason for Bill Woodworth's resignation? Did Farber share that mystery with you?"

"Of course. Woodworth resigned to pursue other interests."

He smiled again. I wanted to push his face in his coffee. Not very professional, but it would be satisfying. However, it was just the type of mistake Farber wanted to provoke me into making so he had a legitimate reason to fire me.

"Sillus, do you know what those interests might be?"

He said nothing, looking down at the table again. "Pursuing other interests" was one of the oldest corporate lies. This resignation puzzled me. Woodworth's salary and bonus was twelve million dollars a year, plus stock options. If he stayed five more years, he could retire with a lifetime pension of 85 percent of his highest annual compensation. *Why would he suddenly throw that away?*

"Do you know where Bill is now? We should give him a call, get a quote about why he recommended Farber for the job."

"Woodworth left on a very long vacation. He can't be reached. Not even by you, Gorman."

I punched the talk button on my conference table to speak with Cathy. "Cathy, please call Bill Woodworth. Try his mobile number first and then his home. If he does not answer, try his other numbers until you reach him. Thank you."

Sillus smiled broadly, sipped his coffee, and waited. Several minutes later, Cathy reported that she had called all the numbers she had, including his private phone numbers and the phone at his weekend getaway place, but no answer. She said she had left messages on each of his voicemails.

"Sillus, I'll write the section announcing the resignation and mention Woodworth's years of contribution to the company. It should be clear, simple, truthful, and short."

"You have to include the information about Mr. Farber."

"You'll have the privilege of writing that stuff."

When I read Sillus's page of horse crap, I felt queasy. But I handed the papers to Cathy, saying, "Please type this up so Farber can review it. He wants the press release and internal announcement to all employees out by noon today. Breaking news for the TV shows."

Cathy read the document and then stared at me in shock. When she finished typing, Sillus and I took the draft to Farber. He added several more sentences about himself and said, "Have it released by the PR department before noon. Make sure they call all major media. This should have maximum coverage on breaking news tonight!"

After the announcement was made public at noon, several of our employees came by my office and either crumpled the letter and threw it in my trash can or turned the press releases into airplanes and threw them into my office. Cathy walked into my office and announced, "Channel 4 news is on the phone. Any additional information or comments?"

I picked up the phone and wanted to say, "Buy EDGE Corp stock" but held my temper and put down the receiver without comment, saying, "No more calls." I put on my jacket and walked out of my office.

Cathy stopped me. "Ryan, where shall I say you're going if Mr. Farber calls?"

"Tell Farber I'm going to put out an APB on Bill Woodworth."

Instead, I walked the few blocks to the St. Francis hotel on Union Square and took a seat at the bar. Halfway through my beer, I was starting to eat a pastrami sandwich when a hand rested on my shoulder and startled me. It was Paul.

"Mind if I join you?"

"You shouldn't. I'm not going to be good company."

He sat down anyway and ordered a beer and sandwich. "Has Bill Woodworth really resigned? To seek other adventures?"

"The only things I know are in the company announcement."

"But how do you feel about it?"

"Let me summarize the week. One friend, more like a father than a friend, suddenly resigns and disappears. Another friend is murdered. Oh, and someone tried to kill me. Did I mention the pleasant meeting with the FBI? How in the hell do you think I feel?"

My answer was intended to put an end to our discussions. But Paul did not back away. We sat in silence for several minutes. Paul looked straight ahead, not looking at me, not responding. I glanced at Paul and could see my outburst disturbed him. In what I hoped was an apologetic tone, I said, "I'm sorry. I shouldn't have struck out at you. You've known Bill Woodworth as a family friend all your life. His resignation must be hard on you."

"Ryan, we've had a lot of bad news to process in a very short period. I know Jack was a good friend of yours. I have seen more than one of my buddies killed. I know how you feel."

"Yes. But in the service, that risk was part of the job. Here, in civilian life, on a ferry to San Francisco, that is not supposed to happen!"

We sat sipping our drinks. Then Paul held up his, and we clicked glasses. "Ryan, were you ever deployed undercover, alone, where your life was always dangling on a thin thread of chance?"

"Not alone. I wanted to deploy with a SEAL team I trained with, but the Navy only allowed that a few times. It was like a team of brothers, and you knew everyone on the team had your back, just as you had theirs."

"It was always a privilege to be part of a team."

"So, you were sometimes out there solo?"

"Butt naked and alone in the Middle East, and elsewhere, several times."

"I know you speak Arabic, but you don't look anything like an Arab."

"You have never seen me in a hijab with a veil across my face. The cool thing about that outfit is that soldiers and terrorists would not dare approach a properly dressed woman. Of course, if some guy had asked me for my phone number, it would have been all over."

I laughed. "I'll remember that. If the company ever has a Halloween party, I'll look for you."

"I'm glad you had our IT department up our computer security. Thank you for taking my concerns seriously."

"Well, you were right. It needed improvement."

He studied my face and cautiously asked, "How will Farber's promotion affect you and Linus?"

"Life is full of uncertainty and challenges. That makes it interesting."

"Are you going back to the office today?"

"No. I think I'll check out Bill Woodworth's home and condo, see if he's there or if there's any explanation as to where he has gone."

Paul smiled and reached for his briefcase, opened it, and handed me a bag.

"Ryan, I called all the phone numbers I had for Bill but couldn't reach him. That worries me. You just saved me some work I planned to do this evening. You should know how to use the presents I just gave you. Now I can hit a nightclub instead."

I put the bag in my briefcase after Paul left.

• • •

As I entered the company parking garage to check out a company car, I called Anne.

"Hello, princess. I love you too. Listen, I may be late tonight. Do me a favor: tell the boys to pack their bags after school and put them in the van. As soon as I get home, let's drive to our 'retreat' and start Thanksgiving early. No, everything is not okay. But I will be fine. I'll explain when we get there tomorrow. No, I did not resign."

I drove to Bill Woodworth's penthouse and rang the doorbell. No answer. I opened the door with a spare key Bill had given me. The luxury place was on the top floor of a high-rise in San Francisco. It belonged to the EDGE, designed for company entertaining of VIPs with a breathtaking view of the city and the bay. Bill kept some clothing there, including a tuxedo, and often used it for business parties. Bill was not there, nor was anything indicating where he had gone. A company laptop sat on his desk in the bedroom. Because it was the property of EDGE, I put it under my arm, turned off the lights, and left.

Bill's house was in Hillsborough. It had been his grandparents' home, a large, gated, California Spanish house. I put in the key code for the gate and drove in. Only a single porch light was on.

I knocked at the door and rang the doorbell. No answer. I pulled out another key Bill had given me many years ago. When Bill was out of town, sometimes he asked me to locate documents he had in the house and either review them or send them to him. This time I was afraid of what I might find. Turning to close the door after me, I noticed men inside a black SUV parked in front of my company car.

I studied their vehicle, took out my phone, pushed the camera icon, and zoomed in. I saw one man in the driver's seat and two more in the back seats. They were watching and recording me with a video camera. The license plate had a *G* on it—a federal vehicle. I put one hand on my car keys and pushed a button. My headlights came on and illuminated the SUV, just to make it perfectly clear I had spotted them. I was in no mood to play.

But why are the feds watching Bill Woodworth's empty house? Is it the FBI? Or has the web interest in EDGE been a red flag to the SEC?

Walking into the entryway, I shouted, "Hello." There was no answer. The house was dark and silent. From my briefcase I pulled out the sack that Paul had given me, removed the mini motion-activated cameras and audio bugs, and planted them around the house. With the feds watching the exterior of Bill's house, I decided I might as well look at the interior. Hopefully I would have the opportunity to explain and apologize to Bill later.

Behind a signed Andy Warhol lithograph of Marilyn Monroe in his bedroom, Bill had a secret wall safe that required both fingerprint and retina scans. Thankfully, since the documents he sometimes had me fetch were in this safe where he kept the most confidential business documents, usually about acquisitions or future dividends, I had access.

Inside the safe was a stack of files, computer discs, two flash drives, and $100,000 dollars in cash, bound in stacks of $100 bills. The two discs read Linus 66. The documents were all Linus and EDGE business documents. I placed those in my briefcase. I replaced the money after inserting GPS tracking devices in a couple of stacks. Then I placed a motion-activated video camera in the room with a transmitter to send me the picture of anyone who opened the safe.

The black SUV was nowhere to be seen when I left the house, but I assumed it was close by. Five minutes later, I spotted it tailing me on the freeway. By the time I crossed the Bay Bridge, I had lost the tail, so I drove to the ferry terminal in Tiburon and pulled into the parking lot. It was well lit.

After waiting a few minutes to make sure I had not been followed, I opened my briefcase and started thumbing through the documents I had removed. They were all copies of documents I had already seen; one was about our two nuclear power plants and the feds' continued failure to develop a needed safe disposal site for nuclear waste. Nothing there could explain Bill's sudden disappearance or resignation. The more I considered it, the more I was convinced that Bill Woodworth was in danger, the resignation letter notwithstanding. My mobile phone rang.

I did not recognize the number but decided to answer. "Hello. Who is this, please?"

"Don't you recognize my voice?"

"General Kathy, what did I do to deserve this call? I thought you were in Washington. Did the Pentagon file bankruptcy? Billions of dollars just aren't what they used to be?"

"I'm out here to meet with state officials about counterterrorism. Ryan, we should talk. Can we meet in thirty minutes, someplace near your office?"

"I'm in the parking lot of the ferry terminal in Tiburon. I was about to drive home."

"Do not leave. I'll meet you there. It's important. I'll get there as quickly as possible."

Then the phone went dead. When Kathy was in the Bay Area,

she often had dinner with me and my family. Anne particularly enjoyed her company and greatly admired both her intellect and strength of character. They texted and traded reading lists. Over the course of a dozen years, Kathy had become one of our closest friends.

After about fifteen minutes, I heard rotors. A minute later, I spotted a black military helicopter coming down for a landing in the parking lot. When it touched down, two young, armed Marines jumped out and did a 360 scan of the area. Then one of them waved to someone still inside the chopper. An officer stepped out. He gestured for me to approach.

"Sir, please get in the helicopter. The general is waiting. We are detailed to take you there and bring you back after your conversation."

I boarded the chopper, and it rose quickly. It landed at the Palace of Fine Arts, a good location for a meeting with defined controlled points. Five identical black SUVs were parked in a row, with two motorcycle police officers at the front and two at the back of the line of SUVs. I was directed to one of the vehicles. When I approached, a window rolled down. It was General Kathy.

"Ryan, it's great to see you. I'm sorry we had to meet like this, but my security detail thought my plan of landing in Tiburon was too risky."

Primarily because she was a female general and very good at her job, terrorists had placed a $10,000,000 bounty on her, preferably alive but payable even if dead. I knew the offer had been presented to a few Mexican cartels.

"Not a problem, Kathy. I understand."

I was surprised she had come to San Francisco without letting me know—but not as surprised as I was at what she said next.

"Ryan, you're a good friend and a good patriot. There are circumstances around EDGE that could be extremely dangerous and may rise to a national security level threat. We lack a clear understanding of the people and the purpose behind what we see. We are also concerned there could be some internal, high-level US government support. You must be very careful. Trust no one except Paul and Kalie. We will do all we can to get to the bottom of this and protect you. Now is not the time to go off half-cocked. Promise me?"

"How do you know about Paul and Kalie?"

"Many of the Linus projects are for me. I keep a folder on everyone close to Linus. They are good people you can trust. Now, promise me you will be careful and not do anything impulsively."

"You know me, stoic and always under control."

"Right, unless you think your family, a friend, or our country is at risk."

"Good point. So, tell me, as one friend to another, what is really going on? Why are people dying, and why is someone trying to kill me?"

"I wish I could tell you more."

"Kathy, this is me you're talking to. Someone just murdered one of my best friends. Someone shot at me. 'That's all I can say' just doesn't cut it. I know about the internet chatter on the dark web, the interest in Linus and EDGE, and our senior officers. What is that about? You know more about this, and you are not telling me. For God's sake, Kathy, my life is in danger!"

"I will do everything in my power to protect you. I promise to push the right buttons to get to the bottom of this. But beyond that I cannot comment. Please be careful. Give my love to Anne and the kids."

The window of the SUV rose, and I watched the convoy of SUVs and police escorts drive away. Two Marines escorted me back to the chopper. Five minutes later, it landed in Tiburon, and I was standing alone in the parking lot. When I reached my car, I took out my mobile phone and texted Farber. The message was simple. I was taking the vacation time Bill had approved before his resignation and could be reached on my mobile phone twenty-four seven. I did not expect Farber to miss me.

· · ·

When I pulled in the driveway of my house, Anne and the boys were putting our suitcases in our old, converted Chevy van. It had four rear captain seats for the boys and ran beautifully. Anne looked up at me with both a smile and a look of concern. "Hey, babe, you looked very stressed. What happened at the office?"

"Today was a clusterfuck."

The boys came down the driveway, waving. I shouted jovially, "Men, get your butts in the van. We're going to Grandma's, then skiing. Shawn, with your leg just healed, you are confined to the beginner's runs."

"But, Dad!"

"No 'But Dads' or you can stay home and weed the garden."

Anne put her hand on my chest to get my attention. "I've rescheduled my appointments and packed my things and yours. Kozlov is at the kennel for boarding. We're ready to go."

This trip was not a surprise for the boys. The news of Woodworth's resignation just pushed up our departure a day. I called my mother on my cell. "Hi, Mom. Yes, we will be . . . Yes, I know it's early, but we're anxious to see you. I'll call you when I can see the Sangre de Cristo Mountains. Yes, Mom, we can get pastries at the French Bakery. Okay. I love you too."

I got into the driver's seat. Anne sat in the front passenger seat while the boys climbed in the back. Anne looked at me, waiting for me to answer her lingering question about my day. I smiled half-heartedly and said, "Tell you later."

CHAPTER 7

The Ranch

My father and mother never made any money before he was killed. He had joined the Marines out of high school and proposed to my mother right after he got back from the war zone. He had been wounded, twice, but was eager to settle down with his high school sweetheart and start a family. After he died, my mom and I lived for a few years in a trailer park. To support us, she worked as a seamstress and cook at a retirement home in Santa Fe. Her uncle had inherited her family's ranch, but he never married and had no children. He died when I was six and left the ranch to my mother. I grew up there. It was well off the reservation, which suited my mother, who liked to avoid tribal politics as much as possible. The ranch was 640 acres of beauty, nestled between two mountains with a small lake in the valley behind the ranch house.

On the way there, Anne and I took turns driving through the night. While the boys slept in their reclined captain chairs, I briefed Anne about Bill's resignation.

• • •

We reached Mom's just as the sun was rising over the red-streaked hills behind the ranch house. I had forgotten how beautiful it was. The boys were still asleep in the van as we walked up to the porch, where my mother greeted us. Smiling broadly, she said, "Come on in. You must be exhausted. Coffee is ready, and your beds are made if you need to collapse and sleep for a while. Where are the boys?"

"They're still asleep."

"Go straight to bed. I'll make breakfast for the boys when they wake up."

Anne and I followed her advice and went to the bedroom. I noticed the picture of my dad still on the desk in my room. My mom used to say to me, "Make him proud." That became my personal motto. I stopped and stared at the photo. Anne put her hand on my shoulder.

She looked concerned and said, "Ryan, I can hear you thinking. Let it rest for a while. There is plenty of time to think about your Byzantine court, Count Dracula, and where you want to work the next twenty years."

We lay down on the bed with our clothes still on and immediately fell asleep. Three hours later, we woke. Mom was sitting in her blue, bentwood rocking chair, reading a book in the family room. She looked serene. A fire crackled in the brownstone fireplace. When I went to my mother and kissed the top of her head, she looked up from her book with a puzzled smile.

"Son, you know I always love it when you find time to come and visit me. But something is troubling you. It feels like you are running from something. What it is?"

I poured Anne and me a couple of French press coffees. Anne went outside to check on the boys, and I sat next to mom to talk. I went through the office situation, sparing some of the worst details, while my mom sat listening and watching me intently. I didn't mention that Jack had been murdered or that someone had tried to kill me. When I finished, my mom took a deep breath.

She was deeply spiritual and always had a grace, elegance,

and kindness about her. I don't remember her ever raising her voice at me, although I surely deserved that many times. To me she was always patient, tolerant, and wise. I had never heard her say something negative about anyone. If someone was truly horrible, she might call them "a very little person."

"Ryan, do you know what you want to do? Are you going to stay there and be mistreated? It's not a football game or a war you must win. You have a family to consider. You must be happy at work to be truly happy at home. It's unfair to Anne and the boys to work for people who make you miserable."

"You sound like Anne. I know you are both right. But I have never quit at anything. I learned that first on the football team and then in the Navy SEALs. Mom, I wouldn't be happy if I was running from a challenge. When I took over the law department, it was very tough. But now it's the best corporate law department in the state. The attorneys I work with are exceptional people, smart, hardworking, and very ethical. It is a privilege to work with them. If I leave, what will happen to them? What if Farber is free to put one of his flunkies in as general counsel?"

"Son, I understand how you feel. Just do not make a rushed decision. Relax here with Anne and the boys. This is still your home. The answer will come to you if you wait and listen to your heart."

Without thinking, it just burst out: "Bottom line, I work for a guy who is at least an a-hole, probably evil."

My mother looked at me with disapproval written across her face and in her eyes. "Ryan, your job is to be the best person you can be. It's God's job to judge people. Do not try to do God's job."

I realized I needed to explain the full situation to make her understand why I was on edge. "Mom, you remember Bill Woodworth?"

"Yes, your boss. I met him once at your home. A very nice man."

"He has disappeared."

"What do you mean?"

"He just vanished. I have no idea where he went. He wrote a resignation letter and then vanished."

"That seems strange."

"And our friend Jack Names—I mentioned him to you before."

"Yes, the nice man you knew in the government."

"He was murdered last week."

"Oh my God! What is going on?"

"I don't know. I just do not know.

• • •

It took the boys and me a full day to paint the entire porch of my mom's home, but it was time well spent. The porch looked great. Then we started on the fence. During the painting process, I learned who was cool at school, which teachers were "great," which were "dumb as dirt," which girls were "hot," which new bands I "must hear," and which movies I "must see." I also learned things about our neighbors that I really did not want to know. Parents wanted to think their homelife could be kept private, but among teenagers there was an active communication network that the CIA could not duplicate. Their social media networks were updated in real time with the constant stream of data they generated.

The next day, the boys and I did the ranch chores early in the morning. At 2 pm, the boys saddled up and rode to the lake to fish, skinny-dip, race up and down the meadow on the horses, and just fool around. Anne and Mom took long walks and talked. By Thanksgiving, Anne and I felt relaxed in a way we hadn't in ages. Mom and Anne put together enough delicious food to feed a small army, or in our case, three teenage boys. The boys left no hostages.

On Saturday, after evening church, we watched a news special again summarizing Mathew's trial and death. They broadcasted the memorial service. According to the commentator, it was believed Mathews had suffered a stroke, probably resulting from the "unfair governmental pressure and persecution he endured." At the memorial, the president read a statement describing Mathews as "a true patriot, a hero, a great American who was unfairly persecuted for purely partisan political reasons." He also read an official general pardon he had issued for Mathews.

My politics were a bit mixed—conservative on national defense and finance but generally liberal on social issues. That probably gave me the label "moderate." I did not vote for the current president. My cynical side noted that with the presidential pardon, the feds would not be seizing any of the assets Mathews had left behind, including his post-mortem political contributions.

The reporter said that according to "highly trusted sources," Mathews had left half a billion dollars to his favorite PACs, $275 million to his favorite political party, and $150 million to the future reelection campaign of our current president. In the end, he put his money where his mouth was.

My mother turned towards me, concern and puzzlement on her face, and she asked, "Ryan, that's so much money. What do people do with that kind of money? Surely at some point they know they have enough money to take care of themselves and their families for the rest of their lives. What do they do then?"

"I think people with great money or great power work hard to have more of it."

She thought for a while and said, "According to the Bible, I think it is in Isaiah, 'Greed is idolatry.' Money and power are not divine."

"Mom, money and power can be as addictive as heroin."

• • •

Watching my three sons do their chores and mostly horse around the ranch, and seeing my mom and Anne spend hours talking and laughing together, I knew the ranch was a special place, a place where Anne and I could decompress and withdraw from the tensions from EDGE, a place where we could think through the issues in front of us. I told Anne that if we ever needed to escape from our life in Tiburon, we should come to this "retreat." She agreed. I wrote and rewrote my résumé several times. Anne was pleased. It reminded me I could have a life away from Farber.

Towards the end of our trip, Anne said, "Your mom wants us to move here and for you to take over the ranch. That's not such a bad idea."

"Anne, there's too much unfinished business in San Francisco. If I leave EDGE now, I'm afraid the investigations will be shelved. I must be there to keep the pressure on. I owe it to Jack to find his killer."

• • •

By Sunday morning, I still had not heard from Bill Woodworth. That concerned me. Every few hours, I checked the cameras and GPS devices that I left at Bill's home with my phone. None had been activated.

Sunday afternoon, we were planning to take the boys skiing at Taos. The boys were getting into their ski clothes when Farber called. The only other time he had called me personally was to share his good news that Bill Woodworth had resigned. Considering Farber's preference to see and speak with me as little as possible, I was surprised by his call.

"Gorman, you need to get your ass back here immediately."

"What's up?"

"We can't talk about it over the phone. Too confidential. Just be in my office as fast as possible. Monday afternoon."

He hung up abruptly. After I calmed down a bit and digested Farber's aggressive order, I told Anne, "That was Farber."

"What did he want?"

"He ordered me to return to the office. Now."

"Really? Is it worth it? Farber treats you like dirt. How can you tolerate that man?"

"As they say, I've grown seven layers of skin on my back. Anyway, I must go back."

"Well, explain that to your sons."

CHAPTER 8

The Return

We drove through the night and reached home Monday morning. After taking a quick shower and putting on my best corporate gray suit, I caught the ferry to San Francisco. At the office I learned that the day before Thanksgiving, Farber had taken the corporate jet to DC and had not returned. That explained why he had called me rather than having his secretary or executive assistant call me. *What a complete jerk!*

I picked up the phone and called the FBI, then Captain Marks. Neither had any additional information. Same with the police in Tiburon. *What are these people doing? Nothing?*

I plunged into my work. It was good to be lost in meeting other people's demands and scheduling catch-up sessions next week with my staff. By noon, Farber had still not contacted me. I left several messages for him via email, on his office phone mail, his mobile phone, and through both his secretary and executive assistant. No response. Obviously, he had not ordered me back to the office to talk with me. But this was odd even for Farber. I wondered if he was okay.

I looked at the picture of Anne and my sons that was always on my desk. *Why am I doing all this? What am I trying to prove? Do I have a death wish?* Anne thought I was acting like a testosterone-poisoned teenager, all guts with a sense of invulnerability but no judgment. She was right; she usually was. I needed to stop acting like a kid and get out of here in one piece before it was too late.

• • •

At home that evening, while dinner was in the oven and the boys were in their rooms doing homework, or at least supposed to be doing homework, Anne poured two glasses of wine and motioned for me to follow her out into the backyard garden. She sat in the lawn swing and handed me wine. I noticed she did not sip hers but instead was studying me. I sensed she was deciding how to discuss something. Then she spoke.

"Tom's wife called me."

"What did she want?"

"She told me that a young analyst who worked for Jack Names at Linus had been kidnapped, murdered. The Mexican government found his body, or parts of it, floating in a river. She knew someone tried to kill you and Jack was murdered. Tom thinks you should resign, get away from EDGE and whatever danger is there. She said they worry about us and the kids."

Tom Smith worked in the law department but had once been my boss.

I was surprised Tom's wife had heard about an employee kidnapping before I had. *How could she know that?* I tried to be calm when I said, "What did you say?"

"I told her I had no idea, but she did not believe me. Tell me, Ryan, the truth. What is going on?"

All I could think to do at that moment was look at my wife. I kissed the top of her head, which only made her angry. Then I admitted, "Anne, I do not know what's going on. This is the first I've heard about an analyst being murdered."

"Any other good news at that dreadful company that I haven't heard yet?"

"Agents from the FBI dropped by my office to say hello. They refused to say what they were investigating. They knew Jack was murdered."

"Do you know what's going on but can't tell me?"

"Honestly, I don't know. I feel like an idiot. It's not that I can't tell you, it's just that I have no clue."

"Ryan, we both need better answers."

"I'm trying."

"I'd rather you resign and get away from there now. It's poison."

After dinner, I opened my computer and redrafted my resignation. By the fifth attempt, I had shortened it considerably and phrased it the way I wanted it to be remembered by the board.

Dear Mr. Farber,

Your abusive conduct, and other relevant circumstances, have made it impossible for anyone in my position to fulfil the legal and ethical responsibilities of general counsel of this great corporation. As a result, I have concluded that the appropriate option for me is to resign effective immediately.

On behalf of EDGE Corporation,
Ryan Gorman
cc. Board of Directors

Short, sweet, and honest. Just what I wanted. I printed a copy and placed in it my briefcase. It felt like a safety net to know that I had the resignation letter on hand, ready to go if I decided to pull the string and quit EDGE.

• • •

The next morning, when I arrived at the office, it occurred to me that I needed to talk with Kalie and Paul. Once I sent the resignation letter that was in my briefcase, that might be impossible. I particularly wanted to talk with Paul and find out if he knew why a picture of a church had spooked Farber so badly. I strongly doubted that Farber was a regular attendee at any house of worship. I called Paul and Kalie, but they were on vacation and would not be back for a few days. I would have to wait.

Farber still hadn't returned to the office, but I decided that a day without him was a good day. I could get used to that. At 5 pm, I slowly walked down California Street to Market Street, then to the ferry building. I listened to the seagulls on the pier and gazed over the beautiful San Francisco Bay as if for the first time. On the ferry, I sat in the upper-deck lounge, sipping a beer. I did not know what the future held, but surely it would be better without Farber.

• • •

Dinner was already waiting at home. I sat down in a great mood, joked with the kids, and kissed Anne on the cheek, thanking her for a great dinner and for being my wife. I told the boys they did not need to clear the table or do the dishes; I wanted to do that. Anne looked surprised, but the boys asked no questions and escaped the kitchen before I changed my mind. As I picked up the plates from the table, I suggested Anne go relax, have a glass of chardonnay, or soak in the tub. She studied me for a moment and looked as if she was going to ask me a question, then decided better and left the kitchen. I hummed to myself as I rinsed the dishes and put them into the dishwasher. Life was beautiful.

Half an hour later, when I got back from my walk with Kozlov, my mobile phone rang. It was Paul returning my prior call. Lots of voices in the background suggested he was in public.

"Paul, the day you brought some material to the officers' meeting, what were the documents you put in his folder?"

"The packet I brought was our analysis of the proposed acquisition of the energy company in Chile. Why do you ask?"

"I was just wondering."

"Is there something else you want to discuss?"

I considered whether I should tell Paul about my resignation plans but quickly discarded the idea. I had not even told Anne that I had prepared a final-draft resignation letter in case Farber pushed me beyond my level of tolerance.

"Nothing urgent. By the way, have you heard anything about our Linus analyst who was apparently found dead in Mexico?"

Paul took a long time to answer. He must have walked out of a party or bar because when he answered, I no longer heard other people's voices.

"Ryan, we need to talk. My instinct is that the danger to you and Linus is somehow related. When you have spent twelve years of your adult life like I have, you tend to see conspiracies where other people see coincidence. On a happier note, my old buddies are throwing a thirty-third birthday party for me, so now is not a great time to talk. I am not at my best, cognitively. Let's catch a racquetball game when I get back. Maybe I can figure out why my instincts are on high alert. Okay?

"Okay."

I thought about the only two things always on my office desk: a picture of Anne and our sons and a framed copy of the letter my father wrote me shortly before he died. I knew whenever I decided to pick those up and put them in my briefcase, my decision to resign would be final. The resignation letter in my briefcase gave me a sense of comfort. There was time to send it later. It was important to learn as much as I could before I resigned. *Why was Jack killed, and where is Bill Woodworth? If those mysteries are not solved, will I be safe even if I leave EDGE?*

CHAPTER 9

Farber Returns

The next morning, Farber was back in the office. I sent him an email asking when he wanted to meet. There was no reply. I learned Paul had taken three additional days of vacation. Must have been a great birthday party. Our meeting on the racquetball court would have to wait. I called Captain Marks.

"Good morning, Captain. Just calling to find out what you folks have discovered since our last discussion."

"Nothing new, Mr. Gorman. Nothing I can report."

My temper rose. I took a breath and tried to calm down before I replied but failed.

"Captain, I'm not trying to do your job. But you have command over one of the best police forces in the country and have the assistance of our venerable FBI. So how is it possible that none of you have learned anything relevant? Forgive me for wondering if anyone is doing their job."

As soon as the words left my mouth, I regretted it. It was never possible to take back what was said in anger, frustration, or stupidity. But at least an apology needed to be made.

"Captain, I apologize. You do not deserve that. I am very frustrated. I don't know what is going on or what I should do to fix it."

"Mr. Gorman, I understand your concerns. We are doing

everything we can, turning over every stone. Our best officers are assigned to this. We have a weekly status call with the FBI. As I promised you, I will let you know the minute we have something concrete."

"Thank you, Captain. Again, I apologize."

"Have a good day, Mr. Gorman."

That was not going to happen, not until I left this place. If he only knew what it was like having to deal with a CEO who would love to see my guts explode in front of him.

I noticed an email from my old friend Farber. *What now?* I opened the email, expecting some new unpleasantness. It was worse. His email stated he was attaching an "excellent" analysis that the genius Sillus had prepared that demonstrated the law department attorneys were paid too much: "Salaries and bonuses must be dramatically reduced immediately." The so-called "analysis" was only two pages and labeled Summary of Critical Findings.

I'll be damned if I let that asshole Farber and his idiot lackey destroy the department I helped build. Not on my watch! If I resigned now, he would slaughter the law department. No doubt about that. My resignation letter could wait a little longer.

After reading Sillus's summary sheets, I sent back a good defense of our pay system and offered to sit down with Sillus and explain the deficiencies in his analysis. I did not expect a reply.

Two hours later, Martha Cohen, the head of internal audit, called Cathy and asked to get on my calendar, the sooner the better. Cathy scheduled her for 4:45 after Martha told her that Farber had ordered a forensic audit of my expense accounts for the past twenty-four months. I stifled my anger.

This was a declaration of war. *No way that bastard is going to drive me out of the company so he can put Tom Smith in as general counsel and cannibalize the attorneys! Never! My dad never ran from a battle, and neither will I!*

Martha was a woman I admired and liked. She was smart, thorough, and very professional. She knew her stuff. I had worked with her on several of the dozens of internal investigations I had conducted. She always impressed me. Martha took her responsibilities very seriously, but she was fair and not pompous. She never tried to abuse her position.

When Martha arrived at my office, she looked nervous. Martha typically displayed the calm self-assurance of an NFL quarterback. She clearly did not want to do this audit. I felt sorry for her and said, "Martha, what is this all about?"

"An hour ago, there was an anonymous tip to Mr. Farber claiming there are numerous irregularities with your expense account during the last twenty-four months. A whistleblower call."

"Why did this alleged whistleblower call Farber, rather than our company hotline?"

"I don't know, Ryan. I know that's not the way it's supposed to happen."

"Did you listen to the recording of the call?"

"No. Only Farber did. He erased the voicemail after he heard it to keep it confidential and not embarrass you or hurt your reputation."

Highly unlikely.

"Thank you for letting me know. Normally you would have just picked up the accounting records and then made your report. Why the courtesy call to me and this visit?"

"That is another difficult thing. All your expense reports are missing from the accounting department files. No one seems to know how that is possible. The whistleblower claimed you had someone destroy those files to hide your thefts."

"Interesting," I said softly, although I wanted to yell.

"Ryan, under these circumstances, I must make a report to the finance committee of the board of directors. I just wanted to let you know in advance. I hope you understand."

Now I was angry. It was one thing to be audited. It was entirely another thing to be called a criminal and have that trash sent to the board. I smelled Farber's pawprints all over this. I dialed my secretary on my speakerphone and asked her to come in and join us. She did.

"Cathy, you know Martha."

"Of course."

"Please show Martha all my travel, hotel, and other expense reports for the last twenty-four months. Then please go with Martha so she can witness them being copied. Let Martha take the originals with her, and you keep the copies."

Cathy looked puzzled but nodded agreement. I turned to Martha and explained: "The protocol here is that Cathy prepares my expense accounts, not me. I just turn over receipts. She then makes two copies; one she sends to accounting for reimbursement, and the other goes to our office manager."

"So, Cathy has the originals in her files?"

"Yes, we keep the originals of the reports and receipts. Accounting can inspect the originals if they wish. It is a system established long before I even joined the company. Apparently, it was thought that the expense reports of the general counsel could contain confidential information that should be protected. The general counsel is supposed to remove confidential or sensitive information and forward only the redacted copy. When I became general counsel, Cathy just continued the historic practice of my predecessors. It is a strange coincidence, but our office manager's file cabinet was broken into during lunch hour, and his copy of my expense reports was also stolen. He already reported that to security."

Martha looked both puzzled and relieved. Then I said, "Martha, please go with Cathy. I want to make such we have a good chain of custody here."

Martha understood what I meant. But my secretary still

looked puzzled. The two of them went first to Cathy's files and, after loading a pushcart, took the documents to the copy room. Then someone from the internal audit department picked up the originals, sealed them, and took them to Martha's office.

Martha returned to my office and nervously said, "There is something else you need to know."

"What now? Don't tell me Farber wants a body cavity search?"

Martha looked down at the floor, choosing her words carefully. "No, of course not. But he has canceled your company American Express card for the duration of the audit."

I stood up. It was not possible to hide my anger. "What's the purpose of that?"

"I am sorry, Ryan. I guess you'll have to use your personal credit cards for a while. I really am sorry. But I'm just following orders."

"I hope accounting can promptly reimburse me."

"Another thing, accounting will not be able to reimburse you until the audit is finished."

"What? How am I supposed to pay for business expenses? Airlines? Hotels? Out-of-town meals? For God's sake, next week I have an important trip to South America and Asia. Now I'm supposed to finance the company? My last two months' expense accounts are still sitting on Farber's desk, waiting for his review. We're talking about more money per month than this place pays me!"

Martha explained, "I have a lot of documents to review. Each receipt must be verified with each airline, hotel, cab company, and restaurants, etc. Farber's orders. Verification of hundreds of receipts will be very time consuming. Farber insisted I personally verify each expense item with each separate vendor for each charge."

"This just gets better and better."

"I promise, I'll finish the audit as soon as possible. Normally we would divide it up between several people, and that saves time. But Farber insisted I do all the work personally. I don't know why."

"I do. But it doesn't concern you. Please give it top priority. I know you have a lot of other things on your plate. "

"Ryan, it will be the only thing on my schedule until the audit is completed."

"Thank you. I appreciate that."

I knew my conversation that night with Anne would be interesting. After telling her this good news, I would also have to tell her I needed to max out all my cards and borrow hers. She would not be a happy camper. I readied myself for another discussion about whether it was worth the pain to continue to work here.

After Martha left, I sat down, closed my door, and asked Cathy to hold my calls. Farber had a strong personal dislike for me. He was turning up the pain dial in the hope I would jump ship so he could replace me with a sycophant.

On the ferry to Tiburon, I tried to be philosophical and detached about the situation. It did not work. My mobile phone rang. It was Paul. "Hi, Ryan. I just landed at the airport here in San Francisco. My voicemail had a message from my secretary that said you came to my office looking for me."

"I thought you were not coming back for another couple of days."

"Actually, I thought I would just go to bed and rest."

"How was your birthday party?"

"Great. My birth certificate claims I'm thirty-three, but after that party I feel like I'm seventy-five. Did you need me to come into the office tomorrow morning?"

"We'll catch up when you recover from your bad behavior. Thanks for calling."

I hung up.

With all the things happening, I didn't know if I could trust Paul. He had been a spy, trained in deception. *Could he be working for Farber?* Maybe his apparent concern and attempts at friendship were just a charade. But my instincts, and the instincts of General Kathy, were to trust him. Maybe.

• • •

When I got home, the wonderful smells of Anne's cooking floated through the house. It even had the three boys anxiously waiting at the kitchen table, although it was at least half an hour before the meal would hit plates. I fixed myself a short single malt scotch, neat. My new struggles with Farber flashed to my mind, uninvited, and I added more scotch.

The phone rang, and Anne picked it up. At first, she looked shocked. I thought perhaps someone else we knew had died. She stared at me while she listened. Then her expression changed to anger, and she slammed down the phone. The boys jumped and looked between Anne and me. She took a deep breath and turned, her face rigid with anger.

I asked her what had happened. The boys noticed this interchange and moved in concern towards their mom, who was shaking with anger. They were highly tuned to our relationship. Several of their friends' parents had divorced, and anytime they sensed tension between their mother and me, they worried we might be next.

She tried to calm them, saying, "Boys, it's just something your dad and I need to discuss in private, after dinner."

I could tell that the boys did not buy that. Shawn kept quiet, but his mouth opened as if he wanted to talk. Matt patted me on the shoulder and smiled at his mother. Aaron made the sign of the cross. But they were not alone with their concerns. I too was wondering what this was all about. Anne and I had made a pact to never discuss business or tense personal matters in front of the kids. I gave Anne an inquiring look but got no response.

It was an almost silent dinner, except for the blessing, which Aaron led. Hardly anyone spoke after that. The five of us seemed to have lost our appetites and mostly rearranged the delicious food on our plates. The boys kept glancing at their mother and me, waiting for some explanation. Although I had no appetite, I ate a little and told Anne the meal was fantastic, which it was. The boys quickly joined the praise. But Anne remained silent.

Eventually, Anne told the boys they could be excused; they did not have to do the dishes. She would do them later. Our three sons looked at each other and slowly left the room.

"Ryan, let's go to our bedroom where we can talk."

In our room, Anne began to cry, threw her arms around me, and said, "I love you."

"Anne, I love you too. But what happened? What is wrong?"

"It was a man on the phone. He said he had to be anonymous. I could tell he was trying to disguise his voice. Maybe it sounded a little like Tom Smith. He said you were having an affair with someone in your office, that you got her pregnant and insisted she have an abortion or you'd fire her."

"What the hell!"

"Ryan, lower your voice. The boys will hear. I know he was lying."

"You're damn right he's lying!"

"I know he was trying to hurt you, hurt both of us. He claimed he was a friend and only wanted to help. He said I should get you to resign and get away from the temptation before it destroyed our marriage."

"I can't believe this crap!"

"Promise you won't do anything or say anything to Tom or Farber. They want you to do something they can use against you. We cannot prove it was Tom. The most important thing is that

I know it is a lie. But this confirms my view that they will go to any lengths to hurt you and get you to quit."

We discussed this latest attack for another hour. After that, I had two single malts, promised Anne that I would follow her advice, and we went to sleep. Well, I went to bed, but I didn't get much sleep. I was too pissed.

CHAPTER 10

A Caution

Captain Marks called first thing in the morning at seven, just as I was getting ready to head for the office. The good captain said he wanted to touch base and let me know that they were still working with the FBI. They had just finished their weekly conference call. Although there was nothing to report, they were still working hard. He added, "Also, I was just going through our background files on you and your friend Jack. I noticed your military record and that you have a license to carry a concealed weapon."

"Yes, so?"

"Do you routinely carry it?"

"No, I don't. I keep it locked in my gun safe."

"Well, Mr. Gorman, if I were you, I would carry it. Just in case."

His words sent a shudder through my body. Obviously, he believed the threat to me was real and, worse, continuing. After I hung up, I went to the safe in my closet, took out the weapon and holster, and left for the ferry. My rides on the ferry and walks from the dock to my office were no longer going to be peaceful moments.

CHAPTER 11

A Board Meeting

It was the first Monday of the month, our scheduled date for monthly board meetings. The December meeting was primarily devoted to year-end discussion and the dividend. My name tag had been removed from its traditional place next to the CEO and put at the far end of the table. Another childish prank. Some of the board members noticed the change, with Sillus in my traditional place next to the CEO. This seemed to puzzle them, but they said nothing.

As I waited for the other attendees to enter and take their assigned seats, I thought about the phone call to Anne. Surely neither Farber nor Sillus would make such a call. But I wondered if they had encouraged Tom to do so. When Farber came into the room, talking to Sillus, I instinctively patted my side to confirm my weapon was there, though I couldn't imagine Farber or Sillus shooting a rabbit, let alone me. *I'm getting paranoid. How long can I live and work like this? Sometimes I feel like I could jump out of my skin.*

Farber thanked the board for their support and guidance, then proudly announced that an internal survey confirmed that the employees were "thrilled" with the board's decision to make him CEO. I wondered what employees, if any, were questioned, because that was not what I had been hearing. Sillus had not asked me or anyone I knew for an opinion.

Just before our noon break, Farber mentioned to the board that he had been studying the corporate structure and would be presenting a reorganization plan next quarter. He told the board that it was clear that some corporate departments had been allowed to grow too large, become too costly to maintain, and were inefficient. Worse, they had been allowed to become internal political machines, independent fiefdoms undermining senior management. The board should anticipate substantial cost savings. In closing, he said the reorganization would also include changes in the senior officer ranks to bring in new blood, new energy, and new constructive ideas.

Dianna Waterson, the chair of the executive committee and the board, cleared her throat. Dianna was a corporate lawyer in one of the biggest law firms in the country. She had been asked twice, by both a Republican and a Democrat administration, to chair the SEC. More recently she had been offered a cabinet position in the prior administration. She declined all these offers, saying she did not want to live in Washington, DC. But I thought there might be personal reasons. Her four kids were all in a local school, and her husband was the general counsel for a local company. I suspected she put her family before her résumé and power. Besides, any government salary would look very thin compared to what her law firm must be paying her.

She slowly rose to her feet and said, "Mr. Farber, please remember, it is the executive committee that must approve any significant reorganization. Also, the board must approve the election or removal of any senior officer. That is required by the bylaws of EDGE."

Farber was visibly uncertain how to proceed. After a short pause, he forced a smile at Dianna and the rest of the board but tried to ignore me. We both knew exactly which department and officer were his targets. In a calm and controlled voice, Farber replied, "Dianna, of course you are right. I only wanted to alert the board that this topic would be on the agenda next quarter."

As usual, we adjourned for lunch. The board huddled around a table in the adjoining room, working their way through the lavish buffet Farber had ordered. When Bill Woodworth was CEO, the board meeting lunch offerings were simple salads and sandwiches. The officers, of course, waited until the board members had served themselves and returned to their seats. Dianna passed me on her way back into the boardroom and motioned for me to follow her.

She whispered into my ear, "Ryan, what the hell is going on?"

"He's just trying to figure out how things work here. Remember, he's still relatively new at EDGE."

"Well, the board did not have many options. We all received Bill's resignation letter delivered to our homes at 7 am. We needed to act quickly. The board did not want to panic the market and suffer a hit on the price of the stock."

"I understand, Dianna. What I don't understand is why Bill suddenly resigned."

"No idea. We were as shocked as you were."

I lowered my voice and said, "Have you heard from Bill? I've tried to reach him, but no success."

"I don't think any of us have heard from him. Farber said Bill told him he was going to be traveling for several months and might resettle in Europe for a year or so. It doesn't seem like Bill. I always thought he loved this company and would never want to retire."

"Me too."

Dianne seemed to evaluate something and then said, "You know, he had a bout of cancer last year and did some chemo. Maybe it came back."

I was considering whether to bring up Jack's murder and the attempt on my life, but Farber came up to us, his plate piled high with extra-large prawns.

"What were you folks discussing? Maybe I can help."

I turned to get some lunch. Dianna smiled and turned to Farber. "We were discussing how surprised we both were that Bill had resigned." Farber responded that he shared our surprise. I wondered if someone as smart as Dianna believed that. After putting some salad on my plate, I returned to the boardroom.

Our corporate secretary, Mike Brackett, was seated next to me. I sensed Sillus standing behind us, holding his plate of food and eating, probably listening to hear what Mike and I might say. Mike looked up from his plate and saw me playing with my food. "You seem deep in thought, Ryan. Penny for your thoughts."

"I was just thinking about Anne and the boys. We bought the boys new skis and snowboard equipment and rented a house for the week after Christmas in Tahoe. I need to pick up some new snow chains."

After the board meeting, I went to my office, returned a half dozen calls, and checked my email. An hour after the board meeting, I received an email from Sillus.

Dear Mr. Gorman,

Mr. Farber asked me to inform you that he will be out of the country from December 24th through January 14th. As you can appreciate, Mr. Farber believes it is essential that our general counsel be present, in town, in our office, for the duration of Mr. Farber's unavoidable absence. He asked me to inform you that he, therefore, has withdrawn the prior approval for your vacation. He asked me to convey his regrets to you and your family.

Sincerely, Sillus.

Mike knocked on my door, then entered with his first draft of the minutes of the board meeting. But I could not look away from the computer screen. I was too busy thinking about the adjectives that best described Farber and Sillus. Many came to mind.

"Ryan, is something wrong?"

"Farber told me to stay local and cancel my vacation. He had Sillus tell me."

"You mean the Christmas ski trip for the family? Why?"

"Yes. First the Thanksgiving trip and now this. Anne will be furious. The house in Tahoe is nonrefundable."

"Why would Farber make you cancel?"

"Apparently he's going to be out of the country."

"What difference does that make?"

"I don't know."

We finished our review of the draft minutes in silence. I felt restless, wondering what to expect next, and decided to take a walk. As I exited the building on California Street, I patted the pistol in the holster under my left arm. But I did not feel any safer. In a few minutes I found myself walking through the Chinese Gates across Grand Avenue and into Chinatown. All things Asian seemed slightly mysterious to me, a bit romantic, although I avoided the first set of stores near the Chinese arch. They were actually owned by people from the Middle East and sold nothing authentically Chinese.

In a few blocks, Old Saint Mary's Cathedral appeared on the right. I paused and decided to enter. As my eyes adjusted to the dark, I saw that the church was empty. Candles flickered, and the mild, lingering aroma of incense relaxed me, gave me a feeling of safety. I sat in the third row, looking up at the crucifix above the altar and the statues of saints on either side. I decided to say a prayer for Jack, for Bill, for me, for my family, and for the people I wanted to protect in the law department.

When I rose and turned, I froze. A few feet inside the front door, in the dark vestibule, stood a man, staring at me. Instinctively, I put my hand on the left side of my coat, feeling the comfort of the pistol. The man did not move, and his hands hung at his sides.

What should I do? Take out the pistol? Run? Maybe it's some old man who just came to say some prayers. Maybe it's the priest. The bullshit from Farber was getting to me. *Just walk slowly towards him and watch for any sudden movements.*

As I slowly headed for the door, the man cautiously moved towards me. He raised his right arm, then his left. I could see his hands were empty, but I kept mine on my pistol under my coat. He waved to me.

"Hello, Ryan. Paying a visit to the Creator?"

"Paul? What the hell are you doing here?"

"Wow, that's a strange greeting in the house of the Lord."

I kept my hand on the pistol until I was four feet away and could see his face. He was smiling. "Can I buy you a drink or some chow mein?"

"Let's step outside."

On the street outside the church, I relaxed, concluding Paul was not a threat—at least, not immediately. *But why is he there, out of nowhere?* Paul said, "Ryan, there is a place just up the street. It serves Great Wall beer from China, and the tables are all booths with curtains for privacy."

"Okay."

I knew the place. It was a landmark for city residents and a destination for tourists. A hundred years ago, it was a favorite place for politicians and those seeking to influence politicians, as well as an afternoon rendezvous for elicit lovers. We walked into the restaurant with its high ceiling, dark mahogany wood, golden dragon, and display of jade carvings. It was almost deserted. A hostess showed us to a booth. We sat. Paul pulled the curtain across the front of the booth. I put my right arm across my chest, close to the pistol, and leaned slightly forward on the table, looking Paul directly in the eyes. Waiting.

"Ryan, do you want anything in addition to the beer?"

"No."

Paul pushed the discrete button on the table, a light outside the booth went on, and a waitress appeared and took our order for two Great Wall beers. She quickly brought the beers and closed the curtain again.

"Ryan, I wanted to follow up on your call when I was out of town. What do you have on your mind?"

"How did you know I was in the church? Were you following me?"

"I was coming back from the gym when I saw you bolt out of the front lobby. I called out to you from across the street, but you marched off as if you were racing to a fire. I decided to catch up and see if you still wanted to talk."

I examined his smiling face for several seconds and said nothing. I wanted to believe him. My instincts said he was telling the truth, but they also said something was missing in his explanation. He took a sip of his beer and waited for me to reply. I said nothing, letting silence pervade the booth. His expression was puzzled. He pushed his beer away and stood up.

"Sorry, I thought you wanted to talk about something. I'll go back to the office."

He pulled the curtain aside and stepped out of the booth. I reached and grabbed his right elbow. "Paul, wait. Come back."

Paul hesitated for a moment. "Ryan, when did you start packing?

"Advice from the San Francisco PD."

Paul stepped back into the booth and pulled the curtain closed. Standing, he took several sips from his beer, studying me. Then he sat down. "Ryan, talk to me."

"Captain Marks has been working with the FBI on two murders, Jack and the analyst, as well as the attempt on my life. He called, said there were no new developments, then advised me to carry a gun."

"Shit! The word around the office was that the guy who shot at you in the parking lot either mistook you for someone else or it was an attempted robbery. But certainly not connected to Jack's murder. No offense, but you're just a corporate lawyer. Nobody goes around trying to kill corporate lawyers. Divorce lawyers, yes. Why would anyone do that?"

"My question exactly."

"Is that what you wanted to talk about?"

"No. It was something else. But it is not relevant now."

We sat there for a few minutes, Paul waiting for me to go on.

"Paul, CEOs of major publicly traded companies do not simply go missing. Your dad is close to Bill. Has he heard anything from him?"

"I asked my father. He's heard nothing, which is strange. They roomed together at Yale, pledged to the same fraternity and became like brothers. They kept close after graduation. My father said that Bill was supposed to join my father and mother in Davos but never showed up. My father contacted several of their mutual friends, but nobody has heard from him."

I thought about this update for a moment, then added, "I went to Bill's house and picked up some company property. I felt like a spy but installed the surveillance devices you gave. No one has been there since my visit."

"My father will be devastated if something has happened to Bill. With the attempt on your life and Jack's murder, you and I both know it's possible Bill was killed. EDGE is the common denominator."

"What does that tell you, Paul?"

"Besides the fact that EDGE is a more dangerous place to work than Russia or the Middle East?"

"Besides that."

"The implication is that you and Jack, and maybe Bill, are

obstacles or threats to someone big and powerful, someone who has the assets and need to hire professional killers."

"Do you believe there is a national security threat here?"

"Ryan, we both know that the FBI is concerned about that."

"Well, Paul, what do we do now?"

"I wish I knew."

We finished our beers, mostly in silence, and then walked back to the office.

• • •

When I got home, I told Anne that Farber had canceled my Christmas vacation. As I expected, she was furious. She immediately rejected the idea of going to Lake Tahoe and leaving me alone. But after we discussed how that would ruin the boys' Christmas, particularly after opening their new skis and snowboard, she relented and agreed to take them. I promised to call every day.

I told myself that I would not let Farber drive me to resign, but I was not sure how much more I was willing to take.

The next day, I learned that Farber and Sillus were taking the new corporate jet to Switzerland on a "working trip." Sillus sent me a note with instructions to call Farber's secretary if anything "very, very important" needed his immediate attention. The note made it clear that under no circumstances was I to interrupt his "hard work" in Switzerland. I was sure Farber would be working hard on something: Sillus.

Captain Marks, who had now become sort of a friend, assigned a plainclothes officer to meet me at the San Francisco ferry terminal and accompany me each day between the ferry and office. The fact that there had not been another attempt on my life had become as big a question as why someone shot at me in the first place.

CHAPTER 12

Christmas

Christmas came. Nothing at the office changed. I started to hope and tried to believe that the shooter had mistaken me for someone else. The absence of any additional attempts on my life seemed to support that hypothesis. There were plenty of opportunities to shoot me every day of the week. I still carried my mobile phone, which of course was a tracking device, as was the GPS system in my car. But nothing. I ceased carrying my weapon and felt relieved that at least one threat to my happiness and longevity had disappeared. If Farber would just get a job offer he couldn't resist, my life could return to perfect.

We decorated our house to the fullest. The boys and I went to a tree farm and cut a beautiful fir tree. When we brought it home, we discovered it was too big to fit in the house. We had to cut off almost three feet at the base. Anne laughed and made some remarks about men's obsessions with big things, which the boys and I ignored.

Our sons sensed something special was planned and started asking questions, like why mom had washed everyone's ski clothes. Part of the surprise was out of the bag. We celebrated Christmas by going to midnight Mass where Father Slade—their uncle and Anne's brother—was assistant pastor. On Christmas morning, we opened presents. The boys loved their new ski equipment and could not wait to get to the snow. Although the boys were disappointed that I could not go with them, none of them suggested we cancel the ski trip. Anne was a good sport about the whole thing. I tried to be unruffled. Work paid the bills. But inside, I could not get over how much I disliked Farber and Sillus.

As my family packed into the Chevy van, I kissed everyone goodbye. It was my habit to kiss the boys on their heads, which they claimed to dislike, saying it reminded them of when they were little kids. But I did it anyway. It was something I wished my dad could have done, a simple sign of love. After they left, I played with Kozlov for a while in the front yard, then went inside, poured red wine, went up to my hot tub, and felt sorry for myself. I slept with my weapon tucked under the mattress. It was some comfort, but after a couple of days, I forgot it was there.

Two days later, I tore up the resignation letter in my briefcase. My resolve to not let Farber make me run from my job had become stronger than ever. I no longer cared why he hated me. I concluded his reasoning was probably simple: (1) the relationship I had with the board was something of a hindrance to whatever he wanted to do at EDGE, including making Tom his general counsel; and (2) he knew I would always speak truth to the board and alert them if I thought someone was not being honest with them.

Sorry, Farber, you are not going to make me quit. I don't run away with my tail between my legs. I knew what kind of damage he would do to the law department people and the company if I left. Firing me would be risky for Farber, unless I did something stupid and gave him some reason the board would accept. Punching Sillus and Farber and kicking them in the balls—assuming they had any—was probably out of the question.

• • •

Anne and the boys returned home New Year's Eve, two days early. Anne said they didn't want me to be alone on New Year's Eve. It was so good to see them, although I suspected the boys would have been happy to spend another day or two on the slopes. I was sure it was Anne who wanted to spend New Year's Eve with me. We had a turkey with all the trimmings, a fire in the fireplace, Andrea Bocelli over our surround-sound stereo system, and board games with the boys after dinner. Then everyone watched the ball drop at Times Square. The boys retired to their end of the house. Anne and I took a bottle of good champagne to our bedroom to have our own private celebration.

After we showered, Anne took a felt pen and wrote on my chest This guy is mine! It reminded me of when we first got married and I was in the Navy. Anne bought "body paint" that was guaranteed to easily wash off. She wrote all over me, little messages including I love to love this man, and a couple of messages that were off color. But in the morning, we discovered the product label lied. It did not wash off, no matter how hard I scrubbed. After PT in the morning, my SEAL team hit the showers, and I quickly became a major joke in the locker room.

• • •

I had used the time during Christmas to start drafting my year-end report on the law department's activities. Each corporate department and subsidiary did the same. SEC regulations required an annual report to the shareholders, and these department reports served as basis data for that. Of course, Farber had already made it clear that the law department was merely a "minor" service organization and a major pain in his ass. His words, not mine.

I was wrong in suspecting that Farber and Sillus were not working hard in Switzerland. Mike Brackett told me that Farber had added a new matter on the agenda for the January board meeting: "Downsizing excessive service departments in headquarters." Obviously, Dianna's admonition at the prior board meeting did not derail that project. It was another petty attempt to get me to resign. It did not surprise me, and it would not work. I wondered what pretext he would fabricate. Sillus called me from Switzerland and bragged about the great skiing and the lavish cocktail parties with the rich and famous. Then he asked me to confirm last year's budget for the law department. I did.

I understand the games you play, Farber. I do not quit. I have had to work through serious punishment. You and Sillus are amateurs.

CHAPTER 13

The Corvette

The following Friday, I lingered over coffee with Anne. We talked about how lucky we were. We laughed about things in the past. Reluctantly, I picked up my car keys and kissed Anne goodbye. I headed out to my 1981 black T-Top Corvette in the driveway. A beauty. It looked like a car from a Batman movie.

I had not taken the time to put it in the garage the night before because I got home late, quickly picked some roses from the garden, and then hurried into the house for dinner. It was our anniversary. Either that night or early morning, the boys had written Newlyweds with soap on the side windows and attached a string of cans to the back license plate. Both were Shawn's idea. I took off the string of cans and decided to wait to wash off the soap message until I got home. I got into my car and started down the hill.

As ours was the last house on the street up the hill, there was usually little traffic to start with. After the second turn going down the hill, I pressed on the brakes to slow the car. Nothing happened. *Shit! Where are the damn brakes!* I frantically pumped brakes again. But the car gained speed. I pulled back on the hand brake. It had no effect.

Damn it! What the hell is wrong?

My Vette raced faster down the steep hill, gaining speed every second. I almost hit a small dog running across the road and swerved to avoid it, and then swerved again to miss a tree on the right side of the road. The mounting speed made it almost impossible to steer. I lowered the gears, but it did little good. I pulled on the hand brake again, but to no avail. The tires screeched loudly at every turn.

My God, help me!

As I went around the next curve to the right, the increasing speed pushed the Vette into oncoming traffic, and I knew I had to make a final effort to gain control. I saw a Tudor-style redbrick house to my right. Its large, green front lawn sloped up at least a hundred feet to the house. The yard was planted with a host of rose bushes and trees. It was my best chance. I steered the car up onto the yard, barely avoiding crashing into the rear of a black SUV in front of me. My Vette plowed through the rose bushes. When I realized that the car would not stop before it hit the Tudor house, I turned the wheel sharply to the left, crashing into a ten-foot-tall pine tree. That stopped the car.

"Thank you, God. Thank you."

My injuries were minor, but my beautiful Corvette was in ruins. Both the front and left side of the body had broken apart. The front window had shattered, but thankfully the safety glass kept the pieces in place and protected me. The police were summoned by the furious property owner, who demanded the police make me take a sobriety test, which of course I passed. The police politely and disbelievingly listened to my story about how the accident happened. Then one of the officers looked under the car. He reported that someone had cut my brake lines. The police were suddenly sympathetic. They taped off the site and called for assistance, having decided it was a crime scene.

My crumpled Vette had to be towed away. The police dropped me off at my home, recommending that I see a doctor, just to be safe. Anne had already gone to her office, and the kids were at school. I called Anne and left a message on her voicemail saying

I had been in an accident but was totally unharmed. Then I called Cathy, my executive assistant, saying only that I would not be in until tomorrow.

An hour later, there was a knock at my door. It was two detectives. They were in their twenties and looked nervous. The apparent senior officer was the first to speak. "Mr. Gorman, may we come inside and speak with you about the car accident today?"

"Of course, come in."

Once we were in the den and seated, they went directly to the point. The senior officer did all the speaking. "Mr. Gorman, we checked out the car. There is no question about it. The brake lines were all cut, including the hand brake. It was not an accident. In fact, not only were they cut, but part of one segment had been removed. In addition, our folks noticed that all but one of the bolts on the differential had been removed, probably a backup in case cutting the brake lines was not enough. We found the bolts in the rose garden next to your driveway."

I was shocked. With the two detectives confronting me with the cold facts, it quickly dawned on me that someone still wanted to kill me. I just sat there, unable to understand why this was happening.

"Mr. Gorman, we are now investigating an attempted murder. Two attempts to murder you. It's critical you tell us who might want you dead."

The younger officer took out his pad and pen and sat a tape recorder on the coffee table. I told them we had normal politics at the office, but nothing that could justify what had just happened.

"Tell us about any and all employees who might be pissed off with you."

"I don't believe any of my employees could have done this. I have a great team. They get along well. I haven't had to fire any law department employee in three years."

"Outside the law department?"

"That does not seem likely."

"Could some other company feel threatened that you are going to acquire them? Do you have any contentious business deals, unhappy competing companies, something like that?"

"Not that I can think of. We're always in the process of evaluating new acquisitions, and at any given time, we probably have more than a dozen big, active business deals around the world. That is the normal situation. However, people don't commit murder because they think their company may be bought. And companies compete aggressively. They must. But it doesn't mean a company eliminates senior people in a competing company. This is not a Mafia war."

"Mr. Gorman, what might connect the attempt to kill you today to the shooting at the ferry parking lot?"

"I don't see any connection."

"Really? How about both were an attempt to kill you."

"Right. But I don't know why."

"What about other corporate officers? Have you recently stopped someone else's career or had them censured? We understand you are also the company's chief ethics officer."

"Nothing like that in the last couple of years."

"Mr. Gorman, we know that one of your fellow employees, a Jack Names, was murdered on a ferry you were both riding from Tiburon to San Francisco. Let's talk about that."

"Officers, you probably know more about that than I do. Jack was a very talented, very intelligent, and very nice person. I did not see who killed my friend, but I would certainly like to know. The FBI is investigating a possible national security angle."

"We've been in touch. We'll talk with them again today. Do you see a connection between today and his murder?"

"Only that we work for the same company. Jack worked for Linus, and I'm its general counsel."

"Any other EDGE officers killed, or shot at recently?"

"No. But our prior CEO, Bill Woodworth, suddenly resigned and disappeared. Nobody knows where he is. He completely vanished."

"The FBI informed us of that. They're investigating."

"Good."

"We are treating this as an attempted homicide. Forensics will check for prints around the brake line area, but we're not optimistic. If you think of anything that might be helpful, no matter how silly you think it is, please call me immediately."

"Okay."

The senior detective looked a little exasperated when I had nothing to add.

"Mr. Gorman, we are talking about murder here, attempted murders, and a major CEO disappearing. The FBI also briefed us on the work Linus does for the government. You need to be truthful with us and not hold anything back. What are you not telling us?"

"I am not trying to be circumspect."

"Then tell us what came to your mind when we asked our questions. I noticed you looked away and hesitated for a moment."

"I think something serious has happened to Bill Woodworth. I do not believe he would resign and disappear without telling me first or reaching out to me afterwards. He is, or was, not just my boss. He was my mentor and a very close friend."

"Thank you for that info. But what else is on your mind that you have not shared?"

"Our new CEO, Rick Farber, has for some time tried to get me to resign. His harassment and insults are harsh. He would fire me, but our board won't permit that. I don't know why he hates me, but he does."

"And?"

"My wife had a call, an anonymous call from a man trying to

disguise his voice. She thinks it was a lawyer in my department, but she's not certain. He tried to convince my wife to make me resign after claiming I'd had an affair with one of my attorneys, got her pregnant, and forced her to have an abortion."

"Did you?"

"Absolutely not!"

"Mr. Gorman, be very careful. You are in danger."

• • •

When Anne got home, she asked me to go to our bedroom, away from the kids. She closed the door, threw her coat and briefcase on the bed, and turned to me.

"I heard your voicemail about the accident. I'm glad you were not injured. But your voice cracked when you said you were unharmed. Tell me what is going on."

"Anne, the car crash was not an accident. Someone cut the brake lines. The police are treating it as an attempted murder."

"My God!"

"No one seems to be able to find Bill Woodworth. The FBI is investigating. It looks serious."

"Ryan, that company is poison. It's hell! You need to get out of there now. Now!"

"Soon, but not now. I can't."

"Why? Because you're stubborn? Because you're pigheaded? Too macho to retreat from danger?"

"When I accepted the job as general counsel, I agreed to accept the responsibilities that went with the job. If I resign, the people I hired will be seriously abused by Farber, and I believe the company would also suffer. It would be my fault. And whoever's behind this will never be caught if I am not here to keep pushing so the investigation moves forward. It must be stopped."

"Damn it, Ryan! How do you think this affects your family?

What about your wife? How do you think I feel, not knowing from day to day whether you'll be the next EDGE employee to be murdered? How do you think that would affect our sons? Do you care how all this is hurting me? Grow up!"

With that, she stormed out of our bedroom, slamming the door shut. I knew I deserved everything she said. She just couldn't understand that I would never quit, never give up. I knew I was inextricably tied to everything that had already happened; there was no leaving that danger behind. It had to be stopped, or I would never be safe!

The phone rang. My insurance company gave me the bad news that the repair shop found no parts available to repair the Corvette. It would be totaled. A complete loss. I really did not need to hear that. Not now.

The next morning, getting into a rental car, I had a bit of a panic attack, got out of the car, and checked it out, looking for signs of leaking brake fluid, then checked the differential and examined each tire. I felt quite stupid. Paranoid. Anne saw me giving the rental car a thorough check and came outside.

"Ryan, are you looking for a bomb? You do know that someone is trying to kill my husband, don't you?

"Yes. I know."

"You are not paranoid, Ryan. You know you are in danger. You're just too stubborn to get away from that rat trap where you work. Have you considered Farber could be the person wanting you dead?"

"Anne, nothing connects Farber with my car crash. I don't think he would even know how to find the brake lines, let alone cut them. I'm certain he doesn't even know a car has a differential."

"He hates you. Money can buy many things, including killers."

"Anne, I'm trying to do the best I can."

"Well, if you get yourself killed, if you make me a widow, I will never forgive you. Do you understand me, Ryan? God. I love you. I will always love you. But I will never forgive you if you leave me a widow and our sons without a father!"

With that she got in her car and left for her office. Depressed, knowing Anne was right, I drove to the ferry, wondering when and if the police would find any useful evidence that could resolve the question of who was trying to kill me.

On the way to the ferry, I called the Tiburon police. They were polite and understood my anxiety. They confirmed no prints were found on the Vette. Then they lectured me about the importance of not leaving my car in the driveway at night. Not very helpful. During the ferry ride, I called Paul's office and asked him to meet me in my office in an hour. Paul was there waiting when I arrived.

"What's up, boss?"

"Someone tried to kill me again."

"*What*?"

"They cut the brake lines on my Vette and removed bolts from the differential."

Paul put a hand on my shoulder. "Ryan, how are you? Really?"

"My wife thinks I'm nuts not to resign. Sometimes I think I'm falling apart. Sorry, I shouldn't have said that to you. Forget it."

"You are under a lot of stress. I understand that. What can I do to help?"

"I don't know. Nothing. I just needed someone to unload with. I shouldn't do that to you."

"Ryan, I think you are one of the most honorable men I have worked for. If there is something I can do to make things better, you only need to ask me."

"Thank you. I appreciate that. I am just unnerved by the car crash."

Paul looked at me thoughtfully, then nodded and left my office.

I needed to appear calm for Anne and the boys. Inside, I was angry as hell and, for the first time since the service, frightened. Anne or the boys could have been driving the Vette. I could never forgive myself if something happened to them. *God, please keep them safe!*

I made the sign of the cross.

• • •

That evening at home, Anne and I decided we needed to be completely candid with the boys. One of Shawn's best friends was the son of the local chief of police, and he knew about the new attempt on my life before Anne knew. So, we both went down to the boys' end of the house, where they were trying to quietly fit in a pool game before going to sleep. Anne made me do the talking. I showed them the pictures on my phone, the Vette just after the crash. Aaron and Matt looked both shocked and frightened when I told them the Vette crashed because someone had cut the brake lines. Of course, Shawn wanted to find out who did it and "kick their butt." Matt asked everyone to be calm. Aaron said a prayer that night.

CHAPTER 14

The Holiday Party

Every year since becoming general counsel, I held a dinner the last week of January. It was a party for everyone in the law department—attorneys, staff, and their spouses and partners to make it a more social occasion, not an office party. We always held it at our home, tenting the yard and renting heaters to overcome the chill.

That year we had mild weather. The house and yard were packed with over 200 people. Kozlov kept near the front door, meeting every guest as they arrived, trying to maximize the pats and attention. Finally, I took him into our bedroom and gave him a bone to chew while dinner was put out. I did not want him begging for food from 200 people.

During the following four hours, wine and good food were shared, and friendships deepened. At about 11:30, Anne and I stood at the front door and said goodbye to our guests as they left. Everyone was in great spirits, giving lots of hugs. Finally, after our last guest had gone, we went back into the house. We let Koslov out of our bedroom and put him in the backyard. The boys helped us pick up things in the house and assisted the caterers in loading up their things.

Anne stood at the back door and called several times for the Koslov, but he did not come. We looked around the house and then the backyard with flashlights, calling him again. We found him sniffing a plate full of meat by the garage. I picked up the plate before he ate anything, suspicious.

The next morning, I took the plate of meat to the vet. He called me in and said the tests showed the meat was poisoned.

I was furious. Someone at the party had tried to hurt my family in a very personal way.

Who was it? What bastard would do something like that?

I reported the attempted poisoning to the police. The two detectives investigating my car crash came to our home that evening after dinner. This time, the junior officer took the lead in questioning me.

"Mr. Gorman, who do you think tried to poison your dog?"

"It had to be someone from my law department. The only guests were my employees and their spouses or partners."

"You know this is probably related to the murders at your company and the attempts to kill you."

"You sound like my wife."

"It looks like one of your employees could be the person behind the poisoning, the attempt on your life, and the murders at your company. The poison may have been a message that they can get to you and your family. It takes either a lot of anger or a big incentive to motivate someone to do that. You must know your employees better than anyone. Who is the most likely killer?"

"I honestly do not know. These are highly respected people, very professional."

"Hired killers are also professionals."

"I see your point."

Anne was watching, and the senior officer asked, "Dr. Gorman, is there anything else we should know?"

"Yes, when you are talking to my husband, whom I love very much, you are talking to a very stubborn man. I repeatedly asked him to resign from EDGE so he would be safe. But he refused."

"Well, we're not sure that would keep the killer from going after him. We don't know the motivation. Anything else, Dr. or Mr. Gorman?"

Anne put her hand on my shoulder, took a deep breath, and spoke. She told them she had received a frightening call from some man claiming I'd had an affair with a woman in the law department and had insisted she have an abortion. The officers had already heard that from me but appeared to be moved by Anne's recounting of the call.

"Dr. Gorman, did the caller say why he was calling you?"

"Yes, he wanted me to talk my husband into resigning."

"Did you recognize his voice? Was it familiar?"

"He tried to disguise it, but it sounded to me like Tom Smith, who used to be my husband's boss but now works for him. He was at the party last night."

"Mr. Gorman, if you resigned, how would that advantage Tom?"

"Mr. Farber would probably make him general counsel."

"Please explain."

"Farber hates my guts, but he can't easily fire me, so he wants me to resign. He wants Tom as general counsel. It would make his life easier."

"It looks like we may have a possible motivation. But how would that connect to the murder of Mr. Jack Names and your analyst we heard was killed in Mexico?"

"I don't see any connection. It does not make sense."

After they left, I turned to Anne, wanting to ease the tension between us.

"Anne, I just—"

"Ryan, I really do not want to talk with you right now. I'm too tired and don't have the patience."

She went to our bedroom. Fully clothed, she went to bed. We did not speak further that night. I knew that in a way she put some blame on me. After all, it was someone from my department, my company, who tried to kill Kozlov. But that made my resolve to fight back and not quit even stronger. I wanted whoever was responsible to be punished and punished fully.

. . .

The police called me shortly after I got to the office the next morning. As I expected, there were no fingerprints on the plate used to try to kill Kozlov. They confirmed the poison was the type ranchers used to exterminate coyotes. The killer had been careful. And cruel.

CHAPTER 15

Napa

Saturday morning, I packed my suitcase. The first quarter of each year, the company held an off-premises conference in Napa. The corporate travel department always chose Auberge du Solei, one of my favorite places in the valley. The final agenda would be passed out when we got to the hotel. The first two days were always devoted entirely to financial matters. The third and the fourth days were devoted to presentations by each line of business. The morning of the fifth day that year would be devoted to a special report from Sillus, supposedly on the relative costs of centralized departments—that is, the law department.

I had already been alerted by my friend Lloyd Bright, our CFO, that my department was the main target of the Sillus presentation. I expected a very strong recommendation to break the law department into different pieces and send packets of attorneys to each of the subsidiaries. Previously, the president of one of our larger subsidiaries candidly told me he believed that lawyers were like dogs: they licked the hand that fed them. He wanted his own law department. In my opinion, that was a strong reason to have a centralized law department at corporate headquarters.

The meetings plodded through the agenda. I suspected that Sillus, Farber, my officer friend, and I were the only ones who knew what was in the special report. Finally, the long-awaited

Sillus analysis was presented. There were no surprises for me. Several CEOs applauded the law department breakup as if it were a divine revelation. It could have been more accurately described as an attempt to castrate the lawyers. I remained silent, waiting.

After the Sillus presentation, there was an hour-long discussion. Then the CFO chimed in to point out that the full costs of the subsidiary law departments would be in each subsidiary's budget, and they would each have to use a lot of outside law firms because no single subsidiary law department would have all the legal expertise currently housed in our comprehensive corporate law department. Those legal expenses would come out of the earnings of each subsidiary. There was a growing recognition that the Sillus recommendation would reduce each CEO's bottom lines and therefore bonus potential. They also realized that if any of their legal matters went south with no one to blame in the parent company, they would own the blame. When the discussion seemed to have wound down, I spoke for the first time.

"Colleagues, it is time we had a show of hands from our operating CEOs as to their preference on this recommendation. All those in favor of a complete decentralization of the law department, as proposed by Sillus, please raise your hand."

No one raised their hand. I looked around the table.

"Mr. Farber, it appears we have the sense of the operating CEOs. Sillus, thank you for raising this very important issue."

The meeting was quickly adjourned at four. Farber had badly misjudged his audience and was not a happy man. But I was. It occurred to me that after this defeat, he probably hated me more than ever. I was sure he would find some way to make me pay for his loss.

What next?

CHAPTER 16

A Note

After dinner in the hotel restaurant and a few drinks with some of my friends, I retired to my room and called Anne. It was about 11:30 pm, but I knew she would be awake, expecting me to call. When she picked up the phone, her voice was strained.

"Hi, Ryan."

"Anne, is something the matter?"

"Shawn is here. I want him to explain what happened."

The fear that Shawn may have been in a car accident immediately hit me. I knew the stats. At least in our area, the highest cause of death for people under twenty-five was car accidents. Every time Shawn left the house and drove a car, Anne and I would silently say a prayer. But if Shawn was going to tell me what happened, that meant at least he was not badly injured.

"Dad, listen, I was just a few minutes past curfew. I had this date with a new girl I met after the game last week. Well, that does not matter."

"Shawn, tell me what does matter."

"I came home a little late. I parked the car on the driveway, not opening the garage. I was trying to be quiet. I didn't want to wake Mom."

"Of course not. Now get to the point."

"Well, I walked up to the front door and was looking for my

house key. Then I heard a car coming up the street and looked down the street to see who it was. No headlights were on. It was driving on the wrong side of the road, very slowly. When it stopped next to our mailbox under the streetlight, I realized it was a red convertible. This guy got out of the car, looked around, put a letter in our mailbox, then quickly drove away. I mean, he tore out of here. Again, no headlights. That's suspicious, right?"

"Right, Shawn. Go on."

"I went down to the mailbox to see what was there. The guy had put an envelope in it. The weirdest thing is that he looked a lot like that guy Tom Smith in your department. And at your party, he was showing off his new red convertible. I'm not sure, but I think it was Mr. Smith."

"Well, there could be many reasons for that behavior, whether it was Tom or not. Did you bring the letter to your mom?"

"Yes."

"Anne, describe it to me. What does it say?"

"I didn't open it. I wanted to wait and talk with you first. It's addressed to you, no return address. It's a purple envelope, and the printing looks like it was done with one of those old dot-matrix-type printers."

This description relaxed me, and I replied, "It's probably just a thank-you note for the party. It's an invitation. Why don't you open it?"

Anne opened the letter and with relief in her voice described the contents. "You were right, Ryan. The envelope is filled with paper stars—red, white, and blue stars. Inside, there's a pink, smaller envelope, tied with a metallic blue ribbon. It must be an invitation."

"You see, we are just spooked, jumpy. After what has happened recently, I think we're all prone to see threats where there are none. Anne, please open the pink envelope and read the invitation."

Anne opened the envelope. Silence followed. Then I heard

Shawn let out a loud expletive. I noticed Anne did not reprimand him.

"Anne, is there something wrong? What does it say?"

Her voice stressed and angry, she read the note slowly.

Dear Mr. Gorman,

Please accept this short note as an effort to help you and your family. I know you loved that car, just as you love your wife and sons. But we have no faith in you. It's time you resigned. If not, anything is possible. You have two weeks.

Sincerely yours,
A Friend

It took me a few seconds to recover. At first, I could not speak. The threat was too personal, to my family. After a moment I tried to think in a detached manner, as if I were advising a client.

"Anne, is the note handwritten or typed?"

"The same dot-matrix printer that was used for addressing the envelope."

"Anne, I want you and Shawn to not touch the letter, envelopes, or note with your hands again. Go put on some latex gloves. Then come back and pick up the two envelopes, the note, ribbon, and the stars. Put them all in a plastic bag and seal it. I will be home tomorrow morning, very early. We can talk then. Shawn, check to make sure all the doors and windows are closed and locked. I know you sometimes 'inadvertently' turn off the house alarm when you go out on a date, so please double-check, and make sure it is fully armed. Don't say anything to your brothers. Got it?"

"Yes, Dad."

"Anne, there is no threat right now. The only purpose is to try to scare me into resigning. We can talk tomorrow morning. I can't drive right now. It's midnight, and I had a scotch and then wine at dinner. I'll start driving about five in the morning and be home around seven. I'll bring you some coffee in bed. How does that sound?"

"Ryan, I won't sleep tonight. I'll be awake when you get here. Shouldn't we call the police tonight?"

"I need to do something first."

"Drive safely, please, no speeding. You are very important. I'll be up and make the coffee. I love you."

"I love you too."

Anne, as always, was a woman of her word. I could not sleep either and left Napa early. When I got home at 6:15, she was sitting at the breakfast table, and the coffee was ready. I went to her and held her in my arms. She cried, and I kept saying it would be alright and that I loved her.

"Ryan, I know you love me. But this is very serious. These people are not just cruel, they are crazy. They have shown they are very dangerous. You must do something, now."

"I know."

At that point, the boys poured into the kitchen, looking for food. Only Shawn was nervous, so I concluded he had followed my directions and had not discussed the note with his brothers. Once our two younger boys were off to school, Anne, Shawn, and I again sat at the kitchen table. None of us had eaten anything, just a sip or two of coffee. I asked Anne and Shawn to each take a separate tall glass from the clean dishes in the dishwasher and press fingers from both hands all over the glass. Then I used a pair of plyers to put each glass in a separate plastic bag to preserve their fingerprints. I wrote their names on the appropriate plastic bag. The process unnerved Anne. But I think Shawn found it exciting, like an adventure.

Anne took both my hands and pleaded, "Ryan, you need to call the police at once!"

"First, I am going to try to find out if Tom is the one who delivered the note. I can do that more efficiently than the police."

"How are you going to do that?"

"I'll need help. Last night I woke up Mike Waver, the head of Rowel and Associates. They're one of the nation's largest private investigation companies. I've worked with him numerous times. I explained everything to him and asked his advice. We'll meet this morning."

"Why not call the police now?"

"I want to talk with Mike first. If that's what he advises, I'll do that. But the police have had no luck with my brake lines, the shooting, or the attempt to poison Kozlov. Besides, no one has been hurt, and we have no proof it was Tom. I want to deliver this note to the police with the proof they need."

Once Anne and Shawn had left, I called Mike again. His office was near mine in San Francisco, but he lived only two blocks from me in Tiburon. He picked me up, and we drove to the ferry while I filled him in on everything I had previously discussed with the police. He believed we should delay calling the police a little while. He took custody of the plastic bag with the note and the plastic bags with the two glasses from Anne and Shawn.

The monthly all-officers' meeting was scheduled for 2 pm that day. I asked Tom to come to my office at 10 am to brief me on something his people were handling that was on the agenda. Tom and I sat on opposite sides of my conference table. There was a coffee pot and two cups. Tom poured himself a cup of coffee. When he left my office, two Rowel agents stepped out of the restroom in my office. With gloves, one of the agents picked up the coffee cup Tom had used. The other took custody of the saucer and coffee pot. Each was placed in a separate plastic bag, marked for date and time, and signed by the agent. They put these in a box and took them to their offices. Two hours later, at 12:15, Mike called me.

"Ryan, the prints on Smith's coffee cup and saucer perfectly match prints on the outside envelope, the interior envelope, and the note. The only other prints were those of Anne and Shawn. I think we can safely say Tom Smith was the man your son saw deliver the note, and he typed it. His prints are all over it. Do you want me to send you a written report?"

"Yes, please do it. Can you have one of your people hand-deliver it? I want to preserve confidentiality, at least for now. Please keep the original notes, coffee cup, and saucer. When you send your report, please include a photocopy of the two envelopes and the note."

"You'll have that as soon as possible."

"Thank you."

"What do you want to do now?"

"I'll call you later."

When Mike's report arrived, I put the report and pictures in my briefcase. I went to the officers' meeting, which seemed routine to me, although in truth I found it difficult to concentrate on the discussions. At the conclusion of the meeting, I looked up at Farber, took out the envelope from Mike, and said, "Mr. Farber, there is something we need to discuss. Privately."

He smiled. I suspected he was hoping for my resignation. When the conference room had emptied, I sat in the chair next to him and handed him the envelope, which he eagerly opened. He took out the photos of the note and envelopes. He did not look up at me. His smile faded, but he said nothing.

"Mr. Farber, the threatening note was delivered and written by your favorite lawyer, Tom Smith."

Suddenly Farber was visibly angry. His hands were shaking as he shouted at me.

"How can you say such a thing to me! You, an attorney, should know that is slander. Slander! You are totally irresponsible to even suggest such a thing. Yes, I do like Smith. He is a good person, a good lawyer, and he has an important attribute you lack. Loyalty!"

"It was Tom. My son saw him. And there is proof."

"What do you mean proof?"

Then I took out the written Rowel report from my briefcase and handed it to Farber.

He read it quickly, then yelled, "This is outrageous. Are you trying to embarrass the company? Maybe you just want a scandal to hurt the company stock and undermine me!"

Farber was so angry and distraught he was losing control of his emotions. The blood vessel on his neck throbbed. I continued to watch him closely as he tried to determine his next move. He looked away, turning his back to me as he stood there, holding the reports. Then he turned quickly to face me.

His face filled with controlled anger, he rasped, "No one must know about this. No one! As your superior, I order you to give me the original letter and envelopes. You will never tell anyone about this. Never!"

"Mr. Farber, apparently you did not fully understand what I said. Several people at the Rowel agency know about the death threat. They have the original envelopes and note. They have the coffee cup Tom used in my office today. They matched his fingerprints to prints on the envelopes and letter. They prepared a written report. Too many people already know what Tom did. It's too late to pretend this never happened."

Farber almost collapsed into his chair, stunned. Obviously, his next move was not immediately apparent to him. He remained seated, silent, looking down at his feet. Finally, I asked, "Mr. Farber, did you know Tom was going to write the note?"

"Of course not. Why would you ask that?"

"I know you and Tom have a close relationship. I also know you would prefer Tom was general counsel, not me."

"Tom is a good lawyer, and loyal. As for his being general

counsel, he would do a hell of a better job than you. Anyone would be better than you."

"When his note says I am not wanted, is that from you? Or is this the first time you knew Tom had written that note?"

Farber rose to his feet and shouted, "What are you trying to say? How dare you imply I had anything to do with this!"

"If I resigned right now, would you pick Tom to replace me?"

"In a heartbeat. Hopefully that question means you are finally resigning."

"I thought about it but decided I'm needed here."

Farber folded the documents I had given him and put them in his inside coat pocket.

Spitting as he spoke and shaking his finger at me, he said, "Gorman, this is an order. Go directly home immediately. Do not go back to your office. Do not speak to anyone about this. Do not come back until tomorrow. We must keep this quiet."

"Sir, you forget, Tom works for me."

"Don't do something stupid out of personal pride. If this is public . . . if the police get involved, it will be public. The newspapers! God, the newspapers! The company stocks. It will be a scandal. The board could lose confidence in us. Damn you, Gorman! You've created a hell of a mess."

"Tom threatened me and my family. He threatened to kill us. He may even have tried to kill me before. I cannot have him working here."

"I promise he will be gone before you get back tomorrow. Isn't that enough?"

"Maybe. We'll see."

Farber stormed out of the conference room, slamming the door as he left.

But he kept his promise. When I arrived at my office the next morning, there was a note on my desk from HR informing me that Tom had resigned to accept a job in Washington, DC, with a small law firm. The important thing was that Tom had left the department, the company, and was leaving the state. I called the head of HR. She confirmed, "Tom Smith resigned, then surrendered his company ID and phone yesterday at 4 pm."

Twenty minutes later, Farber called me and said, "Gorman, Tom is gone. I fired him. I trust you are satisfied."

"It was the right thing to do, sir."

"As you know, I had nothing to do with Tom's temporary lapse of judgment. Let me remind you, you will never mention this again, not to anyone. That's an order!"

With that, Farber hung up. I called my office manager and arranged to have someone pack up any personal items in Tom's former office and send them to him in DC. That evening, I called Tiburon's head detective, Captain Jim Miller, at his home. "Good evening, Jim."

"Hi, Ryan. What's up?"

"I know your guys are working their butts off investigating my problems. I have an update I want to provide, but it can't be public. If it got out to the media, it could hurt my company's stock price. But I thought I should tell you directly."

"Okay. Talk."

"Two nights ago, a death threat was delivered to my home, a threat against me and my family. I called Rowel and Associates. They lifted fingerprints and confirmed the threat came from Tom Smith, one of the attorneys in my department, my former boss. I told our CEO, Farber, and he fired Tom."

"Where is this Tom Smith now?"

"He is on his way to a new job in DC."

"That seems pretty fast to recover from a firing."

"Well, it's a firm almost three thousand miles away, and that feels good."

"What did Farber say about what Tom did?"

"He said he had no prior knowledge of it and described Tom's conduct as a 'lapse in judgement.'"

"You believe him?"

"Well, Farber and I do not get along. But I can't imagine him involved in what Tom did."

"How do you really feel about Tom being in DC?"

"Very relieved. Like a huge weight has been take off my shoulders. But I told Farber that if Tom threatens me or my family again, is anywhere near me or my family, or has anything to do with the company, I will press charges and turn over the evidence to the police. The evidence may not prove he tried to kill me, or that he tried to poison Kozlov, but it does prove that he has threatened to kill me. If that's not enough to put him away, it's enough to ruin his reputation and get his bar license revoked. It might also tarnish Farber's reputation—at least in the company, because everyone here knows Tom was Farber's boy."

CHAPTER 17

That Evening

Anne got home late that night after a meeting for a women's homeless shelter where she often volunteered. The boys and I were already eating hamburgers and fries that I'd picked up on the way home. Gourmet, as far as the boys were concerned. After the boys had gone to bed, I told Anne about Farber firing Tom and his move to DC. She was relieved. We both decided he probably tried to poison Kozlov and could have been responsible for the attempts on my life. I told Anne there was still no evidence for the police to charge him with attempted murder at the ferry or with my Vette. But if he came back, I would ask the police to charge him with the threat to murder. That made Anne angry.

"That rat should be in jail, not escaping to DC."

"Anne, I agree. But the important thing for us is that he knows we know what he did, and he knows he is the first person the police would go after if anything happened to me."

"What if he's crazy?"

"We don't know that."

"Are we certain Tom acted alone? Fired the shot at you? Cut your brake lines? Murdered Jack? Are we certain of that?"

"Of course not."

"Ryan, I am glad that bastard is gone and out of our lives. But after everything that's happened, how can you still work there?

Give me one good reason."

"I've tried to explain that."

"What? That you care more about your company, your career, and your department than you do about me and our sons? You certainly don't place much value on your own life."

"I owe it to the people I hired in the law department. And I owe it to Jack to find his murderer."

"What do you owe to your family?"

"I am trying to provide for my family and take care of all of you. I'm doing what I think is right. For God's sake, I am doing my best."

"Do you take some kind of pleasure in Farber trying to destroy you?"

"Anne, I think Farber is arrogant, incompetent, and evil. He may have had something to do with Bill Woodworth's resignation. I don't know. But I do know that if I leave now, there will be no one at the company to keep him in check. All this will be forgotten, swept under the rug, and no one will be held accountable! My instincts tell me something significant is going on. Anne, please understand. I need to find out what."

Anne glared at me and asked, "Have you spoken to the police?"

"I called Captain Miller and briefed him. The police have a record of this. I told him that I would press charges if Tom came back or did anything further to threaten me or our family. But the fact is Tom is gone. Out of the picture. So is the danger he represented. And Farber might be more civil at work because he doesn't have Tom waiting in the wings to replace me."

"You believe that?"

"I think Farber will become resigned to my presence and my life at the office will be a lot better."

"I hope so, because I am just about out of patience with EDGE and with you, Mr. Gorman!"

Anne went to bed. I took a long, too-hot shower, my fallback remedy when I felt very stressed. I agreed with Anne that in a perfect world, Tom would be in jail. But this was not a perfect world. I had decided that while Tom might not be crazy, he must be a deeply unhappy, disturbed person. As the Bible said, jealousy is like a cancer. It eats the soul and destroys its host. Part of me wished I had listened to the advice Bill Woodworth gave me the day I was made general counsel. He had recommended I fire Tom, who he said had an unhealthy professional relationship with the brilliant but insecure and arrogant CEO that Bill had replaced.

• • •

With Tom gone, Farber did appear to be less combative the rest of the week. On Friday, the audit was completed, my company credit cards restored, and the company issued my expense reimbursement check, about $68,000. That made Anne a bit more relaxed. At least she no longer had to search her purse for gas money.

CHAPTER 18

Monday's Revelation

Paul and I were in a meeting, listening to a pitch. One of the big Wall Street financial houses was doing their best to get us to cough up several hundred million to buy a company in Mexico. Paul was standing behind me, not senior enough at the meeting to have a seat at the table, which was otherwise full of the senior financial and businesspeople from EDGE, plus the Wall Street pitch team.

An hour into the presentation, Paul leaned over my shoulder and told me, "Mr. Gorman, there is a bust in their numbers. Look at these two cells: line 22, box 12; and line 31, box 19. The correct numbers for those calculations are $805,260 and $2,346,000, respectively. The result of those errors spirals through the rest of the analysis."

The lead gentleman from the Wall Street firm was totally outraged. He jumped to his feet as if he had been shocked with 220 volts. Across the table, I saw the veins in his neck pounding. He shouted, "Who in the hell is this guy? We never make mistakes. Never!"

"This is my assistant. Please humor us and get out your calculators and recheck those numbers. Thank you."

They begrudgingly accommodated my request. After all, they wanted to demonstrate Paul was wrong. More important, they wanted to make the sale and get their excessive commission. For several minutes they huddled together, redoing their calculations twice.

"Mr. Gorman, we apologize. Your assistant was lucky. These are merely a couple of minor typos that do not alter the fundamentals of our recommendation to buy this company."

"Fine. Thank you for your time. We will get back to you. Paul, please stay here. I want to talk to you privately. Everyone else, enjoy the rest of your day."

The Wall Street firm left the room, their tails between their legs. If the basic math calculations were incorrect, what about the underlying assumptions and data? After a couple of minutes, only Paul and I remained.

"Paul, how did you spot those errors? There are at least a hundred fifty cells on that chart."

"I looked at them, and they didn't make sense."

"Then how did you know the correct numbers?"

"I did the math in my head."

"Paul, I consider you a colleague. I think I am entitled to give you both professional and friendly advice. When you are as smart as you are, and new in a middle-level job, you must be careful that others around you do not know how gifted you are. If they do, they will see you as a threat and try to destroy you. This Byzantine court is also a jungle. In the future, if you see something at a meeting that I need to know immediately, please write me a note that we need to talk, and I will take a break. Okay?"

"Okay."

"Good."

When I got back to my office, General Kathy had called and left a phone number. I returned the call. "Hi, General. How is life treating you these days?"

"Frankly, Ryan, I don't have much free time to think about that."

"What's up?"

"I hear that you relieved one of your attorneys, who is now in DC."

"You are well informed."

"You know I told you I had contacted a senior official at the FBI and asked to be kept up to date on matters related to you and EDGE."

"I appreciate your concern. But while it is apparent that this guy threatened my life, and family, he is now out of the picture. I feel much safer."

"That's why I'm calling. The FBI is up to speed on all that. But, Ryan, have you checked your office calendar for the day someone tried to shoot you at the ferry?"

"No. Why do you ask?"

"The FBI has. Your former employee was in Atlanta delivering a paper at the American Gas Association annual meeting at the same time of the shooting. Also, both the day before and the day of your car crash, he was on vacation with his wife in Cabo. He could not have been the one who tried to kill you."

That revelation struck me like a hammer in the gut. I hadn't bothered to parse the logic of Tom being a would-be professional hitman. Even if he was the one responsible for the attempts, he'd have to hire someone. Some unknown threat could still be waiting in the wings.

CHAPTER 19

My Birthday Surprise

The next day was my birthday. My mother always called me the morning of my birthday. Often, she regaled Anne and the boys with new stories of stupid things I had done when a kid. That morning was the same. On a ranch, the day started early, so I was not surprised when she called at 6:15. I had not even showered yet. After she talked with me for a few minutes and sang "Happy Birthday," she asked to speak with Anne and the boys.

While Anne and Mom were on the phone, I went to the other end of the house to the boys' rooms. I told them to get their butts out of bed quickly or I would have to get out my mega super-soaker water cannon and hit them with ice water: Grandma was on the phone. They jumped out of bed and thundered down the hall. Anne put the phone on speaker. I went into my bathroom to shower.

After showering, shaving, and dressing, I joined everyone in the kitchen. The boys had made me breakfast, with a lit candle stuck in a stack of five pancakes swimming in maple syrup and melted butter. I blew out the candle while Anne and the boys sang "Happy Birthday." I ate one of the pancakes. The boys ate the others. Then I went to the office.

At 2:30, Cathy returned from a late lunch with Maggie, Farber's secretary and Cathy's sorority sister; it was also Maggie's birthday. Cathy poked her head into my office and put a piece of birthday cake on my desk with a birthday card. I thanked her.

"Ryan, do you need anything for the board meeting tonight?"

"What board meeting?"

"The special board meeting scheduled for seven this evening. I know it's very confidential. But don't worry: Maggie told me. Do you need me to get anything for the meeting?"

"No. I don't need anything. Thanks."

What the hell? A board meeting? Why wasn't I told? It seemed that just when I thought we had established peace in our time, Farber had broken the truce. This was not just some childish prank. *How would he expect to explain my absence to the board? Why all the secrecy?*

My temper was rising. I needed to keep calm before I did something stupid. I resolved to walk into the board meeting at 7 pm as if I had known about it all along. In the meantime, I grabbed my gym bag and racket. I charged out of my office, heading for the athletic club. Just outside our elevator in the lobby, I collided with Paul, knocking him off his feet.

"Geeze, I'm sorry, Paul. Didn't see you." Embarrassed, I reached down to help him up.

He laughed and said, "I was coming up to talk with you. Are you off to beat the ball?"

"Yes. Think I need a little exercise."

"Want a game? My gear is in my office."

"Sure."

I waited while Paul retrieved his gear, grinding my teeth and muttering to myself. Farber was a total jerk, petty, snide, arrogant, and insecure, but even if Tom was not responsible for the threats against me, it was irrational to see a connection between Farber not telling me about the board meeting and the attempts on my life. Farber did not have the *huevos* to try to kill anyone himself. Certainly, Sillus was not a candidate. Tom was not in town. That meant someone else was out there.

I ran through the list of people I'd had to discipline or disappoint in the law department and came up with zero candidates. I tried to remember any other company employees who might be vengeful enough to try it. But there wasn't anyone. And in my personal life, zero candidates came to mind. I reminded myself it was not helpful to allow my dislike for Farber to color my general judgment and imagine threats that were not there.

Paul emerged from the elevator.

"Got my gear."

We walked over to the club. In the locker room, I noticed that Paul seemed a little tense, and I realized we had not spoken on the walk to the club. "Paul, sorry if I'm a bit preoccupied. You mentioned you wanted to talk about something."

"Yes. I wanted to ask how you liked the high-level analysis we did for the board meeting tonight."

I turned to Paul, visibly angry. Paul seemed taken aback. I said, "You knew about the board meeting today?"

"Of course."

"How?"

"My department spent all weekend working on the project—rather, potential project. Very exciting stuff. We worked over Saturday night and through Sunday until early this morning. The team is really excited about this."

I must have looked completely unglued. Paul took in my expression, his eyes wide, and his jaw dropped. "Ryan, are you okay?"

"Yes, fine! Get your racket, and let's go to the court."

The game was fast and furious. I won the game, to my surprise and Paul's. Fury improved my game. We hardly spoke while playing. After the second game, which I also won, we were both exhausted. But I was no less angry. We put away our gear and headed for the steam room. We sat in silence for a few minutes.

I was still trying to decide how to handle the latest insult and harassment from Farber. He risked heavy criticism from the board, which would find it unacceptable that I was not asked to attend a board meeting. What excuse could he manufacture? Farber must have a very strong reason to take that risk.

"Paul, how long have you known about this board meeting?"

"Late Thursday afternoon. When did you first hear about it?"

I didn't answer. Paul studied my face and silence, and then it dawned on him. "Shit! I'm sorry, Ryan. I don't know what to say."

"Paul, thanks for the game. I think I've sweated off a pound of water. Time to hit the showers."

In the showers, I still was not in the mood to talk about this problem. On the walk back to the office, Paul kept glancing at my face as I clenched my teeth. When we reached the office, he asked, "Ryan, is there anything you want to ask me about the project?"

"No."

"You're going to the board meeting, right?"

"Damn right I am! Wouldn't miss that circus for the world."

CHAPTER 20

Before the Board

Fifteen minutes before the scheduled board meeting, I tried to casually stroll into the room. But my walk was probably more like a Prussian charge. Most of the board was already present, getting coffee and finding their usual seats behind their name tags. Some of them looked at me, probably wondering if I was going to say something about why they had been abruptly assembled. I quickly learned they had only been told the meeting was "essential" and "highly confidential." When Dianna asked me the subject and the need for the emergency meeting, I just said that was for Farber to explain. Otherwise, I stayed silent and kept my poker face.

My name tag was not even on the table—an "unintentional" oversight. But I sat in my now usual spot, ripped a page from my notebook, folded it in half, wrote my name in big capital letters, and placed it in front of me. I tried to pretend I was absorbed in reading something in my notebook.

On the exact minute scheduled for the meeting to begin, Sillus and Farber entered the room smiling, Sillus carrying a stack of papers. They abruptly stopped when they saw me. Farber sat down, then opened his folder. Sillus stood attentively behind him. It was hard to tell who looked more shocked to see me, Sillus or Farber. I felt a perverse pleasure in knowing how upset they must feel. For several minutes, the two of them whispered to each other; then Farber started the meeting.

"Welcome. This is a very important day in the history of this company. Thanks to all of you for coming on such short notice."

When a board of directors is called together in this way, it always makes them nervous. That showed on all their faces, except Dianna's. In her role as a security lawyer, she had been to enough emergency board meetings to not be ruffled. After looking at each board member individually, Farber smiled and continued.

Speaking with pleasure and excitement, he said, "We have just received an extraordinary offer. It is an all-cash offer to purchase both our company and Novation Energy. As you know, Novation is a diversified holding company headquartered in New York City. Its assets parallel our own. Its market cap is almost identical to ours. The proposed deal has two steps. First, we merge with Novation. Second, the merged company is acquired by the ultimate buyer."

I heard the board members' reactions, some gasping and some taking deep breaths. There was nothing more nerve racking and risky for board members than being forced to consider a merger or a sale of the company. Law school textbooks are full of court cases where board members were sued by some aggrieved party or a class-action lawyer-entrepreneur, under precisely these circumstances. Dianna, of course, had been outside counsel on many, many matters like this. She turned to me and seemed to notice for the first time that my usual nameplate was missing. Raising her eyebrows, she mouthed the word "Why?" I shrugged.

She turned her attention to Farber. "Mr. Farber, when was this offer received?"

"Last Thursday."

"Has the staff prepared a preliminary analysis of the offer?"

"Yes, they worked on this over the weekend, turning over every leaf."

Refocusing her attention, she looked at me. "Ryan, have you done a legal analysis of this proposal, the proposed initial terms, regulatory approvals, anti-trust clearance issues, and foreign nation approvals?"

"Unfortunately, Dianna, I have never seen any deal terms or whatever analysis was done by staff. I only learned of this meeting this afternoon and did not know its purpose until now."

The room seemed to explode, with board members all speaking at the same time. Dianna used her position as chair to slam her folder on the table and command silence. She slowly rose from her chair. She was a powerful figure. Even though she was probably no more than five foot two inches and 125 pounds, her presence filled the room. The respect she commanded focused all eyes on her. She stood silently for several seconds.

"Mr. Farber, what possible explanation do you have for keeping this secret from our general counsel?

She stared at Farber with a penetrating look. The room was silent, waiting for Farber to answer, but he did not.

"Well, Mr. Farber, it doesn't matter. The bottom line is that the board will not consider, and you will not present, such a proposal to this board until and unless our general counsel is prepared to provide his initial input and recommendations on legal and regulatory issues. You will be fully involved with our general counsel. Nothing is secret from him. Nothing! Is that perfectly clear?"

Farber cleared his throat and replied, "Of course. We didn't know he was available on such short notice. His schedule is so hectic. It is an urgent matter. We needed to get this matter before the board quickly and—"

Dianna cut him off with a wave and a glare. As I watched the interplay between Farber and Dianna and saw the expressions of other board members, I tried not to smile. I wondered if Farber thought another car crash might make me unavailable next time.

Then I reminded myself not to mix unrelated things.

This board was a very cautious board, but all boards should be cautious. Farber was new to the board and did not understand its style and demands. It must have been very different where he had worked previously.

When Bill Woodworth was CEO, when the board was called to vote at the end of any major presentation by management, Dianna always asked me the same two questions: "Ryan, if you were a board member now and asked to vote on this matter, is there anything, any fact, data, or issue, legal or otherwise, that has not already been discussed today here at this meeting that you would consider before deciding how to vote?" After my answer, she would then ask: "Do you believe the presentations today are legally adequate under existing law, and fulfill all regulatory requirements, for us to now vote on this matter?"

Those questions were designed to provide some legal protection to the board. Initially, they drove Bill Woodworth up the wall. However, after a few episodes, it became clear Dianna was not worried that these questions were causing me problems with my boss, nor was she concerned about making Bill uncomfortable. Fortunately, Bill concluded Dianna was not going to drop the questions, and the result was a close collaboration developed between Bill and me in preparation for such meetings. That developed into a close friendship. Bill even made it a practice to require all senior management to make their board presentations first to me, then to him, before we presented anything significant to the board.

I saw Dianna thinking about her next move, like a master chess player. She looked at me and then Farber and said, "This board meeting is temporarily adjourned until 9:30 pm tonight. Mr. Farber, you will make sure our general counsel is fully briefed, shown all relevant documents, and is prepared when we reconvene. Let the minutes reflect what I have just said."

With that, Dianna put her folder in her briefcase, picked up her briefcase, and walked out of the boardroom. The other board members followed. Only Farber, Sillus, and I remained. I decided not to speak first. I knew Farber was trying to decide how best to make me suffer for his humiliation. We sat a few minutes in silence. If it were possible to feel the heat of hatred, that was what was radiating from the other end of the table. Farber whispered to Sillus. Then Farber got up and left the room without saying a word to me. Sillus looked at me. He seemed a bit unsure of how to proceed.

"Mr. Gorman, Mr. Farber has instructed me to escort you to the strategic planning department conference room. Everything you need to see is there. If you do have a question for Mr. Farber, you are to tell me. Then I will present your question to Mr. Farber. He does not want to be disturbed by you."

We stared at each other for at least a minute. I wondered if and how much Sillus knew about Tom's threat and firing. I considered whether I should mention these matters to Dianna and the whole board. It puzzled me why I was even thinking about those unrelated things at this time. Ultimately, I decided it would be disruptive and certainly had no bearing on the proposed merger. I stood. Sillus did the same.

"Sillus, I can find my way to there."

Nevertheless, Sillus followed me down the hall, into the elevator, and to the conference room in the basement. We did not speak. Of course, the door to the conference room was locked. I knocked. Several of the analysts were waiting inside, including Paul.

"Paul, folks, it's good to see you. The board meeting was adjourned until 9:30. I need your help to quickly understand the proposed merger and acquisition. You'll need to download me with as much information as you can during the next ninety minutes or so. But first I want to read the offer letter."

One of the analysts handed me a two-page letter. It was simple, straightforward. It was an offer to buy both companies with a premium of 29 percent over their market cap at the end of the day. The deal required the agreement of both companies and of course a bucketload of regulatory approvals from the agencies, foreign and domestic, that regulated the numerous subsidiaries of both companies.

What was unusual was the two-step nature of the proposal. The two-step proposal would be structured with a sort of escrow process, much like people used when they bought a home. The funds for the purchase would rest in escrow from the point of initial board approvals until the merger of EDGE and Novation was consummated. At that point, the funds would be dispersed to our shareholders. The next step would be for the buyer of the new merged holding company to be merged into a subsidiary of the buyer.

Apparently, the buyer was the Horizon Energy Foundation, an investment vehicle headquartered in Switzerland. The proposed process seemed unnecessarily complicated. But there must be tax or other reasons for this process. The so-called "social issues" and "synergies" were unspecified—that is, to be negotiated. Social issues could best be described as the struggle between officers about who stayed, who retired, who left, who got the top jobs, what everyone got paid, what jobs were eliminated, where the new headquarters would be established, what executive perks would be granted to whom, organizational structure, etc. Those discussions were never "social" in nature. In other words, our two companies would have to agree on what synergies should take place and how, as well as who would run the new parent combined company. Those recommendations would be sent to HEF to approve or disapprove as a precondition of the merger.

All synergy measures, such as "downsizing," would be finalized and implemented after the merger. The existing two

US parent companies and the combined new US parent company would not be listed on the stock exchange because all their stock would be privately held. There were many hoops to jump through. "Synergy" was a misleading term, probably created by HR departments to obscure what it did to people. It really meant reorganizing corporate departments and functions and firing employees to reduce costs.

It usually ended up that the older staff primarily got severed. No magic there. That generated the highest savings per body, both from a salary and pension standpoint. In my experience, it was exactly this age group that was most challenged to find another equivalent job. Once, I told a good friend of mine who was the VP for HR in another Fortune 500 company that I had concluded HR executives were required to take human sensitivity training at Turkish prisons. She laughed and informed me that I must be thinking of law schools. Over the years, I had witnessed many "synergies." As a lawyer, I had handled about seventy acquisitions and mergers. Only HR executives seemed to enjoy the process and the power it gave them.

Studying the offer letter further, another thing jumped out at me. This was going to be a huge deal, almost fifty billion dollars. Very large by anyone's standards. But I had never heard of the buyer. I wondered if it was for real. "Guys, have any of you ever heard of this investment firm called Horizon Energy Foundation?"

Paul had been silent, watching me and watching Sillus, who was standing behind me and looking over my shoulder. Paul reached for a paper on the conference table and handed it to me. "Ryan, we hadn't heard of it either. So that was about the first issue we tackled. We worried it might be a bogus company, or have Russian oligarchs or even drug money connections. Before Ernst Mathews died, he bought up the remains of Expanse, took it private, and sold off its assets, pocketing multiples of what he paid to buy the company. That landed him well north of at least seventy-two billion; some believe it was over eighty-five billion."

Puzzled, I replied, "What does that have to do with HEF?"

"Mathews formed HEF in the Isle of Man. Its headquarters is in Switzerland with its major office in Paris. We don't know who all the investors are, but its initial cash infusion was Mathews's funds."

"Paul, what is your point?"

"Just before his death, Mathews divided his funds between HEF and various banks in the Cayman Islands. At the same time, several large-wealth individuals invested in HEF. It certainly can afford this deal."

One of the other analysts typed on his computer to check his facts before commenting, "Cayman Island banks are where a lot of wealthy people, including some politicians, drug dealers, terrorists, and others, hide their money. Sometimes to avoid taxes but also to just hide their wealth. Sometimes they create banks and use their bank's debit cards for themselves and family, or bank transfers, and to easily move their wealth into material assets around the world."

I considered that for a moment. It was consistent with what we knew about Mathews. But that left one major question unanswered. "Team, any idea why Mathews put billions in this new foundation just before he died of a stroke? There was some business reason. It wasn't for charity. He could have put it all in his bank in the Cayman Islands."

I surveyed the room; they seemed to be listening carefully, but no one responded. "Paul? Anyone? Any thoughts as to why?"

Finally, I asked, "Do we know who controls HEF now?"

Paul replied, "Not the name of any individual, but it is administered by someone from the Swiss bank. According to an article in the *Financial Times*, HEF's liquid assets are estimated at more than $105 billion."

I figured I had now learned all I needed to know at this point. No question that HEF had sufficient capital to complete the transaction. It could certainly acquire debt for the purchase and reduce the amount of capital drawn out of the HEF fund. The team sat in silence while I considered what I had learned. Looking at their faces, I was certain of three things: they had pulled a couple of all-nighters to develop their analysis, they were eager to help, and that needed to be recognized.

"Team, thank you for your hard work. It is appreciated. Please take turns walking me through your analysis, point by point. Assume I know nothing about the deal, the companies involved, or any regulatory or legal issues you identified."

At 9:15, their briefing was finished. By then I had a decent understanding of the deal and issues. Sillus had stood behind me the whole time, except for when he took out his cell and walked to the far end of the room to make calls, to keep Farber informed of our progress. He took copious notes during the briefing. Before I went back to the boardroom, I pulled Kalie aside. I wanted to confirm my assumption.

"Kalie, when did you first hear about the merger proposal?"

"Last week when Sillus pulled us all together. This afternoon, Paul told me you were not informed. I was shocked. I didn't know that."

CHAPTER 21

The Board Meeting Resumes

At 9:25 pm, I walked into the boardroom. All board members were already seated quietly, waiting. You could have heard a mouse tiptoe on the carpet. Sillus was standing behind Farber and handed him a single page of paper. I assumed it was a summary of his notes of my meeting with the strategic planning folks. Dianna looked around the room. Everyone knew how important it was to have a good written record of these processes in case someone sued over the matter. Dianna looked directly at Mike, our corporate secretary, with his notebook and pen at the ready.

"Let the minutes show that it is 9:30 pm. All board members are physically present. There is a quorum. Also present is our CEO, corporate secretary, CFO, general counsel, and a guest, a Mr. Sillus, executive assistant to Mr. Farber."

Our corporate secretary was already busily writing notes and seemed to be trying not to be seen. I admired how he handled his responsibilities. Again, I noted that his role was far more than the care and feeding of the board.

Dianna looked again at me and then Farber and asked, "Mr. Farber, are you prepared to present the proposal?"

"Yes."

"Ryan, did you have access to all the information you need at this time to provide us with your initial advice?"

"Yes."

"Let the record reflect those responses. Mr. Farber, please begin," Dianna said.

Farber proceeded to read from the page Sillus had given him. Then he fielded questions from the board for ninety minutes. I had to admit he did a good job. But knowing what I knew about him, I could not be sure he was telling the entire truth. When he answered the last question, Dianna directed her attention to me.

"Ryan, please brief us on your initial professional evaluation."

I was still furious with Farber, but it was important to appear calm and controlled. All eyes were focused on me. After taking another deep breath, I began. "Certainly. Thank you. HEF has more than sufficient cash to purchase both EDGE and Novation, even without the leverage of using debt. We and Novation will need to pull together diligence teams. In determining if the exchange rate between the two companies is fair to our shareholders, we will also need to dig deeply into Novation's financials, including the decommissioning funds for their nuclear power plants. EDGE has set aside $414 million for future decommissioning of our two power plants, but we don't know what Novation has done. HEF will certainly want that information from both companies. But in an all-cash offer of this unique type, the fairness issues are defined."

Dianne interrupted, "Ryan, obviously Novation will conduct its own due diligence. How will HEF handle its due-diligence needs?"

"Apparently it will be relying on the due-diligence reports from us and Novation, rather than conducting its own. This is of course very unusual. But HEF has no public shareholders, so it can take that approach if it chooses. Its staff is limited and consists of typical bank and financial employees. A multitude of governmental approvals are required. The proposed premium of twenty-nine percent and other relevant factors justify a serious due diligence and evaluation of the HEF proposal."

There was an audible sigh of relief from some board members. Dianna had been taking notes. At this point she stopped writing and looked at me.

"Mr. Gorman, what do you need to adequately conduct the due diligence?"

"There is a great deal of work to do. With the right company team and full cooperation from Novation, I am cautiously optimistic we could complete due diligence in two to three months, possibly sooner. Also, we will need to retain an appropriate Wall Street company to provide the board with a fairness opinion."

Dianna interrupted again.

"And if both boards approve the merger?"

"If the two boards vote to proceed, we will also need to make formal filings for approvals both in the US and foreign countries, and also have a vote of EDGE and Novation shareholders to approve the first step of the transaction—that is, the merger of Novation and EDGE into a non-publicly traded corporation."

Dianna considered this for several seconds.

"Ryan, at this early point, do you see any legal or regulatory barriers or prohibition that would prevent this merger even if approved by shareholders?"

"No, Madam Chair. I am not currently aware of showstoppers."

The board seemed to explode with an avalanche of questions. After another hour and a half of questions, Dianna called a short recess. During the recess, she went around the table and quietly spoke with several of the board members. When the meeting resumed on the record, Dianna turned to Farber.

"Mr. Farber, is there anything else you want us to know or discuss at this point?"

"No.

"Fine. Ryan, you will lead the due diligence for us, both domestic and international. The company will make available to you all the resources you need, including the individual team members you choose. Mr. Farber will make sure that happens. If the due diligence proceeds as expected, the two senior company managements will need to meet and go into the negotiation phase, officers, structure, synergies. But I am assuming that will be subject to HEF's final decision. That will require heightened security measures to prevent any leaks. Any leak could torch this proposal. Confidentiality will be the joint responsibility of Mr. Farber and Ryan."

Farber eagerly responded, "Mr. Gorman and I will make sure the due diligence is done properly and confidentiality preserved."

Dianna studied Farber for a moment, said nothing to him, and then turned to me.

"Ryan, I want your team to be very thin. We trust you to assemble a team that gives you full confidence the work will be done correctly and confidentially. It is your responsibility to do this as expeditiously as possible. No leaks. No unnecessary delays. Does all that work for you?"

"That is fine with me. Mr. Farber?"

"Fine," Farber replied with a broad smile.

Then Dianna looked around at the other board members, looked down at notes she had taken, and continued, "I recognize that decisions on senior officer selection, corporate reorganization, and synergy downsizing are for HEF to ultimately decide if this deal is consummated. But this board wants to be informed."

Farber quickly replied, "We understand and will comply."

At 12:30 am, the meeting concluded, and Dianna came over to me and whispered, "Ryan, any word from Bill Woodworth?"

"Nothing. I'm worried. I went to his house and the condo, no sign of him. I called and left messages on all his phone, but no response."

"The week after Bill resigned, he was supposed to join me and my husband for dinner at our home. I thought I would find out more about his resignation after a few glasses of wine, but he didn't show. Neither did he call or cancel. That is not like Bill."

"When I hear from him, I will let you know."

"Ryan, I don't want to put you in an awkward position. But are you going to be able to work with Farber?"

"Dianna, from your question I assume you know what I think of Farber. But I am a professional. I know what my job is. I don't have to like the guy to work with him. I will do what needs to be done for the company. That is my responsibility. If I can't, for any reason, I will let you know and resign."

Dianna nodded and left the boardroom. For the first time, it occurred to me that if the merger was approved and I was let go, my employment contract would kick in. It had a change-of-control provision that would pay me six months' salary while I looked for a job in another company. But for now, the focus had to be on the enormous demands of the due diligence.

PART II

CHAPTER 22

Due Diligence Team Assembled

The morning after the board meeting, I called a security firm and gave them my credit card to install a new alarm system at our home. You would have thought our home was CIA headquarters. But I was convinced Anne and I would sleep better knowing our family was now safe in our own home.

Captain Jim Miller of the Tiburon police called me, asking, "Ryan, any more unpleasant incidents at EDGE, murders, or shootings? Something besides the mundane corporate stabs in the back?"

"No."

"That's good news. Glad I don't have to open another file. The best and the brightest of my three-detective investigative department are already assigned to your problems."

"I appreciate the attention. Which reminds me, any developments about how the murder of Jack Names might be connected to my past problems?"

"Our working hypothesis is that the death of Mr. Names and the analyst are unconnected."

"Anyway, with Tom away in DC, I feel much better." I neglected to mention what I had learned about his whereabouts during the attempts on my life.

"You still don't think Farber and Tom were working together?"

I thought about that for a minute before I answered, "Jim, I don't think so. It's a tempting idea, but inconsistent with Farber immediately firing Tom, and it doesn't make sense."

"Why do you say that?"

"No CEO would kill the general counsel or his family just to replace him with a puppet. The risk is too great." I kept telling myself that, but I wasn't sure I truly believed it.

• • •

The following morning, when I got to my office and opened my computer, I found an email from Sillus, commanding me to come to Farber's office as soon as I arrived. I did not relish starting my day with Farber or receiving orders through Sillus. But I had no choice. When I got to Farber's office, the first surprise was that Farber motioned for me to be seated in one of the chairs in front of his desk. That was a first. The second surprise was his general demeanor and attitude. He seemed resigned to working with me. That made me a bit nervous.

He wanted my "proposed" list of people for the due-diligence team. We both knew that in the end our board would ask me if I had full confidence in the team. If my answer was anything other than an unequivocal yes, the deal was probably dead. We quickly agreed upon a team of our employees, including me, Sillus, and Farber. Naturally, Paul and Kalie were core members of that team. Various department officers would be included only if we got to the point of negotiating management and employee issues.

I assembled the team immediately and emphasized the need for long hours, hard work, and absolute confidentiality. Farber and Sillus added their thoughts. Merger due diligence was the corporate version of a special ops mission, maybe a small war. I handed out assignments.

Paul walked the team through the steps of due diligence

and subsequent approval process. Kalie reported that Novation was on the verge of providing half a billion dollars of additional capital to its subsidiary in Colombia. This was troubling. A new half-billion-dollar investment for a Colombian company while working towards a potential merger did not seem appropriate.

Puzzled by the information, I asked Kalie, "Where did you get that information?"

"It was in the *Wall Street Journal* yesterday."

Turning to Paul, still puzzled, I said, "We need to examine the Colombian company very early. I'll ask Farber to ask Novation to put that capital infusion on hold for now."

"Certainly."

"Team, our data room here must be ready for Novation within a week. We have a ton of documents to gather, discreetly. Please contact your counterparts at Novation in New York and make sure we are both on the same schedule."

Looking around the room, seeing the excitement in people's faces, I knew we had assembled a good team. Everyone watched me, waiting for further direction. Smiling, I said, "Paul will oversee all sub-teams and appoint a leader for each sub-team. I expect a weekly written report from each sub-team leader, delivered to Paul every Friday by 4 pm. He in turn will deliver a report to me by Saturday noon. It will be my responsibility to brief Farber."

No one griped about the avalanche of work lying before them. They all wanted to be part of the team that won the game. At the end of the presentation, the only question I got was "How soon can we start?" My answer was "*Now.*"

Yes. Now the real work and real challenges would start.

CHAPTER 23

Bogotá

Over the years, several possible acquisitions in Bogotá, Colombia, had made it to my desk. But we had not pursued those. I was concerned about having a subsidiary there because of the drug trade that was alleged to be rampant in the city. But Farber ordered me to go to Bogotá and "kick the tires" and "turn over every rock." Our Washington, DC, office tried to get me a last-minute appointment with the US ambassador in Bogotá. Unfortunately, on my planned day of arrival, he would leave for a Latin American summit on human trafficking. I was disappointed he and his staff would not be available.

Bogotá was an old city in a beautiful country. I had given a speech on climate change to an international energy conference in the northern city of Cartagena, a true gem, but I had never been to Bogotá. Its history ran deep. I read a short history of the city on my phone before Paul and I boarded the plane in San Francisco. In the centuries before the Spanish immigrated to the Americas, Colombia was the home of diverse and ingenious indigenous peoples. There were still many beautiful older buildings in Bogotá from the colonial era. Like all large cities, there were portions where severe poverty and crime held inhabitants hostage.

Our company travel department booked rooms for us in the Grand Hotel, an older, classic hotel with a reputation for excellent service, lots of history, beautiful rooms, and very good security. It was in a safe, quiet location on a broad, eight-lane street divided by a beautifully planted garden.

I had not been able to sleep on the plane, but after checking in at 7 am and settling in our rooms, we met in the hotel's restaurant for some strong coffee and breakfast. Once we had ordered, I handed Paul the three-day agenda I had developed for our meetings in Bogotá plus a fourth day in Cartagena. We had the morning free before our meetings started in the afternoon.

Looking puzzled, Paul asked, "Why aren't we meeting with the US ambassador, or at least senior embassy staff?"

"Our DC office tried to set that up. The ambassador is leaving at ten this morning, and his staff is busy getting him ready for the summit on human trafficking. He's not available."

"Would you like me to see if I can get us in to see him, for a few minutes anyway? He should be able to give us a few quick high-level comments on the business climate here and his view of the company we are visiting this afternoon."

"Paul, go ahead if you want."

Paul stepped out of the restaurant. The waitress brought hot black coffee. It smelled delicious. I was enjoying my cup of caffeine when Paul returned and said, "Ryan, sorry, but we need to skip breakfast. Better finish your coffee quick. Our meeting with the ambassador is in half an hour."

I gulped some coffee and stared at Paul, who was hiding a smile.

"How did you pull that off?"

"I know people who were helpful. Let's rush. I already called for the security car."

Twenty minutes later, we were ushered into the ambassador's office. There were half a dozen other people with him. The ambassador went directly to Paul, introduced himself, and shook Paul's hand. They spoke in Spanish for several minutes, and then the ambassador introduced his six assistants. As it turned out, they were the embassy section heads. After that, Paul introduced the ambassador to me.

"Mr. Ambassador, this is Ryan Gorman, our general counsel. Please be nice to him. I can't afford to lose this job."

The ambassador laughed and extended his hand. I shook it and said, "Thank you for making time to see us. I know you have a very hectic schedule."

The ambassador was an elegant man in his fifties with a thoughtful, strong, and commanding presence. He was a career State Department employee, not someone appointed as a political favor for making sizable contributions to a candidate. Our DC office told me he was considered a key player in the war on drugs and human trafficking. Previously he had been our ambassador to Brazil, Romania, and Greece. Once we were seated, he turned to me and graciously said, "Mr. Gorman, thank you for taking the time to come to your embassy. We are here to help. What can I tell you that would be most helpful?"

"Mr. Ambassador, thank you. It would be helpful to have your view of the general business climate for American-owned companies."

"Certainly."

The ambassador and his staff gave us an extensive briefing, answering all our questions. At the end of that briefing, the ambassador said, "Paul and Ryan, hopefully this has been helpful."

I replied, "Yes, thank you. This will be very helpful—"

The ambassador interrupted, "One last thing, Mr. Gorman: please be careful about your security. Recently there's been a rash of kidnappings, mostly American and European business executives. The group responsible has infiltrated the US and European travel industry, which provides the kidnapper with information identifying high-potential targets before they even land here. Just be very cautious."

The ambassador stood, as did his senior staff. Paul and I did too. Three embassy Marines entered the room, security detail. The ambassador turned to shake hands. Paul replied in response to his advice, "I have arranged for security guards for Mr. Gorman and an appropriate vehicle. In fact, they brought us here."

"Very good. Mr. Gorman, I hope you have a successful and safe trip."

After the ambassador left the room with the Marines, a staff member cleared his throat and said, "Mr. Gorman, it's important to understand. Kidnapping is a genuine risk here. Not too long ago, a very high-level American businessman from one of our major oil companies got himself kidnapped in the wrong part of town, Bogotá's red light and adult entertainment district. The day after he was kidnapped, his company received a ransom note demanding that five million in cash be paid within forty-eight hours.

"When that was not paid, another note was delivered with his left ring finger, his wedding ring still attached. The new demand was ten million. Payment was due in forty-eight hours. His company hired a black ops company to rescue him. A week later, his wife received a box. Attached to the box was a demand letter addressed to her and to his company. Inside the box was his severed right ear and his penis. The demand was then twenty-five million. His company paid the twenty-five million within four hours. He was released that day."

I wondered if they told all American businessmen this same story as a precaution. But I felt I should acknowledge their advice and express my appreciation for the warning. I assured them, "We will definitely not spend any time in that area of the city."

For the next two hours, Paul and I remained seated in our comfortable leather chairs in the ambassador's office. We picked the brains of his senior staff. After we had looked through their subject-matter due-diligence books and folders, they made copies for us of all the documents we requested. Then it was time to go to our next meetings.

• • •

Finally, at 8:30 pm, we returned to our hotel. After I put my briefcase in my room, dictated a summary of the day to the automatic recording device at my secretary's desk, and spoke to Anne and the boys, I called Paul's room and said I was ready for dinner. I suggested a local restaurant at the end of the block. Paul replied that he would call for the security car and it would only take about fifteen minutes for them to get to the hotel. Obviously, he had swallowed the embassy story hook, line, and sinker. This irritated me, and that showed in my voice when I said, "Paul, that is absurd. It is a waste of time. We can walk there before a car would arrive."

"Ryan, this is my first job out of the government. I need this job. If anything happened to you, that would be the end. I cannot afford for that to happen."

Twenty minutes later, the security car was waiting at the front of the hotel. Besides the armed driver, there were three armed security guards in the car. We climbed into the deliberately beat-up car. I concluded it was all a show, intended to impress me and make money off gullible American businessmen. A minute later, we were at the restaurant. I was glad to get out of the cramped, dilapidated car. Being boxed in with three armed Colombian security men made me feel vulnerable, as if I had a target on my back. I resented the intrusion and anxiety they provoked.

Two guards jumped out and walked on either side of me into the restaurant. I asked for a table by the window, but Paul insisted on a table at the back of the restaurant, for security purposes. Once we were seated, I said, "That was a good meeting with the ambassador. Thank you for setting that up."

"No problem. Here to serve."

"Let's enjoy a good meal and not talk business. This restaurant is too crowded."

"Roger."

After I paid the check, I suggested we cross the street for a drink at the lively bar opposite our restaurant. Music from a great Rolling Stones tribute band was pounding. I figured if the Stones were still performing after their hard lifestyles, I was sure to live to at least 125. Paul immediately took out his mobile phone to call for the security detail.

"Paul, what are you doing?"

"Ryan, down here, like anywhere, kidnappers are looking for a big payoff. They target either the rich or people like you, senior officers from large companies that probably have kidnapping insurance on their senior officers or plenty of cash reserves. Like the embassy said, they usually start off with just a note and demand. If that is not paid quickly, they start forwarding body parts, maybe an ear, or finger, maybe a guy's penis. Do you think Farber would rush down here to pay your ransom? Really?"

"I don't think any part of me, including my penis, will be at risk just crossing to the other side of this street."

"I strongly disagree."

"I don't."

"The car will be here in fifteen minutes."

"Paul, enough is enough. I am not going to climb into that car to just cross the street. Don't be ridiculous. If you insist, the car can take us back to the hotel after we have a nightcap and listen to some good music."

Paul stood and with controlled anger said, "I won't let you endanger your life by doing something stupid. Not on my watch!"

I took a deep breath, trying to control my own temper, and stood up. "Paul, I like you. You're smart, a great analyst, and not a bad racquetball player. But I'm a senior vice president of the company where you happen to work. I am not used to middle-level employees telling me what I cannot do or telling me I am stupid. I am going to walk across the damn street and have a drink! It is entirely up to you whether you join me or not. Frankly, I don't care either way!"

People in the restaurant had turned their heads to stare at us. Having embarrassed myself, I walked out of the restaurant, took a deep breath, noticed how nice the night felt, and tried to calm down. Directly in front of me was the wide, grassy divider planted with jasmine bushes and beautiful, large trees. The mixture of the warm night air and perfume from the jasmine calmed me. The band was doing a great job with "I Can't Get No Satisfaction."

I made a mental note to apologize to Paul at breakfast the next day. I already regretted telling him that he was just a middle-level employee. It was arrogant of me and out of character. Besides, he was becoming a friend. My outburst was a combination of the busy day and lack of sleep, but that was no excuse for being rude. I walked across the four lanes and onto the planted divider, smelling the lavish perfume of the jasmine and hearing the loud rock music. The tribute band was starting "Brown Sugar." Laughter and applause drifted from the bar. It put me in a good mood, and I felt refreshed.

Still on the planted road divider, I noticed a man to my left. He was moving quickly towards me from behind a large tree, dressed in a smart sports jacket and slacks. I decided he must be coming from the same bar where I was going, and relaxed. Then I noticed that close to his belly, he held a pistol in his right hand. Instinctively, I turned towards my right and saw a second man moving towards me, his hand on a pistol tucked in the front of his pants.

I froze. Suddenly a hand firmly grabbed my right shoulder and shoved me forward. Adrenaline and panic ripped through my body. I wished I had been able to bring my pistol with me. I felt very vulnerable.

Then I heard Paul whisper sharply into my right ear, "Just keep walking. Do not slow down. Do not stop. Do not run. Go into the bar. Do not turn around. I got this."

I did as I was told and walked rapidly up the steps into the bar. Once I was safe inside and surrounded by the loud music and happy people, I took a deep breath. I felt I must have imagined the whole scene. But Paul was not next to me. I turned and looked outside. He had disarmed the two men and was pointing a gun at each of them, both lying on the ground. When he said something to them in Spanish, they jumped to their feet and ran quickly away. He emptied the magazines from the two pistols, putting the shells in his pocket and throwing the guns into the bushes.

Paul walked into the bar, looked at me, and walked towards the men's room without saying a word. He motioned me to follow. He was angry. In the bathroom, he tossed the empty magazines into a waste container. When he turned to look at me, I could tell he was very pissed. But the only thing he said was that he was calling the "fucking car" to take me "one half fucking block" back to the "fucking hotel" and I was going to "fucking stay" in my "fucking room." I felt like a recruit at basic training being dressed down by the drill instructor. This time I did not argue. I deserved it.

We did not speak while waiting for the security car. We did not speak in the car or hotel lobby or the elevator. When we got off the elevator, I was still shaken, and Paul was still angry. Our rooms were at opposite ends of the hotel corridor on the ninth floor. Suddenly my room seemed a very long distance from the elevator.

"Paul, I apologize."

He said nothing.

"Paul, I know this sounds weird, but could you walk me to my room? I'm a bit rattled."

We walked to my room in silence. I put my key into the door lock and opened it, saying thanks and good night. But my room lights were already on; I remembered having turned them off before I left.

Alarmed, I jumped back, and Paul pushed the door open. Standing in the room, next to my open briefcase, was a young man, mid-twenties with curly black hair and a large, warm smile. He was nicely dressed and wearing a red blazer with gold braiding on the shoulders. When he turned towards us, I noticed a badge on his chest with gold-braid lettering: Hotel Security.

"I hope I did not startle you, Mr. Gorman. I'm a hotel security guard. Someone reported a person loitering at this end of the hall. I wanted to make sure you were okay. You are one of our VIP guests. But everything looks fine, Mr. Gorman. I even checked in the closet and under the bed. Please make sure you lock your door, just to be on the safe side. Good night, sir."

With that, he smiled again and walked out of my room. I turned towards Paul, who was watching the security guard disappear down the hotel corridor. "Paul, first I want to apologize again, for the way I spoke to you. It was uncalled for. And thank you for walking me to my room. When I saw the security guard checking my room, I almost freaked out. That shows how our imagination can get the best of us."

Paul stared at me for a moment. Then he started speaking slowly, articulating each word as if he were lecturing a young child. "Ryan, do you really think that a hotel in Colombia, a Spanish-speaking country, would have security people dressed in a red blazer proclaiming 'hotel security' in English? Damn it. Get real! Call the front desk and asked them if they have hotel security and what uniforms they wear."

I did as Paul ordered. Of course, there were hotel security guards, but they did not wear any type of uniform. The hotel manager said it was important they blend in with the clientele.

When I put down the phone, Paul looked more concerned than angry. "Ryan, you need to take the first plane out of here, back to San Francisco. We are done here. Please."

After making our flight reservations, I did not feel better. I turned to Paul and said, "We are booked on a 6 am flight to San Francisco, through Miami. Paul, this has been really upsetting."

He continued to look unsmilingly at me, his jaw set and eyes stern.

"Paul, it's already after one. We need to leave for the airport in a couple of hours. Would you mind sitting here and just talking for a little while? I don't think I can sleep anyway. Let's talk about anything other than business."

Paul dropped, exhausted, into one of the chairs and in a tired voice said, "So, I hear you grew up on a ranch in Santa Fe. Sounds romantic Americana. I envy you that."

I replied, "You were born with a gold spoon in your mouth. I envy that."

"Did your dad bust your butt making you work as a ranch hand?"

"I didn't know my dad. It was just my mother and me. Ranch life involves a lot of work, long hours. But learning how to herd sheep, rope cattle, and break wild horses is good preparation for being a corporate general counsel."

Paul laughed and rose again to take two drinks from the mini bar, giving me one.

"Paul, what is your dad like? When we hired you, Bill Woodworth mentioned to me your dad was one of the finest men on the planet."

"Well, I wouldn't know. I wasn't around him very much. When I was seven, I was put in a New York City boarding school fifteen blocks from my home. My mom would visit me every other Sunday. But I was only allowed to come home on holidays. Frequently when I did get home, my parents were gone on vacation

somewhere or my dad was out of town on business, or my mother
was off working on some charity or a fundraiser. I spent more
time with the maids, butler, and chauffer than with my father.
Sometimes I wouldn't see him for two or three months. Seems we
have something in common, both raised without fathers."

We talked until 4:30 when we had to leave for the airport in the
derelict security car Paul arranged. After we boarded the flight, we
continued our discussion about personal experiences and our prior
work in the military. I told him about Farber and his commitment
to getting me to resign, the attempt to kill Kozlov, the phone call
claiming I had impregnated a fellow employee and forced her into
an abortion, the car crash, and Tom's death threat. We also talked
for some time about our mutual frustration that no one had been
able to find Bill. I told Paul I had installed a state-of-the-art security
system at my home to make sure Anne and the boys were safe.

After considering what I had told him, Paul asked, "Ryan, do
you think Tom was working for Farber on this stuff?"

"The police asked the same question. I don't think so. In fact,
Farber insisted on personally firing him. He threw Tom out on
the street within hours of Farber learning about the threating
note. Certainly last night's kidnapping attempt had nothing to
do with Tom. He doesn't possess the connections and experience
to arrange that."

"Ryan, our assumption is that the guys who tried to grab you
were kidnappers. But what if they weren't?"

"What do you mean?"

"Suppose it was another attempt on your life? Suppose their
intent was pure murder and they wanted to make it look like a
kidnapping that went wrong? Or suppose there was a plan for
Farber not to pay a ransom demand quickly enough? No one
would ever know."

"Paul, I really did not need that speculation, particularly as I
was about to get some sleep for the first time in two days."

"I don't like Farber."

"You have good judgment."

I realized I trusted this guy. He had saved my life, and he could have gotten himself killed, unarmed against two gunmen. He didn't have to do that, particularly after I was such a jerk to him. I needed someone to trust, someone to talk things out with without always having to burden Anne.

By the time we had landed in San Francisco, I considered Paul to be a good friend. I felt indebted.

CHAPTER 24

Dinner at My Home

We landed in San Francisco at 2 pm Friday. After retrieving my bags, I called Anne, then invited Paul to come to our home for dinner on Sunday to meet Anne and the boys. He seemed a bit reluctant, but he graciously agreed.

At exactly 7 pm Sunday, our doorbell rang. It was Paul.

"Come in. Welcome to our home."

"Thanks. I brought single malt scotch for us and flowers for Anne."

"Great. Wait, how did you get to my door without me knowing? I set the security system with alarms and the cameras for your benefit. I wanted to show it off. You just slipped through all that?"

"I was testing your system. It sucks."

"Thanks for letting me know."

"Not a problem. Just here to help."

I introduced Paul to Anne. He handed her flowers. She smiled and said, "Thank you for looking after my husband. I told him I invested two decades training him to be the best husband in town. I'm too old to start all over with someone else."

We all laughed. My sons came rushing into the kitchen and introduced themselves. Unlike most of our adult guests, they wanted to meet Paul. I had told the whole family about our exploits in Bogotá, so the boys thought of Paul as a combination of James Bond and a guardian angel. They quickly engaged him in a game of pool while Anne and I finished preparing dinner. Paul won three games out of three. Rather than disappointing the boys, that merely served to enhance Paul's reputation.

Over dinner, the conversation was energetic, with the boys trying to impress Paul with all their athletic achievements. Anne and I enjoyed watching the exchange as Paul patiently listened to them, asking them questions, complimenting them on their triumphs, and encouraging their goals. Listening well to kids is an art that few adults master. I think we forget what it was like when we were children and adults ignored us.

After dessert, the boys started on the dishes. Paul and I walked into my study. He noticed a framed picture of my dad in his Army uniform, medals and all. Below that, in the same frame, was a letter.

"Ryan, I thought you lost you dad before you were born?"

"Well, in a way. My dad was driving to the hospital when my mother went into labor. Before he reached the hospital, he was shot. He survived until the day after I was born, but I never saw him. He wrote this letter to me in the hospital before he died. I have always kept it hanging on my wall here, with a copy in my office at EDGE. I look at it often."

Short and printed in bold handwriting, it read:

Dear son,

Your mom and I named you Ryan after her favorite uncle. It's Gaelic and means "little king." The biggest regret of my life is that it doesn't look like I will see you grow up into a man. But I know you will be a fine man, honest, loyal, and the type of man who never gives up, never runs from adversity, is a leader, and can always be counted on to do his duty. I know you will always make me proud of you.

Love and God bless you,
Your dad

Paul read it a second time, this time aloud, then patted me on the shoulder.

Anne interrupted us. "You boys should have some adult conversation, alone. I must look over some math homework, listen to an oral report due tomorrow, and help Aaron get ready for a quiz. I suggest you take the scotch up to the gazebo and hot tub where you won't be disturbed by Paul's new fan club."

We did as directed. My sons had assembled a redwood gazebo kit to enclose the hot tub as last year's Christmas present. Aaron had made me a sign for the door of the gazebo, which read: Dad's Office, Do Not Disturb. I broke it in while the family was away skiing. It had quickly become a neighborhood man cave, although the boys and their buddies made more use of it than I did.

Paul and I got into the tub, turned on the jets, and sipped our scotch. It was good, peaty—one of my favorite single malts. Paul looked serious. "Ryan, you have a great family. Congratulations. You lucked out with Anne. She's beautiful, smart, and charming. No man deserves such a smart and lovely wife."

"Thank you. I'm very lucky. By the way, I noticed you charmed my wife in five minutes."

"I get along well with women."

"Paul, if I were single, you'd make a great wingman. But I would certainly keep you away from any girlfriends."

"I'm pretty good during the approach. But unlike you, I'm not much good at maintaining a relationship."

"After a while they lose interest?"

"You mean, figure out that I'm an asshole?"

"You said it, not me."

He laughed and said, "Your secretary doesn't like me, does she?"

"I don't think that's her issue. She thinks you are a lady-killer. That worries her."

"I do find most women very attractive, all types of women. Every woman is beautiful in her own way. But I also think women figure out I will do anything they want. Fulfill their darkest fantasies."

I laughed, then replied, "So, you're telling me you're just a cheap slut?"

"Probably."

"By the way, one of the downsides of your being unmarried and becoming my friend is that my wife is already running through her list of the single women she knows, trying to decide who would be the best wife for you—someone who can save you from yourself, cure you from the lonely disease of bachelorhood."

"I'll keep practicing my Houdini escape moves."

I laughed and pushed Paul's head under the water. When he came up for a breath, he smiled at first; then that serious stare came on his face again.

"Ryan, on our Bogotá vacation, you told me that you did not see any connection between Farber and what Tom did or tried to do."

"I don't. He fired Tom right after I told him what happened."

"Would it change your mind to know that Tom was not fired? He was given early retirement, full benefits, and a severance payment equal to two years' salary. He is only fifty-two, but his retirement is calculated as if he stayed with the company until he was sixty-five and received a five percent annual raise each year, compounded. Farber's direct orders. He's making more money from his retirement payments than they pay you as general counsel. Farber got him the job in DC at a law firm Farber used extensively for his prior company. The inducement was Farber's agreement to throw plenty of lobbying work their way. Sounds more like a bribe or payoff than a termination for misconduct."

This news startled me. "How do you know that?"

"I'm resourceful. Trust me, I made some inquiries. It's all true. Tom and Farber signed an agreement shortly after you left the company that day. It's in the HR and accounting records. If you want, I can get a copy for you."

I took a deep breath, studied Paul's concerned face, and finished my scotch in angry silence. I had known that Farber would prefer to have Tom as the general counsel. Per the policy I had established before Farber arrived, all legal opinions had to come through my office. Several opinion drafts from Tom to Farber were drafts I could not approve; they were not legally sound and were clearly tailored to support Farber's objectives.

For a few minutes I sat motionless, thinking, then looked at Paul and said, "That changes things."

"Yes, it does. I know you don't like me to tell you what to do, being just a middle-level employee."

"Paul, I already apologized for that. It was a stupid thing to say. I'm sorry. I consider you a good friend. I hope you feel the same."

"As a good friend, then, I have certain rights too. Including the right to tell you to be very careful. I don't know what game Farber is playing, but it's not pretty. Do you think he had the HEF deal in mind a long time ago and thought it would be easier to get it through the board without you? Is that possible?"

"Right now, I think anything is possible."

"We finally agree on something."

I poured us another finger of scotch, thinking about what Paul had just said. It seemed logical, and it was disturbing. But there was no concrete proof connecting (1) Farber's harassment of me, (2) his generosity to Tom, (3) the proposed merger, and (4) Tom's misconduct. I still did not want to jump to conclusions. The evidence piling up was only circumstantial.

After several minutes of silent soaking, I started unwinding just a bit.

Paul broke the silence. "Ryan, I can feel you thinking like a lawyer, weighing evidence based on your 'beyond a reasonable doubt' or 'preponderance of the evidence' rules. You need to think like a detective or analyst."

That was the second time someone had lectured me on that point. After another period of silence, Paul said, "Ryan, please let me send a friend of mine to check out your security system. He can fine-tune it."

"Certainly. Just let me know when."

"I know Farber has made a career out of harassing you. It's no secret around EDGE. There's a lot of speculation as to why. There's also an office pool, betting on the date you finally tell him to go fuck himself and resign."

I laughed, then said, "He has tried to get rid of me from the week he arrived at EDGE. Sometimes it's petty, sometimes vicious. Sometimes he looks for surrogates to punish me, like trying to disembowel the law department. Paul, you also need to be careful. He will figure out we're friends and might go after you."

"Ryan, I've had drug lords, terrorists, lunatics, and some truly dangerous people, like Washington politicians, try to get rid of me. I think I can handle Farber."

Changing the subject, I said, "I hope Bill Woodworth's resignation turns out to be a prank and he comes back. But I have a terrible feeling about it."

"I checked with my dad's secretary yesterday. My father unleashed some world-class international investigators to locate Bill Woodworth, but no luck. Nada."

We sat for several minutes until Paul broke the ice by changing subjects and asked, "What is the magic of keeping a relationship with a woman, like you and Anne. Why does it work all these years?"

"It was a challenge at first. I was raised in a culture that taught me that as a man, I was responsible for making sure everything in the family worked out well. All things must be balanced. Always strive for harmony. If there was ever a problem, it was the man's job to fix it and get over it. Although my dad was gone, he had three brothers, and my mother had two. My five uncles made it clear to me how they believed a man should act."

"What was the initial challenge you mentioned?"

"Well, you've met my wife. What do you think you know about her now?"

"She's beautiful, very smart, charming, a loving mother, and a very strong person."

"Good. You could have been a psychologist."

Paul laughed.

"That type of woman does not want her husband to act as if he is responsible for everything and must always be in control. Anne believes marriage is a partnership of equals."

"How did you resolve it?"

"I learned to agree with her."

"You're smarter than you look."

"Paul, another rule from Rome, in addition to testifying: The hot tub is a confessional. Nothing said here gets repeated elsewhere. Okay?"

"Absolutely. But I have lots to confess, Father."

"I don't think that's the type of confession I want to hear."

We both chuckled.

It felt good to have shared my concerns, anger, and fears. After Paul left a couple of hours later, I headed to the bedroom. Anne was sitting up in bed, reading one of her psych books. She smiled. "Did you have a good time?"

"Yes. We talked a lot. I think we've become very close friends. He wants to have someone he knows improve our security system."

"Good."

"What do you think?"

"I think you needed to unload with someone other than me. Also, I'm glad we're going to improve the security system."

"He's also concerned that Farber was involved with Tom's behavior."

"So am I. I didn't want to worry you, so I didn't mention it."

Once again, Anne was ahead of me in understanding people. She said, "By the way, the boys wanted to join you two in the hot tub and ask Paul about his time in the military. You know, all the gory details. I told them it was impolite. They are very impressed with Paul."

"I don't think he could talk about it, at least not the parts they would find most interesting."

"Well, I also think you need to relax more."

"I do."

"Ryan, I'm glad you found some guy to talk with, discuss the hellhole called EDGE, and whatever else men like to talk about. But remember, Paul works at the same company you do. I think you can trust him, and that's my professional first impression, but just be a little cautious. Okay?"

"Okay, Dr. Anne."

I tossed my clothes on a chair, climbed into bed, cuddled next to Anne, and slept better than I had in many days.

CHAPTER 25

Novation or Bust

Our due-diligence work went smoother than we had expected. We were significantly ahead of schedule, and it was time to meet. Novation suggested a lodge in British Columbia, on a small private island in the Inland Passage area north of Vancouver. It was luxurious, remote, with a private airport runway, and a place where billionaires partied in seclusion. Farber was euphoric. He told me that only the "best people" stayed there. I thought it was excessively expensive, but it did seem like a safe location for this type of meeting. Farber quickly sent out a memo:

TO: All Attending Meeting with Novation:
STRICTLY CONFIDENTIAL
If you received this hand-delivered, confidential memo, your attendance is required at the above meeting. The company travel department has reserved the necessary company planes. The meeting is expected to last the entire week but could be longer. You are prohibited from bringing any mobile phone or computer device. For security reasons, the location will be kept confidential until you are on board the plane. Further instructions will be delivered to you later this afternoon.

R. Farber, CEO

This memo was delivered by Sillus to each team member. I was interested in meeting Muab Stevens, Novation's CEO. I remembered seeing him on the TV at Mathews's wake and had listened to him give a speech at an energy conference. He was very impressive. I wondered how he and Farber could forge a working relationship. Paul provided a briefing and gave each team member a thumb drive with all the due-diligence material. It could only be opened with their fingerprint and on the laptop already at the lodge in the room assigned to them. The team was both anxious and excited. So was I.

PART III

CHAPTER 26

Playing Life and Death Charades in a Canadian Lodge

If the meeting went well and the necessary approvals were obtained, I would soon need to find another job. Saturday afternoon, I polished my résumé. Anne was pleased. At 5:15 Sunday morning, Farber, Sillus, and I boarded the company's G6. Sillus and Farber ignored me the entire flight, sitting together, reviewing the yellow folder I had seen before, thumbing quickly through part of the due-diligence reports, and sharing other documents. When we landed on the island, Farber was in a great mood.

Putting his arm around my shoulders, Farber enthusiastically said, "Ryan, this is damn exciting. We are making what will be one of the greatest diversified, international companies. I can't wait. And thank you for all the great work you have done on the due diligence. The reports were excellent."

I was shocked and doubted he had read the entire report. He had used my first name for the first time. *Why now?* It was not yet noon, and the day was already full of surprises.

Muab Stevens and Joyce Deer were already sequestered in their third-floor conference room. They would join us at seven for cocktails and dinner. Our company security escorted us to our rooms. Since I suspected Farber would spend a lot more time consulting and working with Sillus than me, I was surprised that my assigned room was across the hall from Farber's suite with

Sillus. Maybe they wanted to keep an eye on me.

After showering and changing clothes, I checked out the sumptuous lodge. It was obvious no expense had been spared to make billionaires feel at home.

A suite was assigned to each officer. Staff shared rooms, four to a room. We had equipped each suite and room with special computers disabled to prevent internet access. This was a security measure. As an additional precaution, the hotel's internet system was entirely turned off. Only Sillus, Farber, Joyce, Muab, and I had been permitted to bring our own laptops and phones with their hot spots.

I walked down to the water and found a blue bentwood bench at the end of the dock. It was comforting and inviting. I sat there. The boat at the end of the dock caught my eye—a beautiful, classic, wooden 1970s Chris Craft, impeccably maintained. A pod of orca whales surfaced as they passed by the island, hunting for prey. I took a deep breath and focused on the natural beauty around me. I remembered my mother's favorite lines from the Navajo chant the Beauty Way:

> I walk with beauty before me,
> I walk with beauty behind me,
> I walk with beauty below me,
> I walk with beauty above me,
> I walk with beauty around me,
> My words will be beautiful.

Reciting this old prayer calmed me.

It was soon time to go to the grand dining room for cocktail hour and dinner with the two CEOs and Joyce. It was never too early to start developing good business relationships.

Muab and Joyce were already there when I arrived. Muab looked bright, strong, and elegant with ebony skin. Joyce looked stern, dressed in a severe, black Nehru suit. I noticed she wore no jewelry, and her hair was cut short on the sides with the top standing up, much like a long crew cut. The hairstyle reminded me of one of my favorite female rock stars. I introduced myself to Muab and was greeted warmly. After we shook hands, he introduced his companion. "Ryan, this is Joyce Deer, our senior VP for Human Resources."

Joyce and I shook hands. Her handshake was firmer than Muab's. There was an intensity about her. As she stared into my eyes, it felt as if she were trying to search my mind. I suspected she was very good at her job. We silently studied each other until Muab interrupted.

"You and Joyce should be relaxed about this deal. Other employees must wonder about their future careers. They don't have your advantage. Ryan, we lost our general counsel to a stroke. We didn't replace him. In my view, we will need your skills going forward. You both are key to our future success."

"Well, Mr. Stevens, there is a lot of work ahead of us before we get to the finish line."

"Please call me Mo. Everyone does. Mr. Stevens was my father. He passed away last year. My parents were both physicians from Somalia and immigrated to New York before I was born. After they became US citizens, they worked with Doctors Without Borders. They never cared if they made any money. Unlike my parents, God bless their souls, my ambitions lie elsewhere."

"I can't say my life goal matches your parents'."

Joyce smiled and said, "Ryan, I hear you are a great racquetballer."

"You folks do your homework."

Joyce again studied me before commenting, "I like to know who we are dealing with."

"I'm afraid my opponents on the court would not describe my game as great."

They both laughed politely. Other than this brief exchange, there was no discussion related to the deal, which was appropriate in Farber's notable absence. Instead, we discussed the magnificent lodge and its famous chef. At 7:30, Farber arrived fashionably late with Sillus in tow. Farber quickly made his way to Mo.

"Hello, Mo, it's a pleasure to see you again."

"Well, Rick, it is good to see you again. Since Mathews's wake, we've only talked via phone."

Farber pointed at me. "I see you've already met Ryan. This is Sillus, my special assistant. I assume I finally have the pleasure of meeting Joyce in the flesh."

Another surprise. Farber had never mentioned he'd had multiple phone calls with Mo and Joyce and had met with Mo. *What else don't I know?*

Mo and Farber studied each other while smiling and laughing. *Preparing for a chess game or cage fight?* I was certain that I would not fall asleep over dinner.

Remarkably, the conversation during the meal stayed entirely clear of the project. A stranger observing us would have assumed we were longtime, good friends without any business to discuss. Mo and Farber exchanged stories about their multiple achievements. Joyce and I mainly observed. Everyone was in a good mood following the excellent food and wine. We retired to the library for after-dinner drinks.

The library, heavy on carved mahogany shelves and leather-bound books, was inviting. The soft glow from the fireplace warmed the room and softened the atmosphere. I looked around, admiring our surroundings. Farber handed Mo a small note. Mo read it, then tossed it into the fireplace.

On the antique, carved wooden bar sat an array of fine beverages. Farber and Mo selected a thirty-five-year-old fine French Napoleon cognac. Joyce and I chose an excellent single malt scotch, but I would not drink before any business discussion.

Sillus chose a Cuban rum and retired to his room. The four of us sat on the two sofas in front of the fireplace. For several minutes in silence, we enjoyed the ambience and sound of the crackling fire. Then Mo brought up the subject of the potential transaction.

"Rick, before our teams of subordinates arrive, there are several things we should resolve. Senior social matters."

Farber smiled and nodded. "Go ahead, Mo. Have you been thinking about our conversation Friday afternoon?"

I wondered what was in the note they'd exchanged and how much of what they were going to discuss would surprise only me.

Farber replied, "Yes. I concluded you are right."

"New York?"

"Mo, San Francisco is my favorite, and it will always be my primary residence. But I agree: New York has Wall Street and is more convenient for flights to our subsidiaries in Europe and Latin America. You win that point. The new headquarters should be in New York City."

"Good."

Farber smiled at Mo and continued, "Of course, I'll require a suitable place in New York, something along the Gold Coast."

"Of course. The company will have to provide something appropriate in the general area of my home. Now, about that eighty-three-foot yacht. Did you see the pictures I sent you?"

"It will be useful for my business entertainment purposes," Farber replied.

They are throwing around shareholder money like pirates at Fort Knox. Is this charade for the benefit of their own egos? Certainly not for the benefit of Joyce and me? They were eating at the shareholders' trough with no guilt about their greed. I wondered what the buyer would say if they heard this.

"Rick, Joyce has been studying senior executive issues. Joyce, what do industry standards dictate for an international company the size of what we are making?"

Joyce slowly pulled an envelope from her pocket, opened it, and took out a single sheet of paper. I speculated that what she was about to say was known to Mo and Faber but would again be shocking to me.

"Yes, we conducted a careful examination of market conditions."

"Have you secured a respected executive compensation firm that will forcefully support these findings, if anyone asks?"

"Yes. I interviewed several and selected the best."

"Joyce, why don't you give us the full packages, salaries, bonuses, and fringe benefits for the top four positions."

"Certainly. We are advised that for the two of you, the annual base compensation should be twenty-one million, with a potential bonus ranging from forty to one hundred fifty percent of the base salary, standard fringe benefits, a prepaid debit card of one hundred thousand without a requirement for receipts, and other typical benefits. Pension to be eighty-five percent of the highest annual compensation."

Without any discussion, Farber and Mo both nodded their agreement.

Unbelievable. Of course, many corporate CEOs make this type of money. But we would soon be deciding how many people to fire to create synergies savings. This made me sick.

Joyce continued, "Now, the two executive vice presidents will start at an annual base salary of four million, bonus potential forty to one hundred twenty-five percent of base salary, same fringes, but the annual debit card should be reduced to forty thousand."

Looking at Farber, Mo asked, "Rick, do you agree with the experts that this approach is reasonable?"

"Yes, I do. Very reasonable. Mo, now I would like to hear your proposal on who should hold the two senior positions."

"I have given that a lot of consideration. My recommendation is that you take the position of CEO for the first three years. I will take the second position, COO. After three years, I will become

CEO, and you continue as chairman of the board for two years. At the end of those two years, we both retire. How does that sound?"

Farber smiled and took a few sips of his cognac while he gave the proposal more thought. After a minute of silence, he sat his glass down on the table.

"Agreed," Farber said with a smile, and they shook hands.

Mo continued, "Now, the two executive vice presidents. I recommend that one have responsibility for the law department, shareholder services, SEC compliance, lobbying, pension plans, and a few other legalistic things. The international operations will also report to that office. The second executive vice president will have responsibility for strategic planning, corporate policies, internal audit, finance, treasury, union matters, human resources, public relations and accounting, plus other service groups."

"I agree."

"Good."

Joyce and I said nothing, watching Farber and Mo enjoy the future they saw for themselves, with all its power and wealth. They each took another sip of their thirty-five-year-old cognac. Then Farber turned towards me and said, "Ryan, I looked at your compensation. We only pay you $177,500. Your max bonus potential is capped at twenty percent of your base salary. I was truly shocked. Obviously, we've been underpaying you. As far as the salary for the general counsel of the future company, that will probably be in the range of $750,000, but Mo and I do not see you in that role."

Farber had always known my compensation. Strangely, Mo was smiling at me while Joyce studied my expression intently. *Is she waiting to see my reaction when Farber says I'll be booted out when the merger happens? No surprise there.*

Mo sat back in his chair, rolled the liquid in his glass, took a sniff, and then let a second taste of his cognac move around his mouth, gazing at me thoughtfully. I decided to take a sip of my scotch. He leaned towards me and said, "Ryan, you should know that Rick and I agree that you have great potential. We want you to accept the future position of the first executive vice president. You will then select a person of your choosing to assume the general counsel position, who will report directly to you."

Shit!

I was so shocked that I gasped and almost choked on my scotch, which would have been a mortal sin. For a moment, I was speechless. It was not just the extraordinary amount of money they were throwing at me; it was also the expanded responsibilities, beyond anything I had imagined. I barely managed to stammer a reply.

"I would be honored to have that responsibility."

Farber smiled broadly, no doubt enjoying himself and the shocked look on my face. Then he turned towards Joyce. "Joyce, we would like you to accept the other executive vice president position?"

"I will be pleased to do so."

Farber cleared his throat before he spoke. "After the first five years, Mo and I will retire. We cannot pick our successors. That's up to HEF. But there is every reason to assume that if you two do your jobs properly, you will succeed us."

I studied Joyce's expression and the faint smile on her face. She was not surprised at all.

Was I the only one here who did not already know what was going to be offered before it was put on the table this evening? Maybe the decision to include me in their little group was made only recently. They certainly showed no doubt this merger would be consummated.

Mo regarded me for a moment, then looked at Farber, who seemed to nod. Mo said, "Ryan, unlike you, I haven't practiced law for many years. I am simply a businessman. I want to pose a legal question to you."

"Okay. Shoot."

"The circumstance we have here is a merger, let's say a potential merger, of our two companies. After the merger, it would be a private company owned entirely by HEF. Now, my layman's opinion is that the social issues we just discussed are not matters for approval by our current boards of directors. They are matters exclusively reserved to HEF. Do you agree?"

"My initial reaction is yes. But I will give it more thought."

"Good. We must therefore keep these things to ourselves. These matters have nothing to do with any of our due-diligence work or the value of the merger to our shareholders. No one other than the four of us should know. Understood?"

Being a lawyer, I had to fill in a missing procedural step. "But, Mo, any so-called social issues would be subject to the approval of HEF. We only make recommendations."

"Yes. We must get this merger done quickly."

Are these matters already approved by HEF? Is that possible?

The evening had gone from surprising to unreal. I felt numb. Joyce continued to study me. Mo stood, poured himself another cognac, picked up two Cuban cigars, and stretched.

"It's been a productive meeting. I suggest we all retire for tonight. Our support teams will be arriving tomorrow afternoon, and we should get some rest."

Smiling, Joyce placed her hand on my knee and said, "Ryan, let's meet for breakfast outside on the patio. Say around nine. We need to discuss logistics before our teams arrive at four."

"Okay."

I realized that I had not finished my drink, but I left my glass there. I was still suffering from a brain freeze, as my kids would say. Mo and Joyce walked quickly out of the room, leaving Farber and me alone.

"Ryan, I am pleased you are on board with us. You have a bright future."

When Farber and I stood, I noticed that Joyce had forgotten to pick up the paper with the salary and bonus information. I folded it and put it in my pocket. Farber and I headed out of the library, and he put his arm over my shoulder and gave me a bit of a bro-hug. "Ryan, I want to apologize for anything I may have inadvertently said in the past. Have a good evening. I'm going for a walk out on the dock. Want to come?"

"Thank you, but I think I'll pass. Too much excitement tonight. I'll get some sleep."

Farber smiled and went outside to join Sillus, who was standing on the porch. I started up the stairs, trying to catch up with Joyce and return the note she had left in the library. When I reached the third floor, I spotted Mo and Joyce walking closely. He had his hand on Joyce's waist. She had her hand on his butt.

I decided to return to the library, finish my scotch, and watch the fire turn into glowing embers. There was a lot to digest. When I entered the library, I noticed the wadded note Farber had given Mo earlier at the EDGE of the fireplace and stooped to inspect it. It read: All is agreed.

Damn it! It's Farber's handwriting. It was all a charade!

I sat there for some time, trying to make sense out of the evening. When the fire died out, I went to my room. I heard Farber and Sillus talking in the hallway and opened my door to give Farber the note Joyce had left. Across the hall, Farber held a tray of fruit he must have picked up in the lobby. His door was open, and Sillus was standing there, wearing red silk pajama bottoms but nothing else. I stood there only long enough to close my door quietly. This had proven to be an evening to remember.

The money they were throwing at me seemed obscene. *Is this some type of bribe? Why?* Our analysis showed the merger would be fantastic for our shareholders. *So why do I feel conflicted?*

CHAPTER 27

Teams Arrive and the Fun Begins

The next morning, I rolled out of bed slowly. I pulled on my shorts, my favorite T-shirt from the SEALs, slipped on my running shoes, and headed for the outdoors. I wanted to run before my spirit weakened and I decided to sleep a bit more. Being outside the lodge at 5:30 in the morning was like waking to the world and being the only person there. From the magnificent lodge porch, I took in the sheer beauty of the morning. No one was in sight. No human sounds broke the silence.

Then I heard the shriek of an eagle up in one of the giant pines. It was a large, powerful bird of prey. It spread its great wings wide and flew, seeking something to feed on. The morning air was fresh and full of the scent of pines and the water, mixed into a pure, honest smell. I started running. As I reached my stride, my heart beat strongly. It hurt to breathe. I watched the eagle dive into the water and catch its meal in its large, strong claws, then lift it into the air. It landed in its nest and tore its prey to pieces.

Thinking about last night was like watching a movie. My thoughts suddenly drifted to the note Jack Names had left for me on his thumb drive, something like "All the world's a stage and we are merely players." *Why would Farber and Mo include me and Joyce?*

I took a short break and sat on a large boulder along the shore, gazing out at the water.

What are my responsibilities as general counsel of EDGE? Should I tell my board about all the money and positions discussed, even though it's not a matter for my board to approve or disapprove?

When I reached my room, dropped my clothes, and stood in the hottest shower I could stand, I was still thinking about the night before. There had been so much "good news." But I felt a deep sense of unease. I dressed quickly, made a short call to Anne's office to say good morning and check on the boys, then walked to the dining room to meet Joyce.

She was already seated next to the front window of the dining room, which looked out onto the dock. We were the only guests. Joyce must have sensed me. She stood and smiled. I noticed she was now wearing a pair of jeans with a blue silk blouse. I wondered why such an attractive and obviously bright woman would wear a black Nehru suit for a business dinner. Then I remembered one of Anne's lectures to me that women in business often needed to downplay their femininity to be taken seriously by men. Joyce extended her hand, and I shook it.

"Good morning, Ryan. Beautiful day, isn't it?"

"Yes, it is. I took a run around the island. Absolutely gorgeous."

"Personally, I settle for hot and cold showers."

We laughed while I took a seat. Last night, I'd felt she examined me like a bug under a microscope. But now she was a completely different person.

"Joyce, do you jog or run?"

"Not if I can avoid it. Although sometimes at the office it feels like I am on a treadmill all day."

"I can relate to that."

After ordering, I remembered Joyce's forgotten note and

handed it to her. She took it without comment and put it in her briefcase. I wondered if she had left it for me on purpose, to let me confirm the offers of the night.

"Do you have a family—I mean, a spouse or partner? Kids?"

"I had a husband once. But one day he told me that he thought I loved my work more than him and our daughter. I agreed and divorced him. That was one of the best decisions I ever made. It freed me to focus only on myself and my career."

"Tell me about your daughter."

"I don't see her much. She lives a few blocks from me, but my work is very demanding."

Joyce reached down under the table, brought up her "golden" Zero briefcase, and removed three separate Excel sheets. One was labeled Headquarters - Synergy. The second was labeled Us Operating Companies - Synergy. The third was labeled Foreign Operating Companies - Synergy.

Synergy was a part of any merger. I detested it. It was too often a quick way to justify an acquisition, or to increase earnings post-merger. Usually, I could escape into all the legal work and issues of a merger. But in this potential transaction, that wouldn't be allowed.

"Well, Joyce, I acknowledge the expectation to find synergies to justify the twenty-nine percent premium. But this case is a bit unique. If the headquarters is in NYC, we will lose a lot of San Francisco employees who will not leave the Bay Area. Besides, shouldn't we wait for HEF to take on this task if the merger is consummated?"

"I heard you're not enthusiastic about the synergy process."

That was an understatement. "See all the saving if we just fire a lot of people!" I quipped, not feeling lighthearted at all.

"We have been given very clear directions from HEF as to the amount of dollars we must cut from the staff budget in the first year after the merger. This is not an option. It is a requirement."

Another discussion with the buyer? Why am I not involved in those? Why do I have to hear this from Joyce? Why doesn't Farber keep me in the loop?

"Joyce, I appreciate these Excel spread sheets. Our HR vice president will be here this afternoon, and she can handle those matters."

"Ryan, all the corporate staff departments will be reporting to either you or me in the new organization. In other words, it is our personal responsibility."

She was right. "I apologize. I see your point. Please give me the number of dollars I'm expected to discover in each of my future departments."

She handed me an envelope. Just as I had expected, the numbers had already been decided. Without comment, I put it in my pocket. No sense spoiling my breakfast now. I wanted to change the subject and said, "Joyce, how do you see the process of restructuring the US and foreign companies?"

"Our teams, under our guidance, will have to work through those matters, and we will revise and then submit that to Mo and Farber. The only guidance we have from HEF is to keep our hands off the power plants. The buyer will address that after the merger."

This whole discussion put me in a sour mood. I was pissed at Farber for several reasons. I knew my next question was insignificant in the scheme of things. But I couldn't resist.

"In the new headquarters, where will Sillus report?"

She laughed. "Sillus is destined for a vice presidency in your utility subsidiaries in Southern California."

"I assume Farber has approved that."

"Of course."

How can I put a dollar value on not having to see Sillus every day?

She continued, "Ryan, one more thing we need to discuss.

When we are going through the synergy process, we need to make sure our results reflect real-world diversity."

"My law department is forty-eight percent women, thirty-four percent minority. The only preference I make in hiring is for veterans, and that is usually for our Linus subsidiary. But I sense you have something else in mind."

"I have put together a chart, which I will send to your room once it is finalized. It shows the percent of employee that should be Caucasian females, lesbians, gays, Hispanic female and male heterosexuals, Hispanic lesbians, Hispanic gays, Black males, Black lesbians, Black gays, and the same for Asians and Native Americans, etc."

"Joyce, what about White heterosexual men? I didn't hear them mentioned. Surely, they make up a sizable portion of the population."

"White heterosexual males are the problem. They are not part of the solution!"

"You actually believe that?"

"We are not running a welfare organization. We will capture more dollars by severing older staff members first. That age group is heavily older, White, heterosexual males. They normally have the highest salaries and greatest financial impact on pension costs. Hence their departure produces the highest savings and contributes to diversity."

"Joyce, these are also the people with the greatest experience and historical knowledge of the company, industry, and their areas of expertise. I agree some younger people may have higher energy levels and new ideas. When we were young, we thought we knew it all. But in fact, we did not know what we did not know. Over time, we gain more experience and some wisdom. That has a high value."

"Ryan, I know enough about your family heritage to know you have institutionalized the idea of elder wisdom. But this is the twenty-first century."

"It is not just a matter of cultural background. My view is based on years of personal experience. I do not believe a bias against people based on age is appropriate."

"I'm not going to debate this with you. We need to clear out the older ranks. Period. We want younger people fighting hard, tooth and nail, to please us and sort out the losers. You must come up with half of the total synergy savings. My approach is the most effective in turning in impressive synergy dollar savings. It also reduces the number of employees who need to be terminated."

"Have you discussed this with Mo and Farber?"

She smiled. Again, she had a sense of triumph or superiority on her face.

"The buyer selected me as the communication channel with Mo and Farber. Trust me. These instructions come from the top person at HEF."

"Madam, you're full of surprises."

CHAPTER 28

Synergy Fun and Games

Back in my room, I opened the envelope Joyce had given me, specifying the minimum dollar amounts to be "achieved" through downsizing. I had not expected to be pleased with what I would see. I was not wrong. I sat on the bed and studied synergy numbers.

Why is Joyce the buyer's chosen conduit? Is she trying to warn me, or threaten me, just to stroke her ego?

The phone next to my bed rang. It was Paul. "Hi, Ryan. How is the lovefest going? Everyone singing 'Kumbaya'? Or has someone already taken out a machete and poison darts?"

"Sort of the former. That's the problem. Or it's not a problem. I can't decide. But where are you now?"

"In the parking lot about ready to turn over my luggage, board a prop plane, drop my mobile phone in a locker, and see your smiling face. Why do you ask? Can I do something for you?"

"It's about Joyce Deer. She is the sole conduit to HEF, not Mo or Farber. It puzzles me. Can you get some more background on her?"

"Can I ask Kalie to do that? I'm due on the plane in fifteen minutes. Kalie is coming an hour behind the rest of us, because the tax data Novation sent us today is different from what they sent us last week. She needs to rerun the numbers before she joins us."

"Okay. See you in wonderland."

• • •

At 1 pm I realized I had not eaten lunch, so I dressed and went to the dining room. Joyce had finished her meal and was seated on the veranda. I gathered fruit on a plate and approached her. She smiled.

"Hi, Joyce. Admiring the view?"

"I was just thinking about how much money people are willing to pay for this type of view. Missed you at lunch. Were you sleeping or working in your room?"

"Reading, working, and thinking."

She opened the file she held in her hand and started reading. I sat in the white wicker chair next to her. After a few minutes of silence, I felt the urge to fish for more information.

"Joyce, I didn't see Mo or Farber."

"They're having lunch together in Mo's suite, preparing for this afternoon. They'll greet the officer group that arrives at four. You and I will do the same with the due-diligence staff teams at five, but we should both be at the meeting with the officers."

"Of course. How do you propose we handle the welcome briefing with our two teams?"

"I think we should talk to them together. You're the lawyer; you should do the confidentiality speech. Then I can talk about logistics and scheduling matters. Does that sound right?"

"That's fine. Our teams have prepared individual due-diligence reports and will update those here but won't exchange them yet. At some point, we should share those with each other, or at least share redacted versions."

"What do you mean by redacted?" Joyce asked.

"Remove any references to individual people in either company. There is no good reason to share any of our assessments about the strengths or weaknesses of each other's management."

With that, Joyce stood and said, "Ryan, let's walk. I don't want to talk about business here."

I thought of commenting that we were alone on the veranda but decided to not press the point. For a few minutes we did not speak, only walked in silence.

As we walked, I considered the players. There was Mo and Farber; Mo and Joyce; Joyce and the buyer; Mo, Farber, and Joyce; Mo, Joyce, Farber, and me. Those were the dominant personal relationships. Joyce claimed she had the closest relationship with HEF. *But is that true?*

"Joyce, you seem to have a good working relationship with the buyer."

"Yes, I do."

"How did that develop?"

"I used to work for Mathews. Before the stock price collapsed, he suggested I broaden my experience. He recommended Novation, and I agreed. Later, he founded HEF. He introduced me to the Swiss bankers who manage the fund. I got along well with them from the start."

"Too bad Mathews didn't live long enough to enjoy HEF and his billions."

"Yes, tragic really. He was like a father figure to me."

"My hunch is that the buyer first came to you with this deal, since they already knew you."

"Of course." Her voice and face showed a high degree of self-satisfaction.

"Why did the buyer also include EDGE in this deal?"

"Maybe they wanted to start off big, all in one bit."

I wondered if Mathews had also recommended to Farber that he join EDGE.

CHAPTER 29

Leopards and Jackals at Play

At 4 pm sharp, two private jet airplanes landed, each with one company's selected senior officers. The officers approached each other, making introductions, while security took their baggage to their rooms. They were ushered into the dining room, where Mo, Farber, Joyce, and I were waiting. They looked restrained and working hard to smile. There was no evidence of enthusiasm, only guarded concern. This was what I expected. No one knew how this would play out. They understood their professional futures were now uncertain. Farber spoke first.

"Good afternoon and welcome. I hope each of you relaxed on the flight. Once you are in your suites, you can load your thumb drives into the laptop computers in your suites and review your company's due-diligence reports. Feel free to discuss your company's reports with officers or staff of your own company. The staff teams will be arriving at five, and we will have cocktails here in this room at six, with dinner following at seven."

Mo stood up, looked around the room, and smiled. "For those of you that don't know me, my name is Mo. I'm Mr. Farber's counterpart and hopefully, if everything goes well, his future colleague. Each of you are the cream of the crop at your companies. We need your assistance in moving forward on this deal. You should also know Mr. Farber and I both think highly of you, or you would not be here. The other two people here are Joyce, my senior VP for HR. Ryan here is the general counsel for EDGE. Joyce, did you want to add anything?"

"Thanks, Mo. Everyone, your luggage has been taken to your rooms. Freshen up, relax, and we will see you here at six."

I stood up and took in the crowded hall, the silent and tense officers trying to look calm. I said, "As Mo indicated, my name is Ryan. As the only one of us that is a lawyer, I get to remind everyone of the extreme confidentiality required. Also, please do not have discussions with members of the other company until notified otherwise. Thank you."

Joyce asked if there were any questions. There were none. Only silence.

• • •

At 5 pm precisely, four prop planes landed with the two due-diligence staff teams. They picked up their own luggage at the planes and walked to the lodge. At the front desk, they were given their room assignments, four to a room, and keys. By 5:15, they were in the dining room for their briefing. Joyce and I were waiting.

"I'm Joyce from Novation Energy. I am the senior vice president for HR. Get quickly settled in your assigned rooms. The Novation folks will be on the third floor. EDGE people are on the first floor. The second floor is vacant to ensure greater privacy. Four computers are in each room with name tags. Dinner is here at seven. Don't be late. Ryan?"

I went through the typical speech about confidentiality, then added, "For EDGE personnel, we are meeting in the first-floor conference room at nine tomorrow morning. Please do not be late. I will lock the door no later than 9:15, and it will remain locked all day. The conference room has its own bathrooms.

There will be box lunches when we get there in the morning. Are there any questions?"

Paul raised his hand and asked, "Ryan, when are we going to be able to discuss our work with the other company?"

"The due-diligence teams for each company will be meeting separately tomorrow. At the end of the day, we will access where we are, and a decision will be made by the CEOs whether joint meetings are warranted. In the meantime, remember we are two separate companies, and each team must keep its work confidential until the two CEOs tell us to collaborate."

When I was back in my room, I took off my tie, kicked off my shoes, and called Paul's room on my mobile phone. "Paul, this is Ryan. I'm in room 114. It's just across the hall from the Empress Suite, which houses Farber and Sillus. Please come down here. We need to talk."

"Can I take a shower first? I'm sweaty from being crammed into that damn prop plane. The air circulation wasn't working. I think I'm a biohazard."

I laughed. "In that case, please take your time. See you in fifteen minutes?"

"Sure."

Paul arrived in exactly ten minutes—his military training at work. Over the next half hour, he briefed me on his thoughts, good and bad, about each of EDGE's due-diligence reports. As he put his papers back in his briefcase, he must have noticed something about my expression. "Ryan, is there something else you want to discuss?"

"I really don't know. That's the irony of it."

"Is Farber being a jerk again?"

"That's the problem. He isn't. In fact, he couldn't be nicer. You'd think he was my best friend."

Paul put down his briefcase. "Then something is wrong. Leopards don't change their spots."

"There is also something strange about Joyce and Mo. I googled Joyce to find out her background. She was a vice president over at Expanse before it crashed. She joined Novation about the same time Farber joined EDGE. She is the interface between the companies and HEF. Joyce and Farber were both at Expanse at the same time, but they act as if they just met."

Paul looked at me thoughtfully and sat again in one of my chairs. "Talk to me."

"Before the planes arrived this afternoon, Joyce and I talked. She waxed on about the synergy exercise and confirmed her close relationship with HEF and the Swiss bankers before the merger was proposed."

"Well, that explains her senior involvement."

"Yes. She said HEF came to her with the deal, but she had no idea why it wanted to include EDGE."

"Do you think it's pure coincidence that two of Ernst Mathews's disciples went to the two companies that HEF wants to purchase?"

"No, I suppose not. What do you think?"

"Ryan, there are more mysteries yet to be unraveled. For now, my advice is we keep these concerns to ourselves."

I nodded agreement and said, "At least Tom is no longer involved."

"Ryan, I know the police closed their files because Tom is back in DC and they have no evidence connecting him to the two murders or the two attempts to kill you. But my instinct is that Tom and whoever else is responsible may not have vanished from the field. They could still be sitting on the bench, waiting."

"That's a disturbing thought."

"I meant it to be. Ryan, be careful and keep me informed. Please."

"Of course."

After the cocktail hour, I went to the dining room. The hotel staff escorted me to a table for only four people. There were large, Gothic-lettered name tags for me, Joyce, Farber, and Mo. I took my assigned seat between Mo and Joyce. Sillus was nowhere to be seen. The officers and due-diligence staff members filed into the room, electing to sit only with members of their own company. I knew that would change by the weekend, assuming the process went as Mo and Farber clearly wanted. During dessert, Mo asked me if I had any feedback about what we had discussed last night.

"I have no expertise about executive compensation. That's Joyce's sandbox. I'm flattered by the offer. You are right. Those matters are not something our current boards need to approve. That would be something for the HEF to decide."

Farber smiled and Mo nodded and said, "Good."

I continued, "Of course, if asked by the boards, we cannot withhold any information we have. Also, the house for Farber and the yacht for you, Mo, is also a matter for the buyer, not the two current boards." My three dinner companions all nodded in agreement. "But I need to think further whether any of these matters need to be disclosed to our boards even though their approvals are not required."

Farber looked as if he wanted to reach across the table and strangle me. Joyce put down her fork and stared at me with a blank face. At first Mo looked as if he would scream at me, but he swallowed and forced a smile. Farber spoke first after slamming his coffee cup on the table and spraying coffee all over. "That is the wrong answer!" he shouted.

The rest of the room went silent, staring at us. Mo leaned forward and in a snarling whisper said, "The yacht and house will be owned by the new company. Nothing is final until after the merger. Ryan, you better decide if you are on board with us, or get off the boat!"

Farber stared at me, carefully considering what he was going to say, and then hissed, "You have always had difficulty being a team player. If you are not with us one hundred percent, we don't want you. There's a great replacement in DC."

"Tom?" I said, and Farber grinned.

Between clenched teeth Mo added, "Ryan, think very carefully. It's time to grow up!" With that, Mo stood and angrily threw his napkin on the table. Farber did the same. Then they both stormed out of the room. Joyce got up and silently left the table, leaving her dessert uneaten. I finished my coffee alone.

When I got back to my room, the phone rang. It was Paul. "Ryan. What the hell happened at dinner?"

"Sorry, Paul. Not now. I want to call Anne and the boys while they're still awake, bring some normalcy into my life."

"Ryan, talk to me first. It's important. I saw the others flee the table as if you'd announced you have the plague."

"Apparently."

"What triggered the theatrics?"

"I suggested I might have to prepare a disclosure statement about their proposed compensation, and they exploded. Well, Farber and Mo exploded. Joyce just gave me the ice queen stare and left. Sometimes silence says more than words."

"Ryan, just a thought. Last night it sounded to me as if you were being bribed. This evening it sounds as if you were threatened. They really want you rowing with them, at least until they land this deal. How do you see it?"

"Like you."

I decided to walk down the hall to the library and raid the open bar. A nice single malt scotch and hot shower might straighten out my mind before I called home. I did not want to sound upset or angry when I talked with my family.

I opened the library door and stepped inside. Joyce was at the bar, pouring one for herself. She gave me a weak smile. I nodded but said nothing, walked over, and poured a glass of scotch, neat.

She studied me for several seconds, then said, "Well, cowboy, you really rocked the boat tonight."

"Guess I did. I didn't think it would cause such a stir."

Joyce approached me and clicked her glass against mine. Then she smiled warmly, patted me on the chest, and said, "There's nothing that adults can't work out. Ryan, you need to relax and unwind a bit. Have some fun."

She loosened my tie. I froze. She laughed, unbuttoned two buttons of my shirt, and slid her hand onto my bare chest. If I read her body language correctly, she had a very different view than I about how I should relax. She wasn't thinking of a hot shower, at least not alone. I was trying to decide what to say, not what to do. Then she kissed me on the check while her hand gently rubbed my chest. I had not seen it coming. I tried to behave as if I were calm and in control, part of my lawyer persona.

Joyce softly whispered, "Ryan, you're a very handsome man. But I imagine a lot of women tell you that." I clicked my glass against her glass again, downed my entire scotch in two gulps, and pulled away. I decided to use the old wife-and-kids' defense.

"Thanks, Joyce. I appreciate your support. I need to get back to my room now. My wife and kids will be calling in a few minutes."

Not very suave, I admit, but it was the best exit line I could come up with. It made the point. Joyce turned away, angry, and went to the fireplace. I briefly considered refilling my glass with another scotch but decided it was more important I exit quickly.

Once I got to my room and shed my clothes, I stood in the hot shower longer than normal. After I toweled off, I got in bed, picked up the hotel phone, and called home. I could not tell Anne why Farber and I were away together, or even where. Nor could I mention we were with Mo and Joyce. That would have to wait until after this deal was either killed or publicly announced. Anne could tell I was not telling her the full story, but she let that be and allowed me to just complain about Farber for several minutes.

"Anne, that's pretty much it. I work for a schizophrenic prick. The pay is okay. The job has upside potential. But sometimes it sucks."

"The only time I ever hear you complain about your job is when Farber is somehow involved."

"Fair enough. My job only sucks when Farber is around. Otherwise, it's great, which is why I haven't quit. At least not yet."

"How do you think our marriage is doing?"

"Great. How do you think it is?"

"Great. Tell me, how do you think our boys are doing?"

"I think they are awesome." I smiled, knowing where Anne was leading me.

"Okay. Now, how's your life overall?"

"Thanks for putting things in perspective."

"Do you feel any better now?"

"Yes. Thanks for the therapy, Doctor. Now that I'm feeling better, why don't you go to our bedroom, close the door, and let's talk dirty, very dirty. I miss you and your beautiful body."

"Now you sound like the man I married."

CHAPTER 30

The Viper vs. the Boy Scout

When I entered the dining room in the morning, I noticed Mo, Farber, and Joyce seated at a table set for only three. They were already eating, chatting to each other in whispered tones. I got the message that I was not invited. I worked my way through the breakfast buffet line. As I picked up silverware at the end of the line, Mo took my arm.

"Ryan, good morning. You look rested. We are just finishing coffee. Please join us."

I noticed a fourth chair had been added to their table and walked over there with Mo, who now had his arm tightly over my shoulder.

Perhaps he thinks I want to break free and escape this place. I did. If Farber fired me, he'd probably order me to swim to the mainland, hoping the orcas ate me for breakfast.

As we reached the table, Farber got up and didn't fire me. Instead, he smiled, patted me on the shoulders, and gave me a quick bro-hug. There was no discussion of our conversation last night. In fact, they acted as if it had never happened.

Are these people schizophrenic or just trying to drive me crazy? I never knew if I was expected to be part of the pack or walk the plank. *How long can I put up with this game before I lose my temper and do something stupid?*

Joyce was silent while I ate but occasionally smiled at me. When we all got up from the table, Mo and Farber both made a point of throwing their arms around my shoulders again, patting me on the back, and wishing me success in the meetings. If they'd slapped me on the ass, I would have thought we were a football team.

A few minutes later, I entered the conference room. All EDGE team members were already there. Kalie motioned for me to step outside the room with her. "Ryan, more due diligence on Joyce Deer. While working with Mathews, they developed a close personal relationship, often traveling together, etc. Her nickname there was Viper. She has never had a security clearance; however, I did learn the FBI recently did a background check on her. But I don't know why."

We went back into the meeting room, and I locked the door. It was time for the fun to begin. All day, the team worked hard. At 5 pm, I reminded our people that we did not know what we did not know, so surprises awaited us, and the process would be fluid and evolving. I took Paul aside and said, "Paul, after dinner write me a summary of our discussions here, including a list of what we still want to learn from Novation."

"Okay."

"After dinner, I'll unlock the conference room so you have access to all the charts and material."

"Good."

"After you finish the report, put it in the safe and shred all the notes and charts."

"Understood."

I decided to go for a run. Finishing up, as I rounded the path and approached the lodge, I noticed Paul sitting on the end of the boat dock, feet dangling over the water, feeding popcorn to several mallard ducks that were busy fighting each other for each precious morsel.

I wasn't sure how I would cope with all the crap if Paul were not here. I needed someone here I could trust completely.

Although I was sweaty from the run, I joined Paul on the dock and sat on the bentwood bench.

Paul spoke first. "Good run?"

"Yes, great."

"Maybe you should jump in the water to freshen up?"

"I saw orcas in the water. I think a shower in my hotel room is a safer option."

"After last night's nuclear attack, I noticed this morning's lovefest. It didn't escape our team either. They asked me what's going on."

"What did you say?"

"I told them I didn't know. Which is the truth."

"Did you tell them I don't know either? "

"Of course not. They think Mr. Gorman knows everything and can handle anything. That makes them feel comfortable, safe. You may not know this, but our team thinks of you as the only adult in the room."

"Thanks. I'll see you at dinner."

Paul had told me that our staff called our table the "table of the Four Horsemen"—a rather apocalyptic name. I would have liked to change tables for each meal and sit with other people from our company, but that was not allowed.

· · ·

At dinner, I was the first to arrive, followed by Joyce wearing another severe, black Nehru suit and black leather boots, apparently her preferred uniform. I assumed there would be no attempted seduction this evening and breathed a sigh of relief. I felt like I was acting in a reality TV show, but with real consequences.

She looked thoughtfully at me and said, "Ryan, I hope you

didn't misunderstand my intentions last night. I was only trying to tell you not to stress so much. Relax. Just go with the flow. Have fun. It's harmless and therapeutic. Healthy."

"No problem. I did not misunderstand. Thank you for your concern."

Joyce studied me for another moment. "Ryan, have you found any showstoppers?"

"Nothing that can't be resolved. But we are still working through several things. Stay tuned."

"Any indication that a merger is not in the best interest of your shareholders?"

"None."

"Good. That's the right answer. Keep focused on the big picture and what this merger will mean for all of us, and for your lovely wife and three sons."

Feeling uncomfortable, I changed the subject. "When do you and I brief Farber and Mo? After tomorrow, we'll be at the point where we have things to share with both CEOs."

"Agreed. Shall we suggest the four of us dine alone tomorrow night and give them our reports?"

"Works for me."

Farber and Mo walked in together and joined us. They were both all smiles.

What have they been discussing? Picking out another yacht? Maybe remodeling the Gold Coast mansion?

Mo asked Joyce, "How are you two getting along?"

"Very well. We were just going over logistical matters for tomorrow's staff meetings."

I felt I needed to say something, so I offered my two cents: "If the staff is as efficient tomorrow as they were today, we should be in a position to brief the two of you."

Farber put down his second glass of wine and now looked intensely interested. "How soon can you both do that?"

Joyce smiled and replied, "What do you think about the four of us having a private dinner tomorrow, maybe in one of your suites, to discuss our findings?"

•   •   •

After dinner, I went to our conference room and unlocked the door and safe for Paul. At 11:40 pm, Paul spoke for the first time since he had started preparing his summary reports.

"Ryan, I'm finished. Would you like to read it and edit?"

I shook my head. "No. I'll read it with the rest of our team tomorrow morning."

"Okay. I made more than enough copies for both our due-diligence staff and our officers. I put them in the safe." Paul studied me for a moment and then advised, "Be cautious. This may be the quiet before the storm."

CHAPTER 31

Changing Lemons into Lemonade

The next morning, I unlocked the safe for Paul. Paul motioned to me to meet him outside. We closed the door behind us. Puzzled, I asked, "What's up?"

"Last night when I put the reports into the safe, I placed them in a particular order, pulled out a single hair from my head, and put it on the top of the stack. The hair is not there. The reports are not in the same order I left. But all copies are here. Nothing is missing."

"What's this about a hair?"

"A security thing learned from my former job. Ryan, the bottom line is that someone has been in the safe."

I was shocked, then said, "Don't say anything. Just pass out the reports, and let's get started. Once the meeting gets underway, you and I need to step back outside and discuss this."

"Okay."

The rest of the team arrived. I asked Kalie to take over the discussion while I went outside with Paul. We ignored the benches set periodically along the path. Instead, we walked to a stone outcropping I had noticed during my runs. Several large granite boulders jutted out into the water about twenty-five feet. We climbed over them and sat on the last boulder offshore.

"Paul, you are the former government security analyst. I

imagine you've dealt with this type of situation a lot more than me. What are your thoughts?"

"Well, breaking into the safe is obviously about the reports and therefore the project. It is not personal to you. It is not an attempt to stop or interfere with our work."

"But the reports could have been copied. There is a fast copy machine in the conference room."

Paul nodded and said, "It was copied. I checked the copy machine this morning while everyone was settling into their seats and getting coffee. The reader shows that the last copy job was at 2:30 this morning and the number of pages equals the number in the summary report."

"What was the purpose?"

"My assumption is that it was just to see or confirm what's in the reports."

Baffled, I asked, "Why would anyone risk being caught to find out what everyone will soon know?"

Paul considered this for a moment. "Could someone want inside information for investment purposes?"

"Maybe a hotel staffer was bribed. But could an amateur break into that safe?"

"Ryan, it would take a professional to pick that safe and the conference room."

We walked silently back to the lodge. As we rounded a particularly densely wooded section of the island, we saw Sillus seated with his laptop open, reading and typing. We quietly walked up behind him. I decided to introduce our presence.

"Sillus, is that you?" I yelled out.

He practically jumped off the bench, shoving the stack of papers back into his briefcase and closing his computer. He turned and looked at us, obviously startled.

"Ryan. I thought you and Paul were in meetings."

"We were, but we just took a brief walk to stretch our legs.

What are you working on?"

"Just some work I brought from the office. Trying to catch up. Got to go. See you later." He scurried away. In a matter of seconds, he was out of sight and well on his way back to the lodge. I turned to Paul and said, "He seemed very anxious to get away."

"That was more like a panicked retreat."

"He doesn't like me. Maybe he walked off only because he would rather drop dead than visit with me."

"Ryan, he did not just walk quickly. He practically ran."

"Did you see what he was reading?"

Paul sighed. "Yes, a copy of our report. But he couldn't know how to break into the safe."

We walked back to the lodge in silence and went to my room. Paul was on high alert. He went through my suite, looking under furniture, behind pictures on the wall, in the light fixtures, behind curtains, even in the wall-mounted shower soap dispenser. Nothing. Finally, he pulled the bed away from the wall. A small audio mic with a radio transmitter was hidden behind the headboard. He did not remove it. Instead, he whispered to me, "Say nothing!"

He motioned for me to step outside onto the porch. "Ryan, it's better to just leave it. If we remove it, they will know we found it. Now it might be useful to us. But watch what you say."

Rather than feeling intimidated, I was angry—furious at the theft and mostly over the invasion of my privacy. As we walked back to the conference room, I tried to calm myself.

Our due-diligence group finished their assignment by 4:15. At 6:45, I walked to Mo's suite on the third floor for our joint dinner meeting. When I arrived, I realized I was a bit early but decided to knock on the door anyway. Mo replied, "Ryan, come on in. We're just having a drink before dinner."

I opened the door and entered. Mo, Farber, and Joyce were already there. So was Sillus. I wondered if he was the one listening to the mic behind my bed. The thought of his smirking face listening to me and Anne infuriated me. I knew this was not the time or place to discuss that, but it was on my agenda for later.

Sillus grinned and said, "Hello, Ryan, good to see you again. Please excuse me. I need to get back to my room and finish some work. Mo, thank you for the cocktail. It was delicious. Joyce, it was a pleasure."

With that little speech, Sillus put down his empty glass. As he passed me, he gave me a quick bear hug and a smirk, and Mo handed me a scotch, neat.

"Ryan, we thought we'd keep cocktails and dinner mostly a social evening between us colleagues. Farber and I are looking forward to hearing the report summaries from Joyce and you, but after dinner. Is that okay with you?"

"Yes, of course."

After dinner, Joyce and I gave our reports. We both stressed that there were no apparent showstoppers. Mo and Farber were obviously pleased. As an afterthought, I mentioned that it seemed odd HEF did not want any due diligence from us on the four power plants. Mo looked angry and glared at Joyce before turning back to me and angrily saying, "Joyce already told you the power plants are not part of your due diligence. You're wasting time and our money even thinking about that."

Farber decided to join the spanking and shouted, "Ryan, don't disappoint us with any more of that type of nonsense. Do what you're told. Do not rock the boat!"

Trying to explain, I said, "I know our shareholders should be relieved to not have those power plants, but I thought the buyer would want information about them, for instance the amounts already set aside by both companies for decommissioning."

Farber erupted to his feet, shaking with anger, shouted, "Don't you dare lecture me! We know what those costs are." Mo clearly enjoyed watching me get whipped by Farber. The experience recalled a severe dressing down during Navy SEAL Hell Week. Not pleasant. Not ego enhancing. In some ways, worse than being kicked in groin.

Before going to my room, I strolled out to the boat dock and stood there, thinking. Paul must have been coming back from a walk because he came down the path towards the lodge, saw me, and joined me. "How was your meeting?"

"Well, Paul, it went great during cocktails, dinner, and the reports. However, when I mentioned the four power plants, they took me to the woodshed and beat the crap out of me."

"That bad?"

"Worse."

"Why?"

I took a deep breath and explained, "Their argument is that our shareholders will be liberated from the burden of owning them. I agree. I was just trying to point out it was odd HEF didn't want us to do any due diligence on those. But when I mentioned that, they came unglued. They also said that the buyer has a plan to use the waste, sort of like changing lemons into profitable lemonade."

"How is that possible?"

"I was told it is none of my business."

"Ryan, if there is profit in the waste, maybe the offered premium of twenty-nine percent should be higher?"

"Interesting idea. But I recommend we leave it alone. My backside can't take another beating right now."

CHAPTER 32

Bombshells

At 6 am, still upset, I rolled out of bed and went for a run. Paul was outside already, stretching for a run of his own. He smiled and said, "Morning, Ryan. Ready to run?"

"Sure, but be easy on me. This morning I feel like I'm ninety."

"I'm always easy on you. I understand that you are much older than me."

"Cram it, amigo. You're speaking to a senior officer who is only in his early forties but just happens today to feels like he's ninety."

The air felt clean, cool, and moist as we ran. A thin veil of fog blanketed the entire island. No one else seemed to be outside. It was a silent pleasure to be there. I pushed myself hard during the run, keeping up a speed that destroyed my legs. But I needed it. Paul kept pace with me, occasionally glancing at me, probably trying to gauge my mood. He seemed concerned.

"You okay, Ryan?"

"From minute to minute, I don't know whether I will be bribed, threatened, beaten, or about to be killed. In addition, the woman I love thinks I'm a stubborn idiot."

"Well, in spite of all your faults, I still like you."

"Thanks for the pity."

"Just trying the Mother Teresa thing."

I laughed. When we completed the circle around the lake and split off, my body hurt all over. I was gasping for breath. Even my lungs hurt. Once I caught my breath, I went out on the dock and sat at the end, dangling my feet just above the water. After several minutes, my heart rate returned to normal, and my breathing slowed. But my muscles hurt from head to toe. I knew from Anne that scientists had found that distance runners got a "runner's high." The stress on their bodies during a particularly hard run caused their brains and other body mechanisms to produce and release hormones, endorphins or something that gave them a feeling of pleasure, a natural high. It could be addictive. But it was not working then.

•   •   •

In our team conference room that morning, Novation's associate general counsel, Kevin Sagamore, was waiting for me. We spent most of the day together, reviewing documents in another room. I was thrilled to meet someone in the other company who was a solid professional.

I was one of the few lawyers in our department licensed in both California and New York, and the law department would need to be in NYC with the head office. Other staff departments in San Francisco would be downsized or eliminated when they declined opportunities to move to NYC. I understood people in the Bay Area well enough to know that many would not leave for New York. I sensed Kevin and I could work well together, which boded well for the future of the law department.

Our meeting concluded at five. We went to the library. No one else was there. I introduced Kevin to the open bar, and sure enough he chose a great single malt scotch. I shared with him how I was introduced to single malt scotch by a US Supreme Court justice.

"Well, Ryan, I don't know how it is in San Francisco, but in

NYC they revoke your bar license if you can't enjoy a single malt."

"In San Francisco, we make an exception if you drink Napa Valley red wine."

He laughed, and we clicked glasses.

"Ryan, I'm glad I've been able to meet you. It was obvious to me that Mo did not want me to be general counsel when he left that position open. If I am not general counsel material, in my own defense, I can be a great wingman."

It was easy for me to reply to the combination of his wit and his plea. "I hope you want to stay with the company after the merger. I think we would work well together."

"Thanks. My wife and mortgage company will be very happy to hear that."

"How long have you known this deal was being considered?"

"Ryan, you undoubtedly knew earlier, but I found out about the proposed merger about eight months ago. Mo briefed me and our former general counsel that he and Mr. Farber had met to discuss the offer. But it was only last weekend that I learned you were going to be one of the four top officers in the new company."

This meant that the merger offers surfaced when Bill Woodworth was still CEO. *Is that possible? And did Kevin really know about the offer to me before I did?* This week, people had tried to bribe me, threaten me, and seduce me. Even Sillus gave me a hug. *What a circus! But I will do my job, protect the company and my family. My dad never gave up, and, damn it, neither will I!*

CHAPTER 33

The Viper

Joyce arrived in the dining room smiling, wearing not her Nehru suit battle gear but instead a pastel silk dress that showed more cleavage than most women would show on the beach. It made me nervous. I was determined to make sure we were never alone. After dinner, there was to be an open bar in the library. The room would be crammed with people and therefore safe territory.

At dinner, Joyce sat across from me at our table. She bent forward and nodded at me to move closer. I felt tense, on high alert. She asked, "How was your meeting with Kevin this afternoon?"

"Very good. He's smart and levelheaded. I like him."

"I agree. We were afraid he would resign when he did not get the open general counsel position. But we convinced him to be patient and see how the future developed."

"Well, I'm glad you were successful. We can use his help."

"Tomorrow, we should focus on the legal, regulatory economic issues of subsidiaries—which to combine, eliminate, or sell. We won't need the entire group for that, just the four of us, our CFOs, COOs, and the heads of our respective international operations. Does that sound right to you?"

"Yes, it does. I think the broader team could use a day off."

"Really? I think they should spend their time doing initial synergy work."

There was that awful word that never disguised the real nature of the process. Good people would lose their jobs. I attempted to be humorous and replied, "Joyce, we'll probably need another open bar tomorrow."

"I agree."

Farber and Mo came into the dining room together. They had our final due-diligence reports. They were pleased and worked in the room briefly, speaking with the people at each table. My cynical side whispered to me that this was just a tactic to soften up the teams before the corporate restructuring and synergy exercises started tomorrow. But this did give Joyce and me an opportunity to talk.

"Joyce, companies that directly compete will cannibalize each other post-merger. The combination of some of our companies will raise regulatory or anti-trust issues. A third group may pose other risks."

"You mean like our subsidiary in Bogotá?"

"You know I almost joined my ancestors?"

"We heard about it shortly after you cancelled your meetings."

"I'm going to recommend selling off your company there."

"Ryan, this is really your area of expertise. You take the lead. I will support your recommendations."

"After you give me any input."

"There won't be."

This was a new side of Joyce I had never seen. Very pleasant and not trying to dominate, intimidate, or flirt. Our professional relationship had improved. The viper had become a colleague. I decided I could work with this persona.

After dinner, we went to the library. It was full of people, the conversations loud, the bar loosening tensions and tongues. Small groups were formed that included people from each company. I spotted Joyce talking with Paul. They were standing alone, next to the fireplace. Joyce was smiling broadly and kept one hand on Paul's chest while she whispered in his ear. He did not seem to be disturbed and with his own smile whispered back something that made her laugh and blush. She slid her hand briefly down, touching his groin. It would take a piece of granite to not understand her intent. I turned away.

Paul, what the hell are you doing? For God's sake, think with your brain—the one on your shoulders!

I decided to ignore them and talk with Kevin. He was engaged in a conversation with our CFO and the head of their international division. I tried to pay attention to their conversation, hoping Paul didn't do something stupid. After fifteen minutes, I went to the bar to get a glass of tonic water with a twist of lime, looked around, and noticed Paul and Joyce were missing. I decided to talk to Paul the next day.

CHAPTER 34

Digitus Impudicus

After a great morning run the next day, I returned to my room at 6:45, picked up the phone, and called Paul. "We need to talk. Come to my room in twenty minutes. We'll order room service and eat here while we work."

"Okay."

Exactly ten minutes later, Paul knocked on my door.

"It's open. Come in. Let's order breakfast first. It takes a good fifteen minutes for the food to arrive."

Paul picked up the menu on my desk. We both ordered coffee, oatmeal, and a bowl of fruit. He yawned as he put down the hotel phone. I could not resist saying, "Paul, you seem tired this morning. Problem?"

"Didn't get much sleep last night."

"That's what I suspected."

My voice sounded harsher than I had wanted. Paul looked surprised, then smiled and replied, "Oh. I see. You want to ask me about last night."

Paul pointed to the area where the mic was hidden behind my bed's headboard. He continued, "I had a great conversation with Joyce. She is brilliant. A great asset for the new company. Also, she is very loyal to her company and cares deeply about its future. She's impressive. I know you feel the same way."

"I share your opinion."

Paul motioned me to follow him. We walked out onto the porch, heading for the dock. When we reached the end, I put my hand on his shoulder, looked sternly at him, and said, "I know you're a bachelor. Your sex life is none of my business. But Joyce is a senior member of the other company. We are in the middle of a major due-diligence exercise. What were you thinking? Going off with her looked like you were jumping ship. Don't you understand how people will interpret that?"

"I was taking one for our team. Look, Ryan, you know me. I love women. They are all beautiful and desirable. Normally a woman in this context would be off limits. I know you don't believe it, but I do exercise restraint and judgment when it comes to women."

"Really? So, what happened to your judgment and restraint last night?"

"Ryan, you told me how she came on to you. When she tried the same thing with me, I decided to let it play out and see what I could discover. It was a recon mission."

"Really? I doubt there is anything about women or sex that you have not already explored. What I am concerned about is pillow talk."

Paul laughed. I did not see the humor. It just made me angrier. He saw that on my face and hurriedly replied, "I've been around this rodeo many, many times. I know the process and how to handle myself. You are right. There was a lot of pillow talk. When we paused, she was full of questions, almost all about you."

This surprised me. I had not thought of their time together as an information-gathering activity. "What did she want to know about me?"

"Her questions were about what I thought was in your head. What are your true views about the pros and cons of the merger? What are your priorities? Are you supportive of the merger? Do you have any concerns? What motivates you? Have you been in contact this week with any of your board members? What are you going to tell the board? Why are you so interested in the power plants? That sort of thing. Those questions were asked several times in different ways, but she was always after the same information. She is very good at what she does. I know several foreign intel services that would like to hire her."

I ignored the implication of that last comment but suspected she had a lot of practice honing her various skills. Still perturbed, I asked, "What did you tell her?"

"Many times, I said that I didn't know. I'm just a staffer you use when needed. A gopher. She didn't seem to buy that. Ultimately, she was able to sweet-talk me into divulging that you had confided in me that you firmly believed this was a good opportunity for our shareholders and an incredible personal opportunity for you. You were very excited about the future. I told her you said it was like catching the brass ring. She liked that. Finally, I got dressed and went back to my room at 4:30 this morning."

"Spare me the intimate details. Just tell me what you think she wants."

"She badly wants the merger to happen. She wants you to strongly support it. If you have second thoughts, she wants to know immediately. She said she could make it very worthwhile for me if I keep her informed."

"I see."

"She is a control freak, likes to dominate, and is into S&M."

"Please don't tell me why you came to that conclusion."

Sometimes Paul could be a jerk. Professionally, I did not care about his love life if it did not hurt the company or his career. If Paul had asked me if he could recon with Joyce, I would have ordered him not to do it. But I was glad for the information. I knew one of the problems between Paul and me was Bogotá. After

Bogotá, Paul had become more than just a colleague. I thought of him as the younger brother I wished I had. Of course, I never said that to him. That would be awkward. Acting like someone's big brother was difficult when you worked together. Particularly if you were the general counsel. But I could not resist harassing him, just for fun.

"Paul, I recommend you wear long-sleeve shirts for the rest of the week."

"Why?"

"To hide the rope burns on your wrists."

Paul gasped, and his eyes darted to his wrists. There was nothing there. He smiled and flipped me a *digitus impudicus*. That's a legal term.

• • •

After Paul and I finished our breakfast, the officers of both companies met together, as did the staff. The officers were anxious to size each other up. The staff people looked as if they had been sentenced to a chain gang. After that meeting concluded, Joyce and I presented recommendations to Farber and Mo. They accepted all our recommendations.

Back at my room, I looked out at the lake. I noticed Paul and Kalie talking on the dock. I watched their body language and concluded this was not likely to result in a violation of company policy about behaviors between employees. I got dressed for another jog around the island. I needed the exercise time to reflect on the meetings before dinner and to unwind. As I walked out of the lodge, Paul stopped me. "Ryan, are you still pissed at me?"

"I was never pissed at you. At least, I wasn't pissed at you after we talked. But please don't tell me Joyce called you for another date."

"No. She already persuaded me to give up answers to all her questions."

"Then I understand."

"I think she is not that interested in men but very interested in using them. I don't mean she's frigid. Absolutely not. I just mean I don't think having long- or short-term relationships with men is important to her. Just occasionally useful."

"That doesn't surprise me. Remember, if the merger goes through, you and Joyce are off limits to each other. I've had to deal with a lot of alleged sexual harassment and broken affairs in the office. I have also seen a few folks fired by a superior who wanted to end an affair to prevent future damage to their careers."

"Joyce's interest in me was part of her due-diligence work. She'll never approach me again, and I promise I won't chase her. If I fall off the wagon, you can kick my ass."

"If you do falter, me kicking your ass is the least you have to worry about."

"I think she may like to physically hurt men. It gets her off."

"Paul, no details please."

"Want to hear something strange?

"No."

"One of the women from her company's due-diligence team told me that Joyce once joked that the ideal husband for a woman executive was an old gay man who was impotent."

"Paul, just be careful."

"I always am."

"Really?"

"Ryan, did I ever tell you about the woman in Peru with a pet python?"

"Please don't say another word!"

CHAPTER 35

Eucalyptus and Disclosure

I decided to hit the gym. After a workout that was at best half-hearted, I made my way to the sauna. Sillus was there. It was a Finnish sauna, all wood and very hot. Sillus had taken eucalyptus branches out of a bucket of water in the sauna and was swatting himself with them. I knew that eucalyptus oil was supposed to increase sweat and "clean the system." I was tempted to ask if he needed help. I would be willing to beat him with branches, though a two-by-four was what I had in mind. But I bit my tongue. When Sillus finished, he lay down on the top level of benches.

"You ought to try a good eucalyptus beating, Ryan. It works. Stimulates sweat. Provided you don't wimp out."

Not wanting to wimp out, I went at it vigorously—probably harder than necessary. Childish. I had to preserve my pride. I beat away. When my skin was red and sweating, I put down the eucalyptus and sat. Several minutes passed in silence before Sillus said, "Is it too hot for you, Ryan?"

"I grew up in sweat lodges. Part of the culture. This sauna has moderate heat. If you like, we can turn the heat up or down, whatever is best for you."

Sillus said nothing and seemed to be studying his feet.

"Haven't seen you around much, Sillus. Been busy?"

"Yes. Very."

"Been reading confidential summary reports, stolen from the conference room safe?"

"I don't know what you mean."

"Sillus, I saw you with the stolen report. Who gave it to you?"

"You can't speak to me like that! I'm Mr. Farber's assistant!"

"Sillus, I know what you are."

Sillus got up, wrapped his towel around his waist, and went to the shower. After waiting fifteen minutes, I went to the shower myself. As I'd hoped, he was gone. One encounter a day was enough. I was thankful I had not bumped into him in the weight room; my competitive macho streak would probably have caused me to lift more than I could handle and given me a hernia. Anne was right. Men never actually grew up. They just got older.

Back in my room, I noticed someone had slid two envelopes under my door. The first contained draft contracts for Farber and Mo. What surprised me was that each of them would be awarded the equivalent of $20,000,000 in stock the day after the merger—which would then be cashed out when HEF acquired the merged US companies. Not bad for a day's work.

I made technical drafting changes in those two contracts to make the terms unchangeable unless agreed to in writing by the relevant senior officer. I attached a note concerning the absence of any language about the new "house" or "boat." Then I turned my attention to the second envelope. It contained the contract drafts for Joyce and me. The language of these were identical except for our names and numbers. Seeing the terms in writing made my breath catch. I made the changes to all four drafts to ensure that no future change could be make without the prior written consent of both parties.

Sitting at my desk in my suite, I opened my laptop and set up a chart. On the left side, I started listing all the benefits to the shareholders from the merger, including being relieved of the potential long-term burden of the power plants. In the right column I listed all the negatives. After two hours of this exercise, the left side outweighed the right side. The facts were undeniable. The shareholders were being offered a very, very good deal.

I called Paul on my cell, asking him to come to my room. I wanted him to tell me what I might have missed. Ten minutes later, Paul was reviewing my work. After he read the lists twice, he turned towards me and firmly said, "Your list is good. I agree with everything you wrote. But I think you missed a few additional positives, which I added in blue ink. Frankly, I can't think of any negatives you omitted. Ryan, this is a great deal for our shareholders."

"It certainly is."

Paul contemplated my uncertain expression, then opened the door to the front porch. We went outside and looked at the lake. Under the green lights of the dock, boats gently rocked in the dark water; the Chris Craft beckoned me, a siren calling. We walked to the end of the deserted dock. For no apparent reason, we boarded Chris Craft's main cabin. Paul cautioned me not to turn on the lights. We sat on the ship's cabin steps as it rocked gently, like a cradle.

"So, Ryan, what's still bothering you?" Paul asked.

"Two things. First, they are throwing a hell of a lot of money my way. Do they want a general counsel, or do they want a prostitute?"

"How much now?"

I told him in detail. He looked shocked and said, "Shit! They either really need you to support the merger, or they think you walk on water. Everyone knows your relationship with the board. If you support the merger, it might not guarantee the board will agree, but it is very likely. However, if you do not support the merger, that could kill the deal."

"Agreed."

"I don't see why throwing money at you should make you oppose the deal."

"You grew up around that kind of money. I did not."

"So, what is the second thing that worries you?"

"Disclosure issues. All the money being offered to Farber, Mo, Joyce, and me is contingent on our boards approving the merger. I was told HEF blessed this and wants to put it in our employment contracts."

"What do you mean?"

"I believe our boards should be aware of the offers to the Four Horsemen."

"Why? It won't be our company's money. It's money from HEF."

"True. But as you told me, when you take big money from someone, it always comes with strings. The same is true of power. Shouldn't the board know that? Could there be a conflict of interest for the Four Horsemen? Shouldn't the board weigh that information when it considers our recommendations? I think the answer is yes, even though the facts clearly demonstrate the merger should be approved. In fact, I believe the board will find their approval of the merger is required by their legal responsibilities to our shareholders. If someone filed a lawsuit challenging the merger, that would come out in the litigation and should be in the record of the board meetings."

"Okay. I get it. What do the other three think about disclosing this stuff to the boards?"

"It felt like Alice in Wonderland. They practically took my head off. They also informed me I could be easily replaced by Tom Smith."

"Shit! Ryan, there is still something we don't know or at least don't understand."

"Yes."

After a couple of minutes of silence, staring out at the water, I said, "I need to disclose the post-merger compensation data so the board can consider whether that has affected our recommendation and due diligence."

"Will the board think your work and recommendation are biased?"

"I don't think so. But our disclosure will probably make everyone glad we already hired one of those Wall Street firms to opine on the offer, the so-called 'fairness opinion.'"

"So, your concern is that in making the disclosure, you are rolling the political dice on your future?"

"Yes."

"Are you going to show Farber, Mo, and Joyce copies of your reports before they go to the board?"

"Of course."

"When they see your disclosure report, it won't be pretty. You might be lucky if all they do is fire your ass. Don't be surprised if they crown Tom Smith and throw you to the orcas."

"I think Farber and Mo will want me fired. If that happens, Anne would be pleased. She hates me working there."

"It's one thing to find another job and then resign. It's another to be abruptly fired without another job offer in place, particularly with a family that includes three hungry boys."

"Good point. Tell that to the folks who lose their jobs if the merger is done."

Paul looked pensive, eventually saying, "Ryan, if getting the merger approved was the motive for the threats to you, maybe you don't have to worry while waiting for board approvals."

"Another good point."

• • •

Back in my room, I noticed my laptop had been moved. With my fingerprint required to open the computer, plus the double password protection and encryption, I was sure the contents were safe. I had a hard time imagining Farber, Joyce, Mo, or even Sillus doing this. *Then who? Professionals?* But there was no one on the island other than EDGE and Novation people, and the hotel staff. I wondered if one of them could possibly be a safe cracker.

I lay on my bed, staring at the ceiling, trying to relax and make sense of it all. After an hour, I fell asleep without resolving any issues but hoped the answers would appear soon.

CHAPTER 36

Miss Bliss

The next morning at 7:30, when I arrived for breakfast, Joyce was already seated with the morning paper. She hummed as she read intently. As I approached, she looked up and smiled.

"Good morning, Joyce. Noticed you humming. I must have missed the good news. Did peace break out somewhere?"

"I was just checking our respective stock prices. Neither of our stocks has moved a dollar in the last two weeks. That means there has not been a leak about this deal."

"That is good news."

"Did you go over the four contracts last night?"

"Yes, I made several suggestions to make the agreements more bulletproof."

"You are the expert on that. I'll turn them over to Mo and Farber."

"Okay."

"Have you finalized your final due-diligence reports for Farber and your board?"

"Just polished my prose."

"We should get your reports to Mo and Farber tomorrow pm. I'm sending my report today."

It surprised me that Joyce used the plural, referring to my "reports," not my "report." The due-diligence report was finished, and it contained a footnote referring to the disclosure report. But the disclosure report was only a rough outline.

Joyce rose, called the room to attention, and instructed the group, "Today will be devoted entirely to synergy issues. You need to look hard at how the new organization can optimize savings by consolidation of efforts, redefining tasks, and eliminating surplus deadwood. Be aggressive. Your work will give some people an opportunity to remake themselves and start exciting new careers."

I almost choked on my coffee. I wondered how many of those people who would be "synergized" would consider themselves to be "surplus deadwood."

On my way out of the dining room, I stopped for another cup of coffee. Paul caught up to me and whispered, "Told you she's into S&M."

"Behave yourself. If she hears you, you'll be back in shackles, and she'll take a wooden paddle to your ass."

"Not funny, Ryan."

"Wasn't meant to be. Just a warning. You could end up reporting to her."

"Trying to ruin a perfectly horrible day?"

• • •

Joyce and I were excused from the meeting while the staff teams worked on their synergy proposals. Last night, I had reserved one of the boats for today. A trip to the mainland might help me forget the merger for a few hours. I of course chose *Miss Bliss*, the vintage Chris Craft. I went to the concierge, who said *Miss Bliss* would be ready in forty-five minutes.

Stepping outside, I saw a man standing on the dock. It was Sillus. I should have guessed. He was the only staffer who didn't have to go to all the damn meetings. When I reached him, he did not take my extended hand and shake it. Instead, he just smiled and said, "Ryan, why aren't you in a meeting or something? I thought everyone was singing '*Liberate Eqalite Fraternite*' while playing guillotine today—you know, cutting off heads, celebrating the French Revolution and all that."

"Joyce and I escaped until late this afternoon. I thought I would take a short boat ride across to the shore over there and have lunch."

As soon as the words were out of my mouth, I regretted it. But it was too late to reel them back in. Sillus seemed to light up. "What boat are you taking?"

"*Miss Bliss*."

"The vintage Chris Craft?"

"Yes, it's a classic."

"It reminds me of the Chris Craft my grandparents had. I just loved that boat. Many good memories."

"That's great."

"Mind if I join you?"

This was not what I had planned, but I did not see a way out. Besides, maybe it would give me an opportunity to cross-examine the little rat—or use him to troll for orcas. I did wonder what prompted him to want to spend time with me, considering how quickly he tried to escape my company in the sauna.

"Sure. We leave in half an hour."

Sillus ran back to the lodge, and I walked to *Miss Bliss*. Her brass rails had been polished and gleamed in the sunlight. Her red mahogany wood had been recently varnished and looked warm and rich. The sky was a beautiful deep blue, and the water was like glass. Eagles circled overhead, watching. It was a beautiful day to be on the water. I resolved to not let Sillus ruin the trip.

As I boarded, Sillus came running up, smiling warmly with his briefcase in hand and a knapsack on his back. He looked around the boat and remarked, "What a beautiful vessel."

"Yes, it is."

"There's a great seafood restaurant right on the other shore."

"Perfect."

"While we're ashore on the mainland, I'm going to briefly meet up with some friends from my university days. I'll step away for only a few minutes. I hope that's alright?"

Now I understood this ride with me was to reminisce about his childhood and give him a lift to a meeting he had already arranged. I replied, "Of course."

Sillus jumped eagerly onto the boat, put on a life vest, and grabbed the wheel. My cell phone rang. I took it out of my pocket and saw it was Anne. At this time, she would normally be at her office with clients. I tensed slightly as I asked, "Hello, dear. What's up?"

"Can you talk? It's important."

"Certainly. What is it?"

"It's about your mom. She's been taken to the hospital."

"Just a moment, Anne. Someone is here. Let me step away."

My stomach dropped. I stepped off the boat onto the dock and put my hand over the phone. "Sillus, this is an important call, personal. You know how to operate this beauty. Why don't you take it for a spin and pick me up in half an hour?"

"I hope everything is okay."

"Thank you, Sillus. Enjoy *Miss Bliss*. I'm looking forward to that seafood restaurant. See you in thirty."

I untied *Miss Bliss*. We waved to each other. Then I went back to Anne and said, "Okay. I can talk. What is her condition?"

"She was mucking out the stable when she felt dizzy and fell. The doctors are running tests. Maybe a heart attack or mini stroke. They don't know yet. She's not worried about herself, just about her animals."

"That's Mom."

"I'm flying down there in a couple of hours. Sharyn, our next-door neighbor, said the boys can stay with her a couple of days. I'll call from the hospital once I know more. I don't think you should rush here unless the doctors think it's serious. I'll call tonight."

"I love you, Anne. And thank you."

"I love you too."

Anne hung up, and I put the phone in my pocket. *Miss Bliss* was cruising offshore, looking beautiful in the water. I waved my arms, hoping to get Sillus's attention. He saw me, waved back. He was smiling broadly, thoroughly enjoying himself and probably cherishing great childhood memories of excursions on his grandfather's Chris Craft.

Then came the explosion.

The fireball *Miss Bliss* produced was massive. Huge red and orange flames burst into the sky, and dark, deadly smoke poured out over the water. The sound was deafening. The force of the blast pushed me back.

Miss Bliss burned fiercely, black smoke billowing from the ruptured vessel. Instinctively, I jumped into another boat, started the motor, and took off towards the Chris Craft. My instinct was to see if I could help Sillus. I hoped that the blast had thrown him into the water. I heard a speedboat start up and knew someone else was rushing to help. It passed me easily and got there first.

The beautiful old Chris Craft had been blown apart. Only the bow half was still afloat, the fire consuming everything. The water was littered with debris, some burning, some smoldering, and some pieces of the boat just floating. Pools of fuel on the surface burned like wildfires. Then I saw a body floating facedown. The other boat slowed and pulled up next to the body, hauled the body aboard, and placed a tarp over it.

I knew Sillus was dead. I turned off the motor and just sat there, shocked and terrified. I was supposed to be on that boat. I knew the young man who had been killed instead of me. My hands were shaking from a rush of emotions—shock, horror, grief, and anger. I let my boat float for a while, too numb to do anything else.

Floating on the water was Sillus's backpack and his briefcase. I fished them out, and when the briefcase hit the deck, its hinges broke. Out came an extra-large, clear ziplock bag, the only contents in the briefcase. I recognized the document on top of the stack inside the bag: it was a copy of the report that had been taken from the safe. I put the plastic bag in my own backpack. The report was company property.

My life again felt like a war zone. *What next?*

I headed back to the dock. The hotel boat returned with Sillus's body. The sound of the explosion had brought everyone out to the dock. There must have been close to forty people staring anxiously, watching the boat carrying Sillus. Some people covered their faces. Some were crying. Others held each other. When I got close, someone pulled back the blue tarp. Farber collapsed to his knees, crying. The crowd parted and allowed the rescuers to carry Sillus into the lodge. Farber, sobbing, walked by his side. The bulk of the crowd followed.

I slowly made my way towards the dock. Joyce, Paul, and Kalie were still standing there, talking. When Paul recognized me, he waved and grabbed the shoulders of Joyce and Kalie. He pointed at me. Kalie waved frantically and yelled, "Thank God you're okay. We were told you were also aboard."

"I was supposed to be alone. Sillus asked to go with me, and he took the boat for a spin. My God, it blew up like a bomb!"

Paul looked troubled. "You were damn lucky."

"I know." Anne's call had saved my life.

Kalie gave me hug, then turned and hurried back to the lodge. Joyce looked puzzled and angry. "Well, you sure certainly know how to disrupt a synergy exercise." She cleared her throat. "Sorry. That isn't funny. I apologize. We are all so shaken. Why was Sillus out there?"

I explained. She frowned and shook her head, then took a deep breath. She seemed agitated rather than alarmed. I thought she was going to say something, but she must have thought better of it. "What is it, Joyce?"

"Farber is really shaken. I guess he and Sillus were not just colleagues but also close friends."

"Yes, they were."

"We should postpone meetings until tomorrow morning. No formal dinner or reception tonight. No one will be in the mood. People can order room service. I'll have the hotel leave a message in every room."

She strode back towards the lodge. I was carrying Sillus's backpack in one hand and his broken, empty briefcase in the other. His family would want them. I handed them to the assistant manager, explaining that they belonged to the person who died in the explosion. He agreed to keep them in his office and have them transferred with the body.

I walked to my room, stripped, and got in the shower. Forty-five minutes later, a seaplane landed with three Canadian Mounties, detectives, and two forensic technicians from Vancouver. Everyone got a message to meet in the dining room ASAP. The senior police officer, Margery Brown, confirmed that everyone was present, including hotel staff. She then addressed us.

"This was a tragedy. I know all of you are shaken. We will interview everyone here. At this point, we believe it was an accident. However, the hotel informed us the Chris Craft was fully inspected last week. Nothing was found to be amiss. Our lift boat is on the scene now to bring up the wreckage. No one is permitted to leave the island until we release you. We will have a full team here by this afternoon. We will be as expeditious as the situation permits. Thank you."

If one had to be under house arrest, this was certainly a luxurious cell. But no one saw this situation as anything but horrific. I would have to tell Anne that my return home had been delayed. But I really did not want to tell her over a long-distance phone call that Sillus had died in what might have been another attempt on my life. She would panic. Besides, it could have been a terrible accident. We had to wait to hear what the police concluded after their forensic examination of the Chris Craft.

After this short talk, Paul approached and patted me on the back. "You okay?"

"Just shaken up."

"Want a drink?"

"I think I'll just go to my room."

"Want me to bring a single malt to your room and talk? Need some company?"

"Twist my arm."

Ten minutes later, Paul knocked on my door.

"It's unlocked. Come on it."

Paul entered with a tray with two glasses, each holding a shot of the best single malt the library could provide. I did respect a man who knew his scotch. We clicked glasses. He stared thoughtfully at me.

"Ryan, you have a question. What is it?"

"Why did people think it was me aboard the Chris Craft?"

"You probably didn't notice the bulletin board by the concierge. It lists all boats by name. If someone has rented one, it says 'Captained by' with the name of the renter. Last night and this morning it read: 'Miss Bliss: Captained by Ryan Gorman.'"

"I see."

Paul pointed to my door that opened to the front porch. We stepped outside and he whispered, "Ryan, from now on, please keep your door always locked. And check to see that your windows are closed and locked. Agreed?"

"Yes."

After another sip of scotch, I picked up my backpack and

poured the contents on my bed. Paul noticed the large ziplock bag with the report inside. He opened it and pulled out the report, then motioned for me to be silent and pointed to the headboard where the mic was hidden.

"Ryan, let's walk while we finish our scotch."

He tucked the report under his shirt. Outside seemed deserted. Everyone else must have retreated to their rooms. We walked for several minutes and stopped at a bench under a giant pine tree off the gravel path.

"Ryan, I think you were the target of the explosion."

"Let's just hope it was an accident."

"If the explosion was not accidental, then it was an attempt to murder you."

"But we don't know the explosion was intentional."

"The local police here are top detectives. I've talked to them. They are going to finish their forensic examinations as quickly as possible. The politics and media attention of keeping high-level American businesspeople under house arrest on a remote but famous Canadian island is not something they relish. But I know a bomb explosion when I see it."

"What should I tell the Mounties?"

"You need to tell them everything. This is your fucking life we're talking about. Tell them about the ferry shooting, about the car crash, about Tom's threatening note. Tell them about Jack's murder. Everything!"

"But I can't tell them why we're all here."

"Why not?"

"Because it's confidential. I cannot break confidentiality."

Paul ground his teeth with a look of disgust on his face. He remembered the report and pulled it out. Thumbing through it, he said, "You know what we have here?"

"Of course; it's a copy of our staff due-diligence report."

"Yes. We knew someone on this island has the professional

ability to break into the safe. Maybe that same person can set a bomb on a boat."

Paul opened the back cover of the report and found a letter tucked inside. After reading it, he handed it to me. It was a letter from the buyer's attorney, outlining the offer.

"Shit! Paul, I learned from Novation's counsel that they knew about the deal before Bill Woodworth resigned. But this proves they were in discussions shortly after Farber joined our company. Why did Farber lie to our board of directors?"

"If you had known of this early letter offer, what would you had said to Farber?"

"That we needed to tell the board immediately."

"Exactly. Perhaps Farber was not ready for that. Perhaps his social issues were still being negotiated. Either of those is possible. There's another interesting thing about this letter."

"What?"

"Look at the cc below the signature line."

Tom Smith had been copied with the letter. We sat there for several minutes. Paul put his hand on my shoulder again, as if he were now my big brother.

"Please be careful, Ryan. Don't do anything stupid like I might do. Do not go outside tonight without me. Do you want me to post myself in your room? I could stay on the sofa. Or I could ask the Mounties to post a guard outside your door."

"No. I don't think that's necessary. I'll be a good Boy Scout and stay in my locked room."

"Call me anytime if you need me. Okay?"

"Okay."

"As soon as you get to your room, lock your door."

"Okay, big brother."

Paul laughed. I went back to my room. Suddenly the elegant lodge seemed like a trap, a prison, a potential coffin.

CHAPTER 37

A Restless Night

Shortly after I got to my room, Anne called. She seemed less tense. The doctors said Mom had high blood pressure and a "mild cardiac event." They were putting her on blood pressure mediation and the daily low-dose-aspirin regimen. Mom was complaining about people treating her like an invalid. We thought that was a good sign. I thanked Anne and told her I loved her. I couldn't get into Sillus's death yet.

After I hung up, I did a visual check of my room. I looked under the bed, in the closet, even the shower, then checked the windows and doors. They were locked and bolted. That evening, I fell asleep in a chair.

• • •

At 6:30 am, I awoke unrested but hungry. I ordered breakfast from room service and opened my laptop. Hotel staff brought me hot oatmeal with nuts and raisins. I asked the server to put the breakfast tray on the bed. He moved the documents I had dumped on the bed and handed them to me. For the first time, I noticed a yellow leather folder. It was the same one I had seen on Farber's desk and on the jet. I put it in my briefcase to return to Farber.

The main story on the local TV news that morning was about a mysterious boat explosion offshore from a luxurious island fishing lodge highly favored by the "rich and famous." The reporter said that reliable sources indicated the explosion was not an accident but rather an attempt to murder an American business executive. I hoped this was another example of "fake news," but I suspected it was accurate. I had hoped the danger to me was in the past, but it had suddenly resurrected like a phoenix. *Why now?*

There was a knock at the door. I assumed it was Paul. But when I opened the door, I found two Mounties. The older one asked, "Mr. Gorman, may we come in? We need to talk to you."

"Come in. I saw the morning news. It sounds as if you've decided it was not an accident."

"Mr. Gorman, forensics has concluded it was intentional. They found remnants of explosives, military grade. The bomb was set to explode at a specific distance from the dock. We found the remote triggering device still attached under the dock. It must have transmitted to the Chris Craft and triggered the bomb to explode."

"Officers, what do you want to know?"

"Who would want to kill you?"

"Sit down."

They did, taking out notepads and placing a recorder on the desk. I followed Paul's instructions and told them of Bill's resignation and disappearance and everything since then.

"Mr. Gorman, why are you and the other folks here at the lodge?"

"It's a business meeting."

"What kind of business?"

"I can't be more precise."

"It may be relevant. There may be some connection with the murder yesterday."

"Officer, if you had asked me yesterday, I would have said maybe Sillus, but he didn't have the skill and personality to carry it out. Besides, he was the victim."

Then I remembered the hidden mic and pointed to it, putting a finger over my lips to signal them not to speak. They looked behind the headboard, took out a small digital camera from their bag, and photographed it from several angles but left it in place.

"Mr. Gorman, I think you should come with us. We set up an office in the second-floor conference room. It would be more comfortable to talk there."

I followed the two detectives up the stairs to the second floor. They asked me to begin at the first unusual event I could remember. I started again with Bill's disappearance and Farber's frustrated attempts to fire me and repeated everything I had told them in my room. Room service brought a tray of sandwiches, and they continued to ask questions while I tried to eat half a sandwich. Physically and emotionally exhausted, I asked, "Officers, do you have any leads? Any thoughts about who or why someone has tried to kill me, repeatedly?"

"Mr. Gorman, we're doing our best. But it's too early for even a theory."

Once the police ran out of questions, they told me not to go outside and to keep my door locked. They suggested posting an officer in my room, but I told them no. Back in my room, I felt like a man walking through the woods blindfolded during deer season with a target on his back. I desperately wanted to talk to Anne. But I couldn't tell her what was terrifying me. My mobile phone rang. I did not recognize the number but answered it anyway.

"Ryan, this is General Kathy."

"Well, General, what a surprise. What's up? Are you back in San Francisco?"

"Actually, I am currently on a satellite phone in an Army tent with my Kevlar vest firmly attached."

I wondered why she had called at this time when I was supposedly secretly on an island and someone had tried to kill me in a boat explosion. "So why this call, Kathy?"

"I heard about the explosion. Don't ask me how. Are you alright?"

"All things considered, actually I feel pretty shitty."

"I just want you to know the government is taking this very seriously. Our best people are working hard. Have you considered taking a vacation from work and staying at your mom's place? Or better, we can arrange a place for you and your family to stay, a safe house, just until things sort out."

"I can't do that, not right now. A lot of good people are depending on me."

"I thought that would be your answer, but I had to try. The feds are working with the Mounties to determine the cause of the explosion."

"Kathy, the cause is obvious. A damn bomb blew up the boat I was supposed to be on."

"I understand. Sorry."

"The bonus questions are 'Who did it' and 'Why me.'"

"Ryan, I understand your frustration."

"My frustration? You mean because we have the best damn intelligence and law enforcement systems in the world, and they are totally useless?"

"I just got off the phone with the director of the FBI and requested the feds treat this as a very high priority. I stressed the FBI, CIA, Mounties, and Bay Area police must coordinate and share information on a real-time basis."

"Well, Kathy, we both know their top priority is figuring out the why and who, not my safety. Tell me, is it possible some agency guy high up is secretly slowing the investigation? Is someone using me as bait to flush out the killers?"

After a moment of lingering silence, Kathy cleared her voice and continued. "Ryan, it does not help to become paranoid."

"I'm not paranoid. But I am cynical."

"You and Anne are my best friends. I'm doing everything I

can. But you need to be very careful."

"Kathy, it's not you I'm criticizing."

Once Kathy and I finished the call and hung up, I bolted the doors and lay down on the bed. I was startled by a hard knock.

"Ryan, want company?" Paul asked through the door.

"No. I'm fine."

"Open up anyway or I'll just keep banging on the door."

"What makes you such a stubborn prick? I'm fine. I just want to be alone."

"Being a good friend. That's what good friends do when another friend is being obstinate, stubborn, and refusing help. Notice I did not say stupid."

I laughed, got up, unbolted the door, and said, "Paul, I'm getting flashbacks to that time in Bogotá."

"So am I."

"Could Bogotá and this explosion be connected?"

"That's possible. I told the Mounties about our fun down there."

"Good. I didn't mention it when I was with them. Didn't think it was relevant. How long are we under house arrest?"

"The Mounties are reluctant to keep everyone on the island, but the US asked them to hold everyone one more day. Apparently, the Mounties and FBI discussed the murder of Jack Names, Linus, national security, etc. That put the brakes on letting us fly away."

"I see. What should we do now?"

"Be thankful I don't have to tell Anne your stubborn ass got blown up. She would have been disappointed if only a few random body parts were brought home. Also, I decided you are the luckiest guy I have ever met."

"What do you mean?"

"Simple. Not only have you survived several attempts to kill your stupid ass, but you are also married to a beautiful, brilliant woman, and you're blessed with three great sons."

"I see your point. By the way, the cops must have removed the mic."

Paul shook his head. "Maybe you noticed the super-attractive female Mountie with the long golden hair and emerald-green eyes? When you were upstairs, she went to your room. When she came back, she told the other officers the mic was gone."

"What does that tell you?"

"Someone removed the mic to prevent the police finding it."

I rubbed my hands over my face in exhaustion. "Something evil is hiding here. I wonder how long I must keep fighting."

"Ryan, you can resign, but there is no certainty that will make the killer disappear."

"Someone suggested I'm paranoid."

"You're not paranoid. Someone tried to kill you, several times."

"Why?"

"That's obviously the big question. You're not a celebrity or politician, but you are general counsel of EDGE. You are high profile enough that murdering you would get a lot of police attention, particularly if they thought there might be a national security connection. That means media attention. That makes murdering you very high risk."

"How can I make this all go away?"

Paul sighed. "Ryan, if it related to this deal, maybe this threat will go away if the merger is approved. But then we might never know who tried to kill you, who killed Jack, and why Bill Woodworth disappeared."

"Everyone knows I support the merger."

"Not sure if it makes any difference."

I got up and moved to the desk, pointing to my computer. "Paul, I just remembered. The night you were looking at my draft report on the computer?"

"Yes?"

"After you used my laptop, you put it down on top of my notebook. When I got back, it had been moved. If someone tried to access the documents on my laptop, they couldn't. But it's disturbing anyway."

"Wait, I thought everyone was required to leave their personal laptops behind and only use the ones put here for the meetings."

"Staff, yes, but I also brought my own laptop. So did Mo, Joyce, Sillus, and Farber. IT hired a private security firm to upgrade mine with additional safeguards."

Paul raised a disbelieving eyebrow and said, "What safeguards?"

"It requires my fingerprint, plus two passwords and then a thumbprint from the other hand. In addition, the stuff there is encrypted. A pass code I have never written down is required to break the encryption. That way I always know its contents are safe."

"Ryan, if you smashed your computer into a thousand bits, you would still need to incinerate it at over five hundred degrees. Otherwise, I could access anything on it."

Somehow, I believed him. Paul opened my laptop, took another sip of scotch, and worked the keyboard. Fifteen minutes later he was looking at my due-diligence report. I was shaken. A few minutes later, he turned to me and showed me the computer screen. It was the outline of the disclosure report. He hit a couple of keys and pointed to a row of numbers.

In a controlled but stressed tone, Paul explained, "This shows that I closed your laptop at 8:42 pm. Then we went outside. Someone opened it at 8:49 pm and accessed your data by 9:33—slow but good work. At 9:34, they downloaded every document on this computer to a thumb drive. Probably so they could look for what they wanted later."

"Shit."

"Besides the due-diligence report and outline for the disclosure report, what else was here?"

"Research on whether I'm required to write the disclosure report."

"Anything else?"

"Some web research on HEF, the investors. Didn't find much. I downloaded everything else before I left for here, just as a precaution."

"Anything on it in addition to what you already indicated?"

"Research on spent nuclear waste. Did you know that France took nuclear waste and silica and made radioactive glass rods out of that stuff? Then they put them in lead containers and buried them on an island in the Pacific."

"It's one of the most expensive beachfront properties in the world, but few tourists go there. Anything else?"

"The rest of the stuff on the computer has nothing to do with the merger, just some preliminary drafts on other projects."

Paul smiled and jokingly asked, "Porn?"

"If I ever want that, I'll just borrow your laptop. I'm sure you have an extensive library."

"All you need to do is ask. I'll share. That's what buddies do."

"Forget it. I want to maintain my mental health."

Paul chose to ignore that comment. But I did notice he did not issue a denial.

"Ryan, we better get ready for the next meeting."

"What meeting?"

"Shortly before the explosion yesterday, Joyce sent an email for the head of each group to meet with her. All the other scheduled meetings were cancelled after the explosion, but not this one."

"Strange. I never got that invite. Paul, I appreciate your help, and your friendship."

"Just before I barged in here, I turned down an invitation from that beautiful blond detective to join her for a few drinks in her room. That should tell you where you and our friendship rank in my list of priorities."

I managed a half smile. "Thank you. I'm flattered."

$$\bullet \quad \bullet \quad \bullet$$

At 4 pm, we headed for the meeting with Joyce. When we entered the meeting room, Joyce acted as if she was not surprised to see me. Could she have just forgotten to invite me, or did she not expect me to attend after the harrowing events? Suddenly I felt overwhelmed with anger and slammed my fist on a table. "Damn!" Everyone turned to look at me, but no one said a word.

CHAPTER 38

The Mounties Take Charge

At 5:30 pm the Mounties ordered everyone into the dining room, then informed us we were all to eat in our rooms and they would hold interviews throughout the evening. I quickly excused myself and went to my room to call Anne.

"Hello, dear. How's Mom?"

"She's still insisting she is perfectly fine and everyone should stop fussing around her."

"Sounds like Mom."

"She says that every hour. But I think she really likes the company."

"I'm glad."

"We spent hours talking about you. She has told me a hundred things about your escapades when you were young—and here I thought she'd told us all there was to tell. The meds the doctors gave her either loosened her tongue or improved her memory. You were not a model teenager, Mr. Gorman. Not a good example for our three sons."

"Don't listen to her. You know she's getting old."

"I'm inclined to believe your mom. She also told me about all the dreadful, sleazy girlfriends you had and how I rescued you from certain disaster."

"Don't be jealous. Those other women only trained me to be

a perfect husband for you."

"Not believable, Mr. Gorman."

I smiled, enjoying the brief reprieve this banter gave me. Then I sighed. "Anne, these meetings are dragging on longer than I hoped. But I think I will be back soon. When will you be comfortable coming home?"

"In two or three more days."

"Good. I really miss you. I've been thinking about all the things I miss about being with you."

"Oh. Thinking about porn?"

"Well, that too. But also, just being next to you."

"I miss you too."

"Ryan, your voice sounds stressed. Are you okay?"

"There's a lot of stress with this meeting, but I'm fine. I love you."

"I love you too."

Before I got in bed, I made sure the doors were locked and bolted, put a chair against each door, locked the windows, inspected every corner and crevasse of the room, checked to see if another mic had been planted, and even checked under the bed and in the closet. I found nothing and felt a bit foolish. Finally, I feel asleep, but I woke several times with nightmares, repeatedly seeing the explosion, the roaring fire, and the charred body of Sillus floating dead, facedown in the water. It could have been me. *What's next?*

CHAPTER 39

Exodus

In the morning, the lodge was crawling with police. No one could leave until everyone had been interviewed. They treated me to a two-hour interview. I did not resent the thoroughness of their investigation. No one wanted the killer apprehended more than me. But I had a feeling the solution to this was not going to be found at the lodge. The answers lay elsewhere.

By 3 pm, the police started clearing people to leave. They recommended to Farber that the company provide me with 24/7/365 security. Farber refused and called them incompetent. I knew I could always rely on Farber to look out for me.

At 4:45, Farber, Mo, and Joyce were driven to the airport runway in two separate, elaborate golf carts. They could have easily walked the seventy-five yards, but apparently that was not five-star treatment. The Mounties told me they needed me to remain "a bit longer" for a wrap-up interview after they had spoken to everyone else.

From the porch of the lodge, I saw that when Mo, Joyce, and Farber reached the airstrip, two private jets were waiting for them. They shook hands, spoke briefly, and boarded their respective planes.

Upstairs in the conference room, the Mounties were spread around the room, waiting for me.

The senior officer politely said, "Mr. Gorman, please take a seat. We'd like to discuss some matters with you. It shouldn't take very long. We asked that one of the prop planes for your staff remain for a while so you can catch a ride with them when we're finished."

"Fine."

"We interviewed all the Novation and EDGE people, as well as the hotel staff. We understand you folks are working on a very large merger. Correct? Mr. Farber told us that, as did others."

"Yes."

"We have also been in contact with your police in Tiburon, San Francisco, and your FBI."

This did not surprise me.

"Mr. Gorman, it is apparent that the attempts on your life are related to you professionally and EDGE. Does that seem logical?"

"Yes."

"The mystery is why and who. That is still an open matter. But our conclusion is that it is related to this potential merger."

"Officer, I am not sure I can discuss the details of the merger with you."

"Then let me just tell you what I think. Is that fair?"

"Yes."

"I think this merger is a big deal. A few people will make a hell of a lot of money if this merger is done. It won't get done if your board of directors does not approve it. Your board is not likely to approve the merger if you recommend against it. If you are out of the way, you can't give a negative recommendation to your board. Is that a fair assessment?"

"Perhaps. But both boards will receive highly positive recommendations. The merger is clearly in the best interest of both companies' shareholders."

"That is our understanding as well. Everyone here knows you will support the merger. But suppose you died in the boat explosion and left behind a written, very favorable recommendation to your board. Maybe if you disappeared, that would eliminate the risk of you changing your mind or writing another report to the board that someone didn't like. Right?"

"I don't know the answer to that."

"We know about Tom Smith's note. We know about the lucrative severance deal he cut with Mr. Farber. We also know about his early involvement with the merger offer."

"Well, Officers, you have done your homework. I'm impressed,"

"We are thorough, Mr. Gorman. We even checked on Mr. Smith's whereabouts, wondering if he had somehow made his way to Canada. But we confirmed he has been in Washington, DC, for the last two weeks in a hearing before your Federal Energy Regulatory Commission. We also confirmed he is still in DC. Even if he had the expertise to break into the safe and set up the explosion of the Chris Craft, he didn't do it."

"I see."

"We are still in the dark as to who is the murderer and why."

After an hour, the Mounties cautioned me to be as careful as possible and to consider hiring a security service. They would continue to coordinate with US authorities. When the interview was finished, I spotted Paul and Kalie waiting in the corner of the room and asked them to join me outside. Walking to our waiting plane, I decided to ask, "Any further information?"

Kalie answered, "After the explosion, Paul asked me to make some calls and have background searches done on all of the Novation employees that were here this week."

"Kalie is in the best position to call in a favor and get it done quickly," Paul explained. "We can pull up the report on your laptop while we're on the plane, see if anything jumps out."

"Thank you both."

On the plane, the three of us sat next to each other in one row.

Paul inserted a thumb drive into my laptop and pulled up the report. There was nothing material that we didn't already know about Mo or Joyce. I did not notice anything unusual about any of the Novation employees and commented, "Kalie, thanks. But there's nothing unusual here."

Paul pointed to two names on the screen. "Ryan, take another look at the two Novation security men. These guys are not Novation employees. They were hired from an international agency headquartered in Liechtenstein. Why did Novation do that?"

I thought for a second and replied, "Maybe they worried their own security employees might leak information about the merger."

"Perhaps."

PART IV

CHAPTER 40

Ballistic

Six hours after taking off from the island, I was home. Anne got home a few hours later. The boys fixed dinner for her. I put flowers on the table. We hung a Welcome Home banner in the kitchen. The boys had chosen macaroni and cheese and chili hot dogs for dinner. Anne loved it. It felt so good to be a complete family again.

That night, when we were alone, I told Anne about the boat explosion and the probability that it was meant to kill me. As I expected, she went totally ballistic. I had imagined a romantic reunion, but instead Anne would not rest until I agreed I was being bullheaded and promised I would seriously consider resigning. I could not yet tell her that we were working on a merger and if it went through, we could be rich; I doubt that would have made a difference, though. I went to bed with Anne glaring at me. She also put on her flannel pajamas, which was a sure sign that any opportunity for a romantic reunion had been frozen out. The next morning, as I got dressed for work, Anne was still obviously angry.

"Ryan, this matter is not finished. I am not going to have my husband killed just because he is too stubborn to do what he needs to do. *Resign!*"

"Anne, I promise to give it a lot of thought and decide soon.

I agree, I am not going to retire from EDGE. But there are some timing matters."

"Timing? What timing? Waiting until somebody finally kills you? Is that the timing you're considering?"

"No, of course not."

"Then what is it?"

"I can't talk about it."

"Really? Really?"

With that she slammed our bedroom door and left for her office.

• • •

By the time I reached EDGE, I had concluded that the money being thrown at me was intended to get me to provide the board with a positive opinion about the merger; but that would be my opinion even if the money were not there and I was told they would let me go the first day after the merger. Paul commented that if the explosion of the *Miss Bliss* had killed me, my due-diligence report recommending the merger would have gone to the board without me, but the second report, the disclosure report about the compensation offers, would never have seen the light of day. That seemed a logical conclusion. But what did that mean?

I put my office letterhead on the due-diligence report, signed it and emailed it to Farber. I knew he would like it. It was truthful, detailed, and an unequivocal, strong recommendation to approve the merger. Then I resumed work on the disclosure report, attaching the four employment contracts. In the first paragraph of that report, I strongly emphasized that these contracts were relevant only from a disclosure point of view and did not affect the merits of the merger. In the concluding paragraph I stated, truthfully, that I believed the merger was fair and in the best interest of our shareholders. I hoped that Farber would not completely decompensate when he read this report. At 11 am, I emailed it to Farber.

Two hours later, I had not heard back. I could tell from my computer that Farber had opened the documents almost as quickly as they had been sent. I wondered why he had not responded.

Just before 5:30 pm, I called his secretary and asked if he had received my two emails about the merger. I knew he had, but I hoped to get some insight from her as to why he had not called.

She whispered into the phone, "Ryan, he got the first report this morning. He could not have been happier. In fact, he was all smiles. Then he got your second report. You would have thought you were a terrorist. I can't repeat what he called you. All afternoon, he was on a conference call with Mr. Stevens and Ms. Deer. I wouldn't disturb him if I were you."

"Thanks for the info. I'll take your advice and wait until he's ready to talk."

It surprised me that he had reacted so strongly to the disclosure report.

When I got home, Anne was in the backyard, reading a book. When she saw me, she quickly assessed from my facial expression that it had not been a pleasant day at EDGE. She said, with controlled anger in her voice, "Looks like you had another great day in purgatory."

"Yeah."

"Ryan, you're being obstinate. I don't want you to go back to work there. Quit that horrible place. For God's sake, are you trying to bait a killer? What are you thinking?"

"Anne, I can't quit now. Frankly, I don't believe that would make me safer. Please trust me. I know what I'm doing."

"I don't think you do. You are not acting rationally!"

Obviously I could not tell her the benefits of being part of the company after the merger or that if they canned me, the change-of-control provision in my employment contract would mean we had a year's nest egg to hold us over while I looked for a new job. But I didn't believe they would change her mind and would probably upset her even more. I could only stare at her with nothing more to say. She got up and slammed her book on the table. Her voice trembled as she said, "Ryan, maybe I need to take the boys to visit your mother, give you some space to think this over and come to the right conclusion. By the way, I've decided not to cook. You can order pizza. I'm going to bed."

With that, she turned and went into the house. I walked out to the hot tub, hung up my clothes on the rack, and got in, turning the jets on full blast. Forty-five minutes in the hot tub did not improve my mood, but it made me tired. The boys and I ate pizza in silence. The boys kept glancing at me, trying to figure out what was going on. After dinner, Shawn, as the oldest, was the designated questioner.

"Dad, what's going on? Is everything okay?"

"What do you mean?"

That was a stupid question. A four-year-old could tell there was some type of problem between Anne and me.

"Like, Mom emptied the dishwasher when she got home, practically throwing the dishes into the cupboard. She even broke a cup. Then no cooking? The health-freak mom who insists on organic foods let you order pizza from a fast-food place that delivers? Then she won't even eat the pizza. This is not normal. Is there another woman or something?"

"Shawn, there is no other woman. There never will be. But married people, even dating people like you and your girlfriends, sometimes have disagreements."

Matt took over the interrogation. "Dad, you and Mom never act this way. What's wrong?'

"It's my work. Mom would like me to change jobs."

Aaron looked up and said, "I thought you liked your job."

"I used to like it a great deal. Now not so much."

Shawn quickly retook the lead. "Get another job. That company doesn't own you."

I tried to explain and change the subject. "It's complicated. A mix of personal and financial issues. But your mom and I will work it out. Don't worry. How about a game of pool?"

Aaron also wanted to change the subject and immediately said yes. His brothers decided to join us. The boys and I played pool for a couple of hours. The mood was lighter. When I went to bed, Anne was already asleep. I did not fall asleep until after midnight.

· · ·

The next morning, I found the boys eating boxed cereal at the breakfast table. Shawn shook his head and handed me a note from Anne. It just read: Left early to the office. No signature. No I love you. Just a short statement.

When I got to my office, James Rooney, the senior FBI agent in San Francisco, was waiting for me. We shook hands and he said, "Mr. Gorman, we have an update for you."

"Agent Rooney, I need some good news."

"We were checking into all the people at the lodge. We also did some research on the security guards. The two Novation security guards were employees of a European security company. Those two guards were in Spain two years ago where they planted a car bomb that blew up some bank official. Both guys had been in the military in Eastern Europe, explosive experts. The bomb in Madrid was rigged to explode when the car reached a certain distance from the banker's office—like the explosion at the lodge. We think we know the names and identities of the men. Spain arrested one of them. He was found to be insane and sent to a mental hospital but escaped a couple of months ago. The FBI,

TSA, CIA, Interpol, and police all have their names and photos. It won't be long before we catch them."

"Thank you. That is a relief."

It felt like a huge weight had been lifted from my shoulders.

I grabbed a cup of coffee and strolled around the law department, stopping occasionally to talk with people, asking about their families and discussing any work items they might mention. *These great people are my biggest professional success. And I think my dad would be proud. I didn't run and hide.*

I reread my resignation letter, made no changes, and put it back in my briefcase, just in case. About 11 am, Farber's secretary called. "Ryan, he wants to see you."

"How's his mood?"

"Ballistic."

"When does he want to see me?"

"Now."

"On my way."

When I arrived, she told me to go right in. Farber was seated at his desk. He stared at me. When I said good morning, he did not reply, just pointed to the chair in front of his desk. At least he was going to let me sit for my whipping. A minute passed. Then he sighed and said, "You surprised me, Gorman. I thought you were a team player. You have not learned anything."

"Have you had an opportunity to read the due-diligence report?"

"I sent it to the board with a package of other documents for the board meeting. Both companies have scheduled their meetings for 10 am this Friday."

"The proxy solicitation material is ready to go to the shareholders the moment the boards approve the deal."

"You told me."

"I assume the due-diligence report was satisfactory?"

"Obviously! I told you I sent it to the board."

"You haven't mentioned the disclosure report."

"I did not send that to the board."

"Mr. Farber, the disclosure report strongly urges approval of the merger."

Farber sneered at me, leaned forward on his desk, and snarled, "Gorman, I know what the report says. I read it! When I read it, I called Mo and told him you were not going to be in the new company. I sent him a copy of your damn disclosure memo. He was even more angry than me. Joyce disagreed with us. Her view is that your memo can be cleaned up, but the contracts are not to be attached. Period!"

"I will talk with Joyce."

"Gorman, you will make every change she gives you. Right now, she's talking to the HEF. Get off your ass and call her as soon as you get to your office, before I change my mind and throw you out of here. Damn it to hell what that stupid board thinks!"

Without replying, I went back to my office. Almost before I could sit, my phone rang. It was my direct line and did not go through the receptionist or my secretary. It was Joyce.

"Well, you certainly know how to piss off CEOs. Nice work, cowboy."

"Joyce, I told everyone that I was concerned about the need for a disclosure. It won't change the board's vote."

"I have a better solution, Ryan. HEF has withdrawn all four draft contracts, effective immediately. I hope you're satisfied. I'm sure Farber and Mo will be thrilled when they get the good news. Want to explain to Farber that you just cost him a truckload of millions?"

Obviously, that was not news I wanted to deliver to Farber. But it did remove the need for the disclosure memo. Joyce slammed the phone down hard. I told my secretary I had a meeting outside the office and went home.

• • •

Friday, I arrived half an hour early for the board meeting to make sure the board books were all in place and my power point had been loaded on the projector. All looked ready. The board started arriving about fifteen minutes later. They were in a good mood. A couple asked me how Anne and the boys were doing. None of them asked me about the merger. Fortunately, no one asked what I would be doing post-merger. Farber joined the meeting, trailed by our Wall Street gurus. No one asked about Sillus's absence. Dianna called the meeting to order.

Our presentations went well; then Dianna commented that just before our meeting, she had been in contact with her counterpart in the other company, discussing logistical matters should both boards approve the merger. She went on to say that she had learned that the buyer would be offering Farber and me two of the four senior positions in the new company, should the merger be approved. When she mention the salaries, the board members did not react, although a few nodded as if in agreement. She said this contingent information would not be a factor in her decision when she voted on the merger, but she wanted the record to reflect the fact that she had received the information.

So, the money and jobs are back. Let's get this deal done!

Farber and I left the boardroom to allow them to deliberate. We sat in silence in the small meeting room next door. After two hours and fifty-six minutes, Dianna opened the door and invited us to join them. We did. After a few more questions, the board unanimously approved the merger.

Now, let's get all the required governmental and regulatory approvals in Europe, the US, Latin America, and Morocco!

Back in my office, I dictated a memo delegating my day-to-day responsibilities to Jane, my associate general counsel. She was very competent, and I trusted her completely. I called our

PR folks to issue the press release, directed the proxy solicitor to start work, and developed a schedule for necessary actions. Joyce called and informed me that HEF had reissued the four original employment contracts with terms identical to what I had reviewed before, including the changes I had inserted while at the lodge.

Life was good. I went home. *Time to talk with Anne and sort through these developments.*

CHAPTER 41

Behind Every Great Fortune Is a Great Crime

I emailed Kevin at Novation and told him I needed his help. Ten minutes later he responded with a short email that said: "Yes Sir!!!!" I briefed my new team, which was Kevin, Paul, Bill Donley from my department, plus three analysts Paul had selected. The next day, we started hopscotching across Latin America. Two weeks later, when my team was in Europe, I decided a courtesy visit with the buyer was appropriate. We were invited to meet "principles" at HEF's Paris office the following Monday.

This was my chance to seize the corporate golden ring. I was sure the opportunity would never come again. I had told Anne of the board's action on the merger but had not discussed the employment contracts that were contingent on closing the deal. I wanted to wait until I was confident this merger would be completed.

• • •

In Paris, HEF's office was just off the Champs-Elysees. Historically an aristocratic neighborhood, it was not a business center, except for the Gucci, Prada, Chanel, Armani, Louis Vuitton, Hermes, and similar boutiques that lined the adjacent streets. HEF's office was located on Avenue Victor Hugo in the former home of a French noble family—a well-preserved eighteenth-century classical mansion.

When Kevin, Paul, Bill, the three analysts, and I reached the front door, four heavily armed security guards asked for identification. Fortunately, Paul was fluent in French and translated. The four security guards were impressed. After showing our passports, we were allowed to enter.

The noble house looked exactly like that: a nobleman's home, built to impress. The elaborate, mosaic marble floor of the foyer was covered with exquisite Persian carpets. The walls were covered with huge, seventeenth- and eighteenth-century handmade tapestries and large oil paintings. Beautiful bronze and marble statutes, Greek or Roman, seemed to be everywhere. The furniture looked like it might have come from the Louvre.

An elegant, elderly man who conducted himself more like a butler than a businessman brought us into the library off the foyer, where we were directed to sit and wait. I would not have thought it possible, but the library was more impressive than the lobby. How did people amass the kind of fortune that built and furnished a place like this? I thought of the saying "Behind every great fortune, there is a great crime." Something to remember but, I hoped, not always true.

Fifteen minutes after our arrival, a middle-aged man wearing a highly tailored black suit with Hermes symbols on his red tie entered the library. We rose, shook hands, and exchanged business cards without speaking. His name was obviously Swiss. His title was "director of financial investment." I wasn't sure what investments were not financial but bit my tongue. In French, he explained that he had been president of one of the two largest Swiss banks for fifteen years but had accepted his current position with the foundation because of its challenges, and, of course, the remuneration was appropriate to the task.

Paul translated. I asked Paul to tell him in French that we had come to introduce ourselves, update HEF on our work, and to pay our respects. Our host interrupted in perfect English without any trace of an accent. "Mr. Gorman, I know who you are. I receive daily briefings on your meetings and progress. We appreciate your work and thoroughness. You may be seated now."

He pointed to the sofa, and we dutifully sat down. It felt like I was back in the military, being addressed by my commanding officer. He ignored the others in our team and addressed only me: "Mr. Gorman, are there any specific questions you have for me?"

"Perhaps you would be kind enough to brief us on the overall workings of the foundation and how you became interested in acquiring our particular companies."

"Certainly. The foundation is an investment vehicle for very high-net-worth entities—sovereign wealth funds, for instance, and of course multibillionaires from various nations who require appropriate vehicles to invest capital. Mr. Gorman, in case you have been wondering, we do not want to run your companies. We expect the managements we hire to do that."

"How do you oversee your investments? I mean, what are your expectations of us?"

"As I said, we want the management we select to run the companies. After the merger is completed, we will be very clear as to our specific quarterly and annual requirements. If your management team fails to produce the results our investors expect, we will immediately remove all four senior managers. If those expectations are significantly exceeded, your team will be appropriately rewarded. It's that simple. Remember, we will be very specific as to our expectations and unforgiving of failures."

"Understood."

"If you have been relying on the internet for your information about HEF, you may think you are our first investment. You may also think our fund manages approximately seventy to eighty-five billion. Both of those assumptions are not correct. You will be our third energy acquisition. The prior two acquisitions have been made without publicity because, unlike this acquisition, they did not require any governmental approval. Also, you should understand, the foundation has significantly larger resources than what the press would have you believe."

"How did our companies become subjects of your interest?"

"We have an excellent research team. We do our homework, as you Americans would say. Let me assure you that other than your wife, Anne, and your mother, we know more about you, Mr. Gorman, than anyone. The same is true for the other three members of the future senior management. You do not need to know more."

This made me uncomfortable. Silence lasted for what felt like a long time but was probably less than a minute. Our host sat studying us as if we were amoeba on a slide under an electronic microscope. It was very uncomfortable. I looked around the library and concluded the ball was in my court. I wanted to change the subject.

"This is a very impressive office complex."

He smiled in a kindly, indulgent way, as if he were about to explain something to a small child, and said, "Yes, it is. It is intended to be impressive. The type of investor we attract would feel at home here. That is the point. We want our investors to be as comfortable with us as possible."

"I see."

Our host abruptly rose. He said, "I assume you have no more questions. Thank you for paying your respects. It was a pleasure to meet all of you."

He coldly shook my hand but ignored the rest of our group. With that, our introductory meeting was obviously at its end. We stood there for a moment until the "butler" entered and ushered us out the front door. We walked a long distance in silence, each of us thinking about the meeting and what it might mean. We finally stopped at a café across from Notre Dame, on the west bank of the Seine River. It was a small place near the Shakespeare Book Store, the famous hangout of Hemmingway, Fitzgerald, Gertrude Stein, and others.

We were seated, admired the dramatically lit view of Notre Dame, and studied our menus. But we still had not spoken. I ordered four carafes of the house wine, two red and two white. Everyone finished their first glass of wine too quickly and then poured themselves a second glass. I waited until they had downed their second glass of wine and decided to speak first. "What did you guys think about the meeting?"

Bill answered first. "What meeting?"

Kevin seemed to ponder what to say and then spit out, "Ryan, that guy was an arrogant prick."

Paul could hardly control himself. "It was shake hands only with the leader, say your names, exchange cards if you insist, and goodbye; don't let the door hit your ass on the way out."

I looked around and said, "Anyone want to elaborate?"

No one did. The three analysts in our group looked away, avoiding being brought into this discussion. It was not the meeting I expected from a buyer that was going to invest $50 billion in our companies. But I was glad we had made the effort to meet with the foundation. HEF was going to be a purely passive financial investor. I liked that idea.

At the hotel, when I got to my room, I called Paul and asked him for more feedback on the meeting. After a pause, he cleared his throat and spoke firmly.

"Ryan, it was cold. You'd think we had defiled his daughter and his poodle. The guy really made me angry. His attitude was 'Hello, poor little people. You peasants should feel privileged to be here in our grand palace, but don't touch anything.' He made no attempt to be cordial or collegial. But it wasn't a waste of time. We now know what it will be like to work for those bastards. They will probably have quarterly meetings with the senior officers and keep a sharpened ax on the board table."

I laughed and replied, "I don't think it was that bad. But it was disappointing. Particularly when you view it as a long-term relationship."

"A long-term arrangement for you. But I'll never see that jerk again. Which is fine with me. Ryan, I want to come up to your room and give you something. But you must promise me you will not ask me any questions about it. It's self-explanatory. Can you promise that?"

"Paul, unless it's something illegal, absolutely."

Five minutes later, Paul knocked at my door. He seemed very tense. He did not smile but silently walked into my room and handed me a flash drive. "Ryan, you need to see this video to the finish. Remember, things are not always as they seem. Trust me. I would lay down my life for you if that was necessary. Destroy the flash drive after you watch it."

A strange introduction, but I took it seriously. When he left the room, I opened my computer to watch the video, which appeared to take place in an old church. I was horrified by the evil and violence. I threw the flash drive on the floor, crushed it with my foot, and flushed the pieces down the toilet. Despite my promise not to ask questions, I called Paul and demanded an explanation. He quickly came to my room.

My voice shaking with anger, I shouted, "Why did you have me watch that shit? Was that the murder of our missing analyst?"

"Ryan, did you watch the whole thing, to the end, like I asked?"

"When I was too revolted to watch any more, I destroyed it and flushed it down the toilet."

"At the end it explains that was a special op mission. They put a latex facial mask on me, and I played the part of the analyst. There was no murder. We faked it. The analyst is at a government safe house with a new identity."

"What was the point in having me watch it?"

"Remember the photo that upset Farber, the man standing in front of an old church, the one that made him charge out of the officer meeting? That video was shot in the same church."

"Yes."

"Did you notice it resembles Farber?"

"You mean it *was* Farber?"

"I mean it might have been Farber. But the facial recognition people could not be certain. The light was very poor, and even when he was taking the mask off and the photo was taken, almost the entire face was obscured. I wanted you to know what we might be dealing with. I put my ass on the line to get permission to show the video to you, so please promise to never mention it to anyone."

After Paul left my room, I did not feel convinced that I knew what was really going on. I certainly did not feel safer. Terror and revulsion better described my mood.

CHAPTER 42

The Mamounia Hotel, Marrakesh, Morocco

Our work schedule continued to be hectic. These meetings were always challenging, our travel exhausting, and our meals quick and without much talk between us other than business. Sometimes I was reminded of the myth of Sisyphus, who endlessly pushed a huge rock up a hill, only for it to roll back down to the base, requiring it to be pushed to the top again. At every meeting in Europe, the Middle East, Asia, and Africa, we encountered problems, challenges, and sometimes hostility. All issues were resolved favorably. Our last meeting was in Morocco. To my surprise, that went more smoothly than any of the others.

In Morocco, we were staying at the historic and lavish Mamounia Hotel in Marrakesh. Churchill, Roosevelt, and Stalin had stayed and dined there during WWII. So had kings, movie stars, and billionaires. Liz Taylor famously had her birthday party there with the international A-list in attendance. Once, Anne and I met Senator Bob Dole and his wife there.

Our final team meal that evening was intended to be a celebratory meeting, a thank-you for their hard work. The food and service were fabulous. The conversation was excited and exuberant. All had gone very well, and tomorrow we would be on our way home to our families. I could not have been happier with the extremely professional work of the team. After the seven-course meal was completed and the last of the aromatic sweet mint tea consumed, the group was exhausted and quickly headed for their rooms. I told everyone to sleep in; our plane home did not leave until 2 pm.

Paul and I were on the same floor. His room was across from mine. We said good night to the rest of the team staying on the floor below. When Paul and I reached our rooms, as I stepped into mine, his hand came to rest on my shoulder. He looked troubled and asked, "Can I come in and just the two of us talk?"

"Certainly."

We sat in the two chairs on either side of the table in my suite. I stared at Paul for a while. He looked at least as tired as I felt. His expression seemed anxious and tense, something I had rarely seen with him. I decided to say nothing and wait until he was ready to talk. After a couple of minutes of silence, he looked up at me, troubled, and said, "Ryan, I just got a call from one of my buddies in the CIA. They traced the two Novation security guards, the thugs, to Istanbul. But before Interpol could arrest them, they fled. It's believed they're back in the United States."

CHAPTER 43

The Yellow Leather Folder

Monday, back home, I stumbled over my backpack on the floor of my closet. It was the one I had taken to the lodge. Unpacking it and throwing aged, dirty laundry into the laundry basket, I realized I still had the yellow leather folder that I had fished out of the water, still in its clear plastic bag. I had forgotten about it. The cover was labeled Project N. I put it in my briefcase to take to Farber. Although I was the general counsel and, at least theoretically, nothing in the company was confidential from me, I felt uncomfortable opening the folder. It could hold something personal for Farber. I decided to call Farber and let him know I had found it. His executive assistant answered and said Farber had gone to New York for the week. I told her that I had found a yellow folder that belonged to him or Sillus.

"What's the folder about?"

"I don't know."

"Ryan, you're the general counsel. Nothing is confidential from you. Open it and let me know. I can tell Mr. Farber when he calls me this morning."

I opened the yellow founder and gasped loudly.

"Ryan, what is it?"

"Please tell Farber to call me immediately. Tell him I have the yellow folder. Tell him we need to talk. Now!"

Then I hung up the phone, called my executive assistant, and told her I would be working from home. I waited for Farber's call. I waited all day, but he did not call. At 5 pm, Anne had not come home. It was her usual routine to leave her office at four and start dinner. I called her office, but there was no reply. I called her cell phone. She did not answer. I knew that if she was with a client who needed help, her phone would be off. I waited. At 6:45, I was beginning to worry when the phone rang. Matt picked it up and called for me. It was the police.

"Hello, Mr. Gorman?"

"Yes."

"This is Captain Grey with the Tiburon police. Your wife was in an accident, but her injuries look minor."

"How did this happen?"

"Two rival Bay Area gangs are having a feud. Our best guess is they mistook your wife's car for that of another gang member. They shot out the tires and two windows but did not shoot your wife. We think it was designed to warn the other gang to keep out of their territory."

"Oh my God! Where is she?"

"She's here with me at the station. The paramedics think she should be checked at a hospital because she hit her head when the car crashed. The car is undrivable. She refuses to go to the hospital unless you go with her. I suggest you come here soon."

"I'm on my way."

Everything was a blur as I raced to find the keys and get to my car. I do not remember even breathing. I turned on the car, but before I could put the car into drive, my mobile phone rang. A male voice I did not recognize came on the line.

"This was a practice run, Mr. Gorman. A warning. Obviously, we did not intend on killing your lovely wife, or she would be dead. Now listen carefully. Make no copies of the files in the yellow folder. Speak to no one about them. Return the yellow folder with all its files to Mr. Farber tomorrow morning by 8 am. Do not speak to the police. Otherwise, next time, people you love will get hurt. Very badly."

Then the line went dead. I was in such a panic that I was unsure whether I could safely drive to the police station. My hands were shaking. In fact, my whole body was shaking. I ran inside and gave Shawn the cars keys to drive me. The police station was only two miles away. When Shawn and I rushed inside, we were taken to the room where Anne was sitting.

I was not prepared for what I saw. Her left shoulder and arm had been wrapped. There was a large bandage on the left side of her neck, smaller ones on her forehead and cheeks. Blood was splattered all over her clothes. Anne looked up at me and Shawn. She smiled. We both rushed to her and hugged her. Shawn discreetly wiped away tears. After a few minutes, one of the detectives motioned me to follow him.

"Mr. Gorman, when the tires were shot out, the car crashed into a lamp post. Your car is a total wreck."

"My God!"

"The paramedics responded and bandaged her arm and shoulder. She has a small cut on her neck as well. She hit her head on the steering wheel. The paramedics think she should be seen by a doctor."

"We'll take her to the ER. Thank you for your help."

"The captain has ordered the gang intervention group to make finding these guys a top priority."

"Why do you think it is a mistaken gang attack?"

"What else could it be?"

What else indeed?

Back in the room with Anne, I was overwhelmed with emotions—sheer joy that Anne had not been killed, anger that someone had done this to her, and guilt because I felt responsible. Shawn held his mother's hand. I hugged her, and she cried out in pain. I let go and wiped the tears from her face.

Captain Miller came into the room. Despite the circumstances, his familiar face was a relief. "Anne and Ryan, I am so sorry this happened. We will do everything we can to catch the people responsible."

Anne tried to smile and weakly said, "Thank you, Captain."

Captain Miller was studying me as if he wanted to say something. "Ryan, before you take Anne to the hospital, can I see you for a minute?"

"Sure. Shawn, help your mother into the car, and I'll be right there."

Captain Miller and I went into his office. He looked troubled and said, "Ryan, I have been on the phone with the FBI. Considering what has already gone down, we are not convinced this was a misdirected gang fight. It may be related to the prior attempts on your life. I am authorizing a squad car to drive past your house every few hours, twenty-four seven."

"Thank you."

"Take Anne to the hospital and have her checked out. Tomorrow, come visit me, and we can talk about options and precautions. Okay?"

"There is a connection. I got a call, anonymous. The caller said it was not an accident. It was a warning."

The captain did not look surprised. "Let's talk more tomorrow morning. First thing in the morning, but for now, take care of Anne."

At the hospital, the doctor concluded Anne had suffered a mild concussion and gave us some instruction for the next twenty-four hours. The physician assistant cleaned up the wounds, bandaged her shoulder, arm, head, and neck, then gave her a shot of long-term antibiotics and something for pain. Anne still looked in shock and had said little. I got into the back seat of the car and sat next to her. Shawn drove. Anne started to cry, and she threw her arms around me.

"Ryan, I was so scared. I thought they were going to kill me. I was afraid I'd never see you or the boys again."

I held her tightly. She sobbed against my chest. I felt her tears. I cried and with a choked voice told her, "Anne, I love you very much. I won't let anything happen to you. I promise."

When we pulled into the driveway, Shawn jumped out to open the door for us. Anne kissed me on the check. I kissed her on the mouth and never wanted to let her go. Shawn held the door and smiled.

"Hey, you kids, get a motel."

"Very funny, smart-ass."

Matt and Aaron ran to the car, tears in their eyes, and hugged their mother. I promised myself—I took an oath to God—that I would protect my family, no matter what it took.

The boys wanted the responsibility of keeping their mother awake for the next several hours, doctor's orders. She was sitting up on our bed when the boys tried to convince her to play videos games, but that was not successful. They settled for a game of Monopoly. Anne enjoyed their attention. Once the game was underway, I went into the other room. For a moment, I hesitated, but I could think of no one else to call for help.

"Paul, I'm sorry to bother you at home. But I need to talk with you. Can you come over?"

"Sounds serious."

"Anne was in an accident, sort of."

"Wait. What do you mean 'sort of' an accident?"

"Just come over, please."

"Be right there."

Twenty-five minutes later, Paul knocked on the door. He had somehow managed to pick up a bouquet of flowers and a get-well card for Anne. She was touched. After a short conversation with Anne and the boys, I signaled for Paul to follow me into the backyard, then to the gazebo.

"We're going to the hot tub?"

"No, to the gazebo. This conversation needs to be private."

In the gazebo, I told Paul about the threatening call I'd received just before I left for the hospital and the FBI's opinion that this was connected to the attempts on my life. He took a deep breath and said, "So, it was not an accident. It was a warning to you to turn over the yellow folder."

"Yes."

"What's in the folder?"

"Documents. Very strange. There are five three-page documents that are identical, except for some of the signatures at the end. Each is titled in English, 'HEF/Investor Agreement.' I can read three of the four signatures on each of the five documents. One is the name of our Swiss friend from Paris. One is Farber's. One is Mo's. There is another signature line on each. Some look Arabic."

"Do you still have it?"

"Yes."

"Show them to me."

"It's in my briefcase."

We went back to the house. I opened my briefcase in the kitchen away from Anne and the boys. I took out the yellow folder and gave it to Paul. He studied each page and after several minutes looked up at me.

"Yes, Arabic. But one paragraph in each version seems to be in numerical code, maybe encrypted. I can read Arabic, but the numerical code will take time to break. There's some special software at my place that I'll need for breaking the code. May I take the folder with me?"

"Yes."

"Ryan, I believe Anne and the boys are in extreme danger."

"So do I."

"Please have them pack suitcases now and go somewhere

safe, as soon as possible. Immediately. Please. Don't tell me where they go. Just promise me you'll do it this evening."

"Okay."

"After your family is safe, you need to stay at my place. It's safer."

"Paul, I think it's better if I stay here. If they discover the house is empty, they might go looking for Anne and the boys. I need to keep the lights on here."

"Are you sure I can't convince you to stay at my place for a few days? Like Bogotá? We could do some more male bonding. I could regale you with more of my life story, or if you prefer, all the women I have dated."

He was trying to make me laugh, unwind a bit, but it did not work. Instead I just replied, "Thanks, but I'll pass on that. I'll be fine here. Your friend installed an upgraded, state-of-the-art alarm system. As soon as Anne and the boys are safely away, I'll turn it on and stay here in the house."

"Just get your family to safety. We'll go to the police tomorrow before noon. I'll stay up all night if necessary to break the code. Then I will contact the FBI and others. But, Ryan, I really do want you to come and stay at my place once you have the family out of here and on the way to a safe place. Please."

Paul continued to try to convince me, but the notion felt like running away. Finally, he left with the folder. On his way out he gave me a stern lecture on personal security, reminding me that all alarm systems could be breached by a professional, so I must be constantly alert to possible danger and call him or the police if anything suspicious happened. Again, I felt like a recruit being dressed down by a drill instructor. But I didn't mind. I knew he was justifiably concerned about my safety.

I walked into my bedroom. The boys were trying to convince their mom to play another round of Monopoly. She was resisting. I asked the boys to go to the kitchen and make a "wholesome" dinner for themselves. Of course, in their minds that could mean anything from chili to boxed cereal. After they left the room, I closed and locked the bedroom door and sat next to Anne.

"Sweetheart, we need to talk."

"About what?"

"You and the boys."

"What do you mean?" Anne bolted up straight and took my hands.

"The car accident. It wasn't a gang mistaking your car for the car of a rival gang."

"What was it?"

"I don't know. But I promise I will find out."

"Ryan, you need to explain this to me. You need to share everything you know or think you know. It's not fair to keep it from me."

I started at the beginning, with the explosion that killed Sillus, finding the yellow folder, and the call I received minutes after the police had called me. Throughout this, she was extremely awake but silent. She squeezed my hand harder as I spoke. Then she took a deep breath.

"That damn corporation! I hate it! Damn it to hell!"

"Anne, I discussed this with Paul. You know he's seen a lot in his previous work for the government. He agrees with me that I am not overreacting. You and the boys are in danger. While the police and FBI sort this out, I need you and the boys to be safe. Paul and I will be meeting with the police and FBI tomorrow, but first, I need you guys to go to our retreat, Mom's ranch. Please do this."

"Ryan, who is behind this?"

"I don't know. Farber and Mo signed the documents, and the caller told me to get the folder to Farber. Paul is translating the documents. Maybe it's the merger or maybe something else. But we won't know until tomorrow. For now, the most important thing is for you and the boys to be safe."

"Ryan, I'm scared. I'm scared for you and the boys. I wish you had left that damn company when Bill retired. Our lives just spiraled down since then. All the money they offered you, it's just a bribe! Whoever they are, they disgust me. I hate them!"

The boys brought us dinner they had prepared. Unsurprisingly, it was mac and cheese with potato chips and popcorn, and chocolate ice cream for dessert. When we finished eating, I reminded them that their grandmother lived alone and had recently been hospitalized. She was weak and recovering, like their mom.

"Guys, I need you to man up and take care of the two most important women in our world. Pack the car tonight and start driving to Grandma's ranch ASAP. After a couple of hours' drive tonight, find a nice hotel. Mom has her credit cards. Stay there and order room service. Do not go out. In the morning, drive the rest of the way to Grandma's ranch. Can you do that?"

Shawn immediately answered, "Dad, I'll take care of Mom and my younger brothers. No problem. It's done." The other boys were quick to add they too would take care of their mom and grandma.

Aaron gave his mom a kiss on the cheek, and I added, "Boys, just focus on helping Mom and Grandma. No arguing. They're in no condition to handle that. When you get to the ranch, figure out what you need to do that is the most helpful. Can you do that?"

They each answered with a strong yes, ran to their rooms, and started packing.

Anne smiled at me. "Ryan, we raised them well. They're becoming such good men."

"Yes, they are."

Less than an hour later, Anne and the boys were packed, luggage in the Chevy van, and on their way after lots of hugs and kisses. I called my mom, woke her, and told her the kids and Anne were coming for a visit. Of course, she protested that she was fine, and nobody had to come to take care of her. I replied that Anne had been in a bad car accident, the car was totaled, and I couldn't miss work to take care of her right now. With that, Mom changed gears and promised to take good care of Anne. After that, I took Kozlov next door, locked the doors to my house, checked all the windows, turned on the alarms, and put my loaded pistol under my pillow.

I didn't know how many hours I slept—maybe a couple added all together. At 5 am, I made coffee and decided to remain inside until Paul came by to fetch me for the meeting with the police. Paul told me that when he succeeded in decrypting the documents, he would send me an email asking me to authorize him a short vacation, probably to Thailand or Amsterdam. That would be the signal for us to meet at his house. At 8:17 am, I received a call from an unknown number. I answered.

"Hello, Mr. Gorman. We understand you may still be a bit under the weather, locked up in your house. But our patience is running thin. You need to return the yellow folder immediately, or you will be very, very sorry. This is the only extension you will get. Put the folder in the rose garden on the left side of your driveway before noon. Do not be late this time."

Then he hung up. I called Paul, who answered immediately. I told him about the call I had just received. Then he said, "Ryan, I just finished translating and decoding the documents. Everything was in Arabic, including the coded section. The signature blocks were a clue. Five different terrorists are the investors. Mo, Farber, and our Swiss friend all signed each agreement."

"So, HEF has terrorists as investors?"

"It's worse." His voice sounded alarmingly hollow.

"What could be worse?" I demanded.

"Ryan, the promised return on their investments is not money. It's nuclear waste—enough nuclear waste to destroy millions of lives and render several cities, like New York, London, Paris, Tel Aviv, and Berlin, forever uninhabitable. The delivery points are the four US nuclear plants. The terrorists must think they have a route out of the US. Or the targets are in the US. Don't think of these as investment agreements. These are sales agreements for nuclear waste to make dirty bombs!"

Despite the surge of terror and the violent twisting in my stomach, I tried to remain calm and logical. "How does it work?"

"Upon delivery of the nuclear material, the investor's interest in HEF is canceled. After the nuclear waste is picked up, the sole owner is HEF. It uses the terrorists' fifty-billion-dollar investment to buy our combined companies."

"Paul, maybe Farber and Mo aren't aware of this."

"Ryan, at the bottom left of each page of each agreement are the written initials of Mo and on the bottom right are Farber's. They signed at the conclusion of each agreement. They're in bed with terrorists. These assholes are all traitors! They never wanted you to get in the way of this deal."

"When I first saw the yellow folder, Farber was reading another loose-leaf page before he signed or initialed each page of the agreements. Then those loose-leaf pages were shredded. They must have been the translation."

"Son of a bitch!"

"I can't wait to confront Faber. That bastard!"

"No! Ryan, I need you to stay at my apartment and keep silent until I can get you into a safe house. I'll call the FBI and CIA now, email them copies of the documents, and then come over to pick you up."

"No. You get the documents to the feds. I don't want to wait here. I'll drive to your place. It will be faster."

"Ryan, listen. You're sounding like you did in Bogotá."

"I'm on my way."

I closed my phone, picked up the car keys, and grabbed my briefcase. I threw some clothes and toilet gear in my gym bag, locked the doors, and got in my car. As I descended the hill in Tiberon, I realized that I had forgotten to set the alarm. But it did not matter. No one was home.

CHAPTER 44

The House of Horrors

My hands were sweaty and shaking, not from anxiety but from anger. *Thank God Anne and the boys are safe!* With the discovery Paul had made and with his contacts, I was sure the FBI and CIA would be all over this and those responsible would quickly be in custody.

Paul's apartment was in Berkeley. About two blocks off the freeway at his exit, four cars moved to box me in on all sides. They slowed down rapidly.

The passenger-side window of the car to my left rolled down. The two men inside were wearing ski masks. One pointed an AK-15 at me and yelled, muffled through my window, "Stop the car now or I'll blow your fucking head off!"

I made a quick assessment and concluded I had no choice. I slammed on the brakes and smelled them burn. The car slid to a stop after laying rubber and crashing into a hedge. Trembling and furious, I tried to think about my options, if any. The two men jumped out of the car to my left, both pointing their AK-15s at me as one yanked open my door. He slammed his weapon's barrel hard against the left side of my head, making me see stars as my vision blurred. He screamed, "Get out slowly. Keep your hands up. You make a mistake, you're dead. Then I'll rape your little wife before I cut her throat. Understand?"

I understood. Feeling wobbly, I raised my hands above my head, slowly swung my legs to my left, and got out of the car. I looked around to assess my situation and saw the other three cars were filled with armed thugs. I could neither run nor fight my way out of this. The gunman snarled, "Now, pretty boy, listen and obey. Put your hands behind your back."

With the AK-15's barrel against my forehead, I complied. Another thug tied on my wrists behind my back. It hurt. A blindfold and a black cloth bag were jammed over my head. They shoved me into one of the cars so hard that I fell across the back seats and onto the floor. When I tried to get up, one of the sadistic bastards slammed me in the gut. It knocked the wind out of me and hurt like hell. I gasped for breath but refused to let them know how much it hurt. I lay still. Waiting. Someone grabbed me and slammed me upright against the back of the seat.

We rode in silence for at least thirty minutes. I could not tell what direction we were going or whether the endless turns were to confuse me or were part of the route. The only other time I had been a captive like this was during training with the SEALs. But then I knew they would not actually kill me. That was not a given now.

I made a conscious effort to show no fear and to control my breathing. Per my training, I made another quick mental survey of my situation. There was a sack over my head with the strings pulled tightly around my neck, cutting into my flesh. But I could still breathe. My hands were now cuffed behind my back, and my wrists hurt. My feet were free, for the time being. At least three thugs were in the car with me, all armed. There were three more cars with more guys and an unknown number of weapons. Not good. The gratuitous smash into my gut after I had been submissive told me at least one of these guys was a sadist. Obviously struggle and escape were not an option at this point. I would have to wait and prepare myself for when that opportunity presented itself.

When we stopped, they pulled me out of the car and threw me on the ground. It felt like concrete or asphalt cutting my face through the bag still over my head. Someone rewarded my passive behavior with another hard kick in the stomach, then pulled me to my feet. I decided they were just trying to loosen me up before they got serious.

I listened to the noises they made sliding a large metal door on rollers. We were in a building. I guessed it was a warehouse or storage building, maybe a shop of some type. They shoved me into what felt like metal fencing. They laughed when I fell. I heard cars drive away. Then there was the sound of someone inserting a key into a door lock. When the door opened, they pushed me inside. Someone roughly thrust a rag under the hood, against my nose. I lost consciousness.

• • •

There was no way for me to tell how long I had been unconscious. When I awoke, my head throbbed with pain, and I felt dizzy, disoriented. The blindfold and sack were off. At first my vision was blurred; then I spotted a metal table with a band saw. The table was about six feet wide, four feet high, and eight to ten feet long. At one end was a large metal box with a sign that read Waste Grinder, and at the bottom of that was a shoot that fed into an opening in the cement floor. This was not good.

A conveyor belt was suspended from the ceiling, ten feet above the floor. It entered and exited the room through a large opening in the wall to my left. Large meat hooks were connected to the conveyor belt every four feet or so. Fire hoses hung on the walls. The room was large, probably fifty feet long by forty. I surmised I was in a former meat processing plant.

As my head started to clear, I tried to stand. Not possible. I realized I was naked in a gray metal chair, my hands tied to the chair arms and my legs tied to the front legs. My knees were spread wide and my feet were tied to the bottoms of the chair arms. I knew that binding a prisoner naked like this was a classic interrogation technique, used for thousands of years. It made prisoners feel helpless and vulnerable—which they were. Being bound this way was also a very, very bad sign.

For several minutes, I struggled as hard as I could to free my arms or legs, but the nylon ropes only bit into my flesh until I bled. I needed to calm down. Not panic. I forced myself to stop struggling and take deep, long breaths. It helped. The only sound I heard was of waves slapping against pillars. I concluded that this room was positioned over the water; waste meat and bones were dropped into barges below or even directly into the water, feeding the fish. The cold, gray floor was cement. The walls and ceiling were metal. There was no warmth. It felt like an enormous prison cell on death row.

The fire hoses on the walls were used to wash away blood after butchering animals. If this room was meant merely as a prop to terrorize me, it succeeded. I decided that as soon as they had whatever they wanted from me, I would be cut to pieces, then fed through the meat grinder into the water below. No one would ever find me. There would be no body to find.

I struggled to fight the terror. The acid in my stomach rose into my mouth, and I tasted the foul bitterness of panic. Again, I tried to calm myself, taking deep breaths with my eyes closed. Sitting there, naked, bound hand and foot to a metal chair, I knew I was helpless, at least for the moment. At this point, my mind was my sole advantage. I could only wait and pray that my family was now hidden and safe.

It could have been an hour, maybe more, that I sat there waiting, fighting the panic that swept through my body. Finally, two men walked into the room, one carrying a toolbox. Both looked Eastern European, maybe Russian. It was hard to tell.

One had short blond hair and the coldest ice-blue eyes I had ever seen. A jagged red scar ran across his left cheek. The other one was dark with black hair, a cruel smile, and gold front teeth. His eyes matched his hair, black and lifeless. Both men could have been rugby players, with hard, muscular hands and bodies. They seemed vaguely familiar. Then it came to me. They were the two Novation guards at the lodge. The blond spoke first.

"Hello, pretty boy. My name is Vlad. My friend here is Gorz. We are glad to see you are awake and comfortable. Surely you know you are in a meatpacking house—not so much packing as butchering. The only way you walk out of here alive is to cooperate. I'm told you're smart. Don't be stupid. Cooperate, pretty boy, or we will send pieces of you to the fish."

His accent matched what I gathered from his appearance. I recognized his voice as one of the two men who initially took me hostage at gunpoint. He smiled as he talked, but there was no warmth in his cold eyes. I studied those eyes for a moment. There seemed to be a void behind them, like he lacked a soul. He took hold of my chin with his left hand, drew his face close to mine, and whispered, "You are going to cooperate. Aren't you, Mr. Gorman?"

I said nothing and continued to stare into his glacier-blue eyes. After a few seconds, with lightning speed, he slapped my face, hard. I felt and tasted blood flowing from my broken nose.

"Mr. Gorman, it is very rude not to answer when someone asks you a question. Now I will politely ask you again. Are you going to cooperate or not?"

Before he could strike me again, I answered, "What do you want?"

"We want to know where you hid the yellow folder. It doesn't belong to you. You need to give it back!"

Gorz grabbed my hair and pulled my head in his direction, saying, "After we picked you up, some of my friends went to cut off your alarm system. But it turns out you forgot to set your alarm. They searched your house; everywhere and everything was searched. The folder was not there. Where is it, Mr. Gorman?"

"I don't have the folder" was all I said.

Vlad struck me again.

"That is not a good answer. We know you don't have it. While you were sleeping here, we also checked all your possible hiding places, every inch of your pretty body, and found no weapons, no folder, no papers, no memory sticks, no keys. Nothing interesting."

They both laughed. Gorz stepped forward and pressed his massive right hand around my throat, choking off my breath. It was his turn to speak again. "The question is where is it? Do not play games with us. We play rough, very rough."

He continued to press one hand hard around my throat and with his other slapped me so hard that my chair rocked to the side. I looked up at the ceiling to avoid looking at him. Then Gorz grabbed me around the throat again and put his face inches from me. "The cat's got your tongue? My friend can help you remember," he growled.

Vlad pulled a chair over and sat across from me, grinning. On the floor was a black metal toolbox. He took out an extension cord. He plugged the cord into a box with a dial, a terminal, then plugged the other end of the cord into the electric outlet on the wall. He was moving intentionally slow, letting me watch every measured movement. He took out two wires and attached a copper metal clamp to each. Then he attached each wire to a separate terminal on the box with the dial and set it between my legs. As hard as I tried, I could not stop watching.

I wanted to close my eyes, knowing what was coming, but I couldn't force myself to do that. Vlad took one wire and clamped it to my right thigh. It cut into my flesh, drawing blood. Pain ran through my leg. Then he took the second wire and clamped it to my left calf. Vlad smiled coldly. Then he slowly turned the dial on the terminal.

Electricity screamed through my legs and body. At first it only tingled, but as he continued to slowly turn the dial, the pain increased. My legs and torso began to shake. The pain was intense. I lost control, jerking forward and sideways in a full-body convulsion, my head flopping back and forth. Vlad turned the electricity on and off, several times. When he dialed down the pain, I gasped for breath and tried to calm myself. Each time he turned the dial up, it was the same. The pain was excruciating. I bit down hard, trying not to scream. My eyes filled with water that ran down my face, mixing with the blood from my nose. After the sixth time, he removed the two clamps. My thighs were bleeding and burnt. My entire body was shaking in pain. They both laughed.

"You see, pretty boy? We are serious. You will answer our questions. No matter how long we must play with you, eventually you tell me where you hid the yellow folder and your family. It is only a matter of time. What does or does not happen to your family is up to you. If you cooperate, they can live. If not, their deaths are on your soul."

My breathing stopped at the thought of the danger to Anne and the boys. Then my lungs suddenly gasped for breath, as if I had been drowning. Gorz held the clamps in his hands. Looking at my groin, he pointed and spoke to Vlad in a language I did not understand. But I knew what they were discussing. Vlad smiled and said, "I hear that macho Americans think with their balls, not their heads. We should talk to your other brain, pretty boy." Both men laughed heartily.

They attached one metal clamp to my belly and the other to my scrotum. Even without electricity, the pain was extreme. When Vlad turned the knob, the pain was so sharp I wanted to scream, but I bit down hard to kept silent, although my body quaked involuntarily. They turned off the electricity and laughed. Gorz held my jaw firmly in his right hand, bending my bloody face up towards him.

"Vlad, I think he likes it this way. We should be good hosts and give him some more."

Vlad turned the knob again. Electricity and pain ran not just through my groin but through my whole body. I tried to keep sane. The convulsions made me jump wildly in the chair. I do not remember screaming, but I do remember hearing a terrible, terrible scream. It must have been mine. Finally, my chair fell backwards. I passed out on the cement floor of the slaughterhouse, welcoming the loss of consciousness.

CHAPTER 45

Fingers and Bones

At some point while I lay motionless on the cold cement floor, they cut the ties off my feet, hands, and knees. I awoke unbound. Powerful cold water from a fire hose pounded against my tortured body, pushing me around on the floor while Vlad and Gorz laughed. I could not protect myself. After they had amused themselves, they turned off the hose. Vlad turned my body over with his foot and smiled down at me. They grabbed my wrists, tied them, and hoisted me up on a meat hook, my toes just touching the wet floor as I dangled by the rope binding my wrists.

Gorz smiled through his golden teeth and said, "Mr. Gorman, now we will leave you alone, give you an opportunity to think. The fun is just beginning, my friend. If you refuse to be a good boy, we will have to get serious." Gorz turned on the band saw, smiled, and turned it off. Their laughter trailed behind them as they left. The saw whirred to a stop.

I hung from the meat hook, heaving, trying to calm my breath while pain flooded my brain and every inch of me. Blood and sweat rolled down my body. After several minutes, the two thugs came back, each with a beer in hand. Despite all the torture and pain, I realized that I was desperately thirsty. They stood admiring their work and sipping their cold beers, occasionally saying something to each other in another language and laughing.

When they finished their beers, Gorz pressed the muzzle of his AK-15 against my head.

Vlad smiled and said, "Now is the time to talk." He opened the metal toolbox and took out a pair of plyers. He smiled. His ice-cold eyes stared into mine, and I shivered. Then he patted my head. "Mr. Gorman, I really don't want to take these pliers and break your fingers. Well, that is a lie. The truth is I would enjoy that. But if you tell me where you hid the folder, I won't be able to do that. You see, the people who hired us have given us strict orders to cease our work as soon as you cooperate. They are merciful. We are not."

Vlad took my left hand and twisted my wedding ring off. It was my dad's simple wedding ring my mom had given to Anne to give to me at our wedding. With the pliers, Vlad gripped my finger hard, crushing the nail and pulling the appendage up and back towards me. I bit hard and concentrated, trying to brace against the additional pain I knew was coming.

"Shall we have a little talk? Or do you want to play some more?"

There was nothing I wanted to say. The pain was horrible. Vlad stopped the pressure and said, "I will stop the moment you start talking to me. I thought you lawyers were trained to speak. Don't you American lawyers charge by the word?"

"Fuck you" escaped from my bloody lips, and I spit in his face.

Vlad squeezed harder and pushed my finger back. I heard the bone crack. The sharp pain shot through my hand and up my arm to my head. It seemed to lodge between my eyes. Gorz turned the fire hose directly in my face. I could not scream. I could not breathe. I held my breath and kept my mouth shut, twisted my head to the side, and gasped for air. My hand felt like it was on fire. I tried to summon the focus and determination that had carried me through Hell Week with the SEALs.

Then it was Gorz's turn to have fun. "This is going to be quite simple. Even you can understand this. I will ask you a question. If you do not answer, it will be my pleasure to exercise my whipping arm on you, back and front—a game I enjoy."

They both cackled. I did not. I watched intently as Gorz picked up a leather whip from the metal table. I knew that eventually these professional sadists would make me talk unless I died before that. I hoped it was the latter. Gorz cracked the whip twice, still looking in my eyes.

"Pretty boy, you don't look so good. But sometimes we must tenderize the meat before it talks." He cracked the whip again. "Personally, I hope you do not answer our questions too soon. Well, eventually you will answer. I just hope you take your time."

Before Gorz could lash out with the whip, Vlad interrupted him, placing his hand on Gorz's shoulder. He took out a syringe from the breast pocket of his jacket and plunged the needle into my neck. "That little special cocktail of meds will make sure you don't pass out or die too soon. It gives us more time for fun. The question of the day is simple. Where is the yellow folder?"

It occurred to me that Paul must know by now that they had me and had taken measures to protect himself. I knew they would kill me eventually. My situation seemed hopeless. The police did not know where I was. Paul didn't know. I didn't even know where I was. I could think of nothing to save my own life— so that was no longer my objective. The longer I could hold out, the better chance Anne and the boys had to reach safety, and the better chance Paul had to protect himself. *Stay alive, keep breathing. Come on! Don't wimp out. Remember your training.*

I did not answer him.

As Gorz raised the whip with a wide grin, Vlad suddenly grabbed his arm and reached inside his jacket, taking out a phone. With anger, he answered the call. "What?"

He listened for a couple of minutes and closed the phone, looking frustrated.

CHAPTER 46

Assault

Vlad put his cell phone in his pocket. His face spoke of anger, disappointment, and resignation. He whispered something to Gorz, who also appeared unhappy. Vlad grabbed my jaw with his right hand, brought his ugly face an inch from mine, and snarled, "Well, pretty boy, this is your lucky day. Your girlfriend just arrived. She wants to talk to you."

He laughed. They walked out of the room. I had no idea what they mean by "girlfriend." I hung there for several minutes, working hard to control myself. The shot they gave me must have taken hold. Energy suddenly rushed through my body, but so did the pain. Then the door opened.

Joyce entered the room and slammed the steel door shut, crossing over to me. She looked furious. She was not wearing her Nehru suit but a regular, blue, pin-striped suit, a white dress shirt, red tie, and black shoes—a Brooks Brothers suit I might have chosen for myself. With contempt in her voice, she said, "You are one of the most stubborn people I've ever known. See what you've done?"

She slapped me in the face. As she walked around my naked, bleeding body, her expression was no longer angry. It settled somewhere between fury and joy. She smiled and said, "I see you've met my two security guards from the lodge."

I managed to gasp out, "Joyce, I didn't expect to see you here. Welcome. I suppose you didn't come here to save me from these sadistic pit bulls."

Laughing, she said, "That would be naïve even for you." She whispered in my ear, "But I did I come here to help you save your family and maybe what's left of you." She paused to let that sink in while she studied my face. I did not for a second believe she had any intention of letting me live.

"Or, alternatively, I could make you a eunuch. Men like you, men who think they're such studs, who think their looks conquer women, who think they're powerful, all of you make me sick! You think your balls make you superior to women? They don't. They make you stupid. They make you easy to deceive. Easy to use. A good woman can train a man like you like a puppy, reward and punishment."

"Why are we having this conversation?"

"Because this is a once-in-a-lifetime opportunity for me. If you don't cooperate, I get to fulfill one of my more erotic fantasies. You see, I am going to ask you only once. If you do not answer, I am going to castrate you, just like I used to castrate pigs on my dad's farm."

I stopped breathing. The excitement on her face told me she was serious. My mind raced. But I could not think of anything to save myself. She reached into the metal toolbox and withdrew a knife. Then she put on a pair of latex gloves. With her left hand, she grabbed my balls and squeezed them so hard it brought tears to my eyes. I even forgot about the pain in my mangled hand. She kept squeezing like she was trying to squeeze juice from lemons. In her right hand, she held the Bowie knife. The eight-inch, gleaming steel blade reflected the florescent lights above. She looked totally absorbed in her fantasy. I was helpless, hanging like a slab of meat. I knew that anyone who was willing to sell nuclear waste to terrorists to kill millions of innocent people was capable of anything.

It was hard for me to speak. Hard to even think. But I needed to keep Joyce talking if possible. I tried to appear calm even while I heard my heart throbbing rapidly, pounding against my chest. I managed to pant out, "Joyce, why?"

"What?"

"I don't understand."

"You don't need to understand anything."

The pain was excruciating. I fought not to scream, not to pass out. I knew if I stopped talking, I would pass out, and she'd cut off my balls. "Joyce, you have the board approvals. Why all this now?"

Joyce stepped back, letting go of my balls. The relief from the pain almost made me gasp. She looked puzzled, then said, "Ryan, your recommendation to approve the merger was to be your last testament. The deal was for Sillus to deliver the signed agreements and a copy of your draft report to the investors. But he stupidly hitched a ride with you, and you survived. Everyone thought the agreements were destroyed. It was decided you would be useful until we got in all the governmental and shareholder approvals. But we learned you had the agreements, and the investors demanded them immediately."

Her telling me this confirmed my belief that she had no intention of letting me live. Among other things, she had just confessed to Sillus's murder. I accepted the fact that I was going to die, but I did not want it to be from the blood loss of being castrated. I tried to swallow, then said, "But why are the agreements important now?"

"If those documents fall into the wrong hands, the investors' lives will be worthless. We must get those agreements back, no matter what it takes."

"I noticed you had Mo and Farber sign and initial. But not you. Was that so you could deny knowledge if this thing went south?"

She smiled but did not answer. To keep her talking, I continued, "But why make me an executive VP? Why throw all the money at me?"

"We needed to keep you in line until we had your written recommendation. Sometimes it seemed better to just remove you from the playing field. But, Ryan, you never had a long-term career ahead of you. You were always going to be the first synergy!"

"Gee, I thought you liked me, even found me attractive."

"Don't be ridiculous."

"Who was the mastermind behind this? Certainly not Farber. Was it Mo? Or the foundation? Or you?"

She did not answer, only smiled.

"Joyce, I think you set this up so that in four to five years, Mo and Farber will both be retired—if they live long enough. After you got rid of me, it would be the Joyce Deer show. Right?"

She sneered and said, "You're smarter than I thought. Any more questions? Ask anything. It doesn't make any difference because you are going to die. Soon."

Most of the pieces of the puzzle had been revealed, except one. "Joyce, why was Jack Names killed?"

She grinned. "Oh yes. He was a friend of yours; I forgot. No harm in educating you now. There was a young analyst who reported to Names. The analyst was working with us to mine data. We wanted to show potential investors that if the merger was done, in addition to nuclear waste, there was a gold mine of data at Linus that was also very valuable."

"So, what happened to the analyst?"

"He never knew who hired him. It just took money to buy him. But I hate loose ends. When he was no longer useful, he was eliminated."

So they don't know the analyst is alive and what they saw was a special op exercise. Well played by Paul.

"How did that affect Jack? He wasn't helping the analyst."

"Your friend Jack started snooping around. He was exceptionally talented. We were watching closely. We learned he was putting together a briefing for you on what he suspected had happened and why. He was very meticulous. He made a calendar entry that read: meeting with Gorman ref. security breach and missing analyst. Right after he made that entry, he contacted the FBI and asked the feds for protection. You may not remember, but the day Vlad fired at you, Jack scheduled a meeting to brief you."

"I remember. We were to have lunch."

"Obviously we had to eliminate both of you. It was not just your connection to Jack. The feedback I got from Farber was that your Boy Scout persona was an impediment that should be removed, sooner rather than later. He was right."

"Let me guess. You sent your two sadistic friend here to do your dirty work."

"Vlad targeted you in the parking lot. We thought he had succeeded. Then Vlad and Gorz reported seeing you on the ferry. They also spotted the two FBI agents. But Jack made a mistake. He was leaving the ferry with the two FBI agents but suddenly broke away and rushed back into the ferry crowd. That gave my team the opportunity they needed."

Trying to control my seething anger and prolong the conversation, I started to ask another question, but she cut me off.

"Ryan, you had your last question. I am going to ask you a question, only once. Then I am going to count to three. If you have not answered by the count of three, you will be eating your own nuts. Understand?"

I just looked at her. I could not speak. I swallowed and opened my mouth to speak, but no sound came out.

"You think I'm kidding? You forgot the question. It is simple. I require only a single-word answer. Where is the yellow folder and its files?"

I did not reply.

"One."

She smiled broadly and stared into my eyes.

"Two."

She slowly brought the knife down against my groin.

Then the door flew open. She turned to look. Vlad and Gorz had returned with grins on their faces. Vlad said, "Sorry to interrupt the fun, Ms. Deer. The two CEOs and your lawyer want to see you right away. And they want us to bring this guy to them. They said to tell you they have exceptionally good news."

CHAPTER 47

Quid Pro Quo

Frustration and disappointment radiated from Joyce's face. She angrily threw the knife on the cement floor, where it clanged sharply as it bounced. Then she smiled at me, squeezed, and pulled on me as hard as she could. I cried out in pain. The thugs laughed. She smiled again and turned to the two thugs. "Wash him off. He's disgusting. Make sure he's dressed when you bring him to us."

She pointed to my clothes piled in the corner of the room. Then she walked out, violently slamming the metal door. The sound was like thunder. Vlad and Gorz took turns having fun spraying me with the fire hose. Then Vlad held his weapon against my head while Gorz untied my wrists and shoved me towards my clothes. I landed hard. They put their AK-15s on the cutting table. Vlad kicked me in the stomach, just for fun. Gorz shouted, "Get up, pretty boy. Put your clothes on. They want to see you looking your best."

The serum they had plunged into me was still flooding major energy through my body. Sitting against the steel wall, I tried to catch my breath. Slowly, painfully, I pulled on my undershorts and stood up. Gorz and Vlad laughed as they watched me struggle to button my shirt with my mangled left hand. I saw no escape option. But I knew that by now Anne and the boys were safe at my mom's and Paul was with the feds.

While I was struggling to put on my socks, the door was kicked open. Paul charged into the room with a .45 in hand. With his free hand, he slid the two AK-15s up the steel table and away from Vlad and Gorz as they tried to decide how to respond.

Paul spoke firmly. "The first one of you who moves is dead. I can shoot both of you between the eyes in one second. If you don't believe me, try me. Put your hands above your heads. Now!"

They slowly obeyed. Leaning against the wall, a flood of adrenaline swept through my body as I realized I might escape. Paul looked at me, swallowed hard, and said, "Ryan, they have weapons in their holsters, under their left arms. Take the weapon away from the blond one first."

Paul was right. When I reached under Vlad's left arm, I found a holster with a Glock. I took it. Then I removed the Glock from Gorz. I looked at Paul and he said, "Point the Glock at the blond moron; aim for his stomach."

Paul, pointing his pistol at Gorz, motioned for him to step away from Vlad. I kept my pistol pointed at Vlad, ready to fire if either of them charged. Paul looked at my jacket, shoes, and socks still on the floor, as well as my half-buttoned shirt. Then, with a smile, Paul said to Vlad and Gorz, "Gentlemen, I noticed you stripped Mr. Gorman of his fine clothes. I think the legal term is *quid pro quo*. Gentlemen, slowly strip. No quick moves or you're both dead."

They stared, motionless, at Paul and me. In an impatient tone, Paul said, "Either take your clothes off and drop them on the floor now or we will shoot you where you stand."

They hesitated. I pointed the pistols right between Vlad's eyes, looking straight at him, and bared my teeth in a smile. "Actually, Paul, I would rather we just blow their brains out. It would improve my mood."

They quickly complied.

"Ryan, cover them with your weapon. If they move an inch,

shoot them. I know you trained with the Navy SEALs. You know how to use a weapon, right?"

"In my sleep."

"Will you shoot them between the eyes if they move?"

"With pleasure."

Paul pointed his weapon at Gorz's belly.

"You, stick your hands out. Now!"

They studied Paul's face and mine, then apparently decided not to take the risk. Gorz held his hands together while Paul tied his wrists. Paul pulled Gorz's hands over his head and tied his wrists to a meat hook on the conveyor belt. Then he did the same to Vlad. We found duct tape in the toolbox and taped their mouths shut. Then we taped their legs together. Paul pulled the wall levers on the conveyor belt. It lifted them until their feet were just off the ground. Paul threw their clothes down the waste shoot.

"Paul, what are we going to do with these guys?"

"Leave them. Our mission is to get you out of here—preferably alive and preferably in one piece. There may be other bad guys around here, and we can't afford to be weighed down by two prisoners. The authorities can deal with them later. I called for reinforcement. Let's move out."

"Great."

"Can you finish dressing?"

"Yes."

My sense of hope came back in force. I would live through this and see Anne and my sons. I thanked God that my family was safe from these sadistic murders. But I knew we would be dead if we didn't get out of there. The only thing I could think to say was "Thank you, Paul."

"No problem."

"How did you find me?"

"I followed Joyce. Keep the Glocks and take an AK-15. I'll do the same. We may need them."

I did as told. Paul cracked open the door. We crept out, low crawling, leaving the two thugs hanging by meat hooks. The next room was huge, about 200 hundred feet long. The exterior walls were metal, as was the ceiling. The floor was cold gray cement with drainage holes every few yards. There were several metal pens where animals once waited to be slaughtered. Between the metal pens stood gray metal cabinets five feet tall.

At the far end of that large room were two more rooms. The walls and door of the smaller room were painted red. It had no windows. The larger one had a glass wall running the twenty-five-foot length of the office, showing a large conference table. We crouched behind a set of cabinets. Two more thugs, each armed with an AK-15, stood in front of the conference room. Fortunately for us, they were watching the meeting inside. Paul whispered to me and pointed at four people in the room: Joyce, Mo, Farber, and Tom Smith. They had not heard us.

Fuck! I should have known!

Paul whispered, "Let's just scope this out for a minute. We need to escape soon, but without drawing the attention of that hit squad."

"Got it. There's a door over to our right, next to the large rollup door."

"See it."

I whispered back to Paul, "We need to get through that door without alerting anyone."

"Agreed."

Then we heard a noise outside the building, which caught the attention of the two goons with the AK-15s. They raced to the door with their weapons ready. One threw open the door and aimed his weapon while the second one took a firing position to the side of the door. We froze. I hoped it was the arrival of the reinforcements that Paul had mentioned. But it was not to be. The goons relaxed and lowered their weapons. They clearly recognized the newcomers.

A man stepped inside, pulling a rope and dragging four people into the room, their hands tied to the rope and black hoods over their heads. Another man with another AK-15 pulled off the hoods. It was Anne, Shawn, Matt, and Aaron.

My heart stopped. So did my breath. Instinctively, I started to leap to my feet. Paul grabbed me and kept me down below the tops of the cabinets. I knew he was right. If they saw us, weapons would be fired. Anne and the boys would be killed. The risk was too great.

God, please help me save my family!

CHAPTER 48

The Viper Strikes

It was excruciating to watch Anne and my boys led past me, only feet away, and not be able to help them. This changed everything. I could never live without them, no matter what. I knew Paul understood. We watched my family being led down past the animal pens, to the windowed office. Mo, Farber, Tom, and Joyce turned to view the procession through the window. When my family reached the office, Joyce opened the door and came out, smiling broadly. Mo and Farber followed. Tom at first hesitated, then stepped out and looked at Anne and said, "Well, Anne, it's a pleasure to see you again."

Joyce stepped forward, taking control. "Greetings, Mrs. Gorman, boys. I'm sure Ryan will be happy to see you. We thought you might want to take a trip, so we put GPS transmitters under the fuel tank of each of your cars. It wasn't hard to find you or Ryan."

I heard Anne trying to respond, but the gag muffled her voice. Joyce smiled, then slapped my wife hard across the face. Shawn bolted towards Joyce but was knocked to the ground by one of the guards. Joyce kicked Shawn in the groin for good measure. The guards pulled my son back to his feet, and Paul had to grab me again.

Bastards!

Joyce turned towards the guards and snarled, "Did you thoroughly search them for weapons?"

The guard who held the rope laughed, then wiped his mouth with pleasure. "Yeah. I personally searched each of them. Every inch of them, head to toe. All possible hiding places. Especially the woman. I searched her twice, just to make sure."

My stomach churned at the thought, and my blood pressure soared. I was not conscious of the pain, but I was conscious of my right hand firmly gripping the trigger of the AK-15. It must have been the combination of the drug they shot into me, pure adrenaline, and my fury. Paul kept his hand on my shoulder and pressed down firmly as a reminder not to jump up.

Joyce smiled before giving her orders to the guards. "Take them into the red room next door. Tie them to the chairs. Then lock the door. One of you, go to the butchering room and hurry the two idiots there. They need to bring Gorman to us. Keep alert. Move!"

Mo, Farber, and Joyce smiled at each other. Tom patted Joyce approvingly on the shoulder. Then they returned to the windowed conference room and closed the door. The guard with the rope pulled it sharply, forced Anne and the boys into the adjacent room, and shut the door. A few minutes later, the red door opened. One armed guard stayed outside the offices with his weapon while the other headed towards the butchering room. The other two thugs went outside to stand guard. All were equipped with AK-15s. The guard by the conference room continued watching the action inside.

When the guard reached the butchering room, he was only four feet from where Paul and I hid. He opened the door and took a step inside. He stopped, startled by the sight of his two hanging colleagues. I charged and tackled him inside the room, something I'd learned playing football. He quickly turned towards me, trying to grab the weapon he had dropped. Paul sprang at him, one foot landing on his wrist just as his hand grabbed the barrel of his AK-15. Paul's other foot landed on his throat, causing him to release his weapon and choke. Paul kicked the AK-15 towards me and put his own pistol in the man's open mouth.

"Do not move or you are dead. Do not speak. If you make any noise, I'll blow your head off."

I pulled the AK-15 towards me and stood. Five minutes later, the third guard hung with his comrades. Watching them hang on the meat hooks brought back horrific flashes of my own torture. I shuddered. We waited inside the room, listening, to see if anyone else was coming.

I knew I had to defer to Paul to determine the best tactic to escape with Anne and the boys alive. My emotional instinct was to charge, firing my new weapon, taking no hostages. But I recognized it was my anger, not my brain, that was speaking. We opened the door of the butchery room a crack and watched. The guard at the office door shouted to the guard we had just bound. No answer. He raised his weapon and started towards us. We slowly and silently closed the door, pressed ourselves against the wall on either side of the door, and waited.

CHAPTER 49

Naked Pigs

The door opened, and the guard rushed in, his weapon raised and ready. He stopped, shocked, when he saw his three colleagues hanging naked from meat hooks. Simultaneously, Paul and I put the barrels of our weapons on either side of his skull. He dropped the AK. Soon there were four bound, naked pigs hanging on meat hooks. I gathered up the clothes and threw those down the waste shoot, then smiled at our handiwork. The four guards looked terrified, probably wondering what we would do to them. Not what they had done to me, although the thought had occurred to me.

Paul motioned for me to join him by the door and opened it slowly. The large room, with its animal pens, was again empty of people. We quietly crawled behind the nearest row of cabinets. Then we slowly moved towards the other end of the room. Thousands of animals must have been forced into this corrugated steel building, killed, cut to pieces, and the waste washed away. I had almost been one of those. If Paul and I failed to rescue my family and escape, that was the fate we all faced. I shuddered as if ice had suddenly coursed through my body.

A hundred feet way, Joyce, Mo, Tom, and Farber came back into view through the window of the conference room. The four of them were pacing, waiting for me to be brought to them so they could threaten to kill Anne and the boys if I did not tell them where the yellow folder was hidden. The truth was I did not know where the folder was, but I was sure Paul had placed it someplace secure, and I assumed the FBI and CIA now had copies.

We watched Mo, Joyce, and Farber for a few minutes. Tom brought their attention to some document on the table. Then they seemed to argue over something. The backs of the men's heads were towards us. Joyce was on the other side, facing the window. She shook a fist at Mo and Farber, apparently very angry. Perhaps she was complaining that they had deprived her of the pleasure of castrating another "pig." I suspected they were telling her she could have the pleasure once I told them where the yellow folder was hidden. *Sorry, Joyce, that is not going to happen.* Maybe the four pigs hanging in the butchery room would entertain her.

Then all four of them bent over the table, studying whatever lay there. The opportunity had arrived. Each time Joyce turned her head away from the window, we crawled towards them. Finally, we were behind a row of black metal cabinets a mere twenty feet from the conference room. Focusing on the red room where my family was imprisoned, I felt determined. I did not know if I could save them, but, if necessary, I would die trying. Anne would be strong for the boys. The boys would try to "man up" for their mom. But I knew they would all be killed unless Paul and I saved them.

Joyce threw open the conference room door. It hit the wall hard. She quickly looked around. Observing the missing guards, she shouted, "Damn it!"

CHAPTER 50

Nest of Vipers

Joyce darted into the red room with an AK-15. My heart sank. She had my family. I knew she had no limits. She would do anything.

I put my weapons on the floor behind the cabinet where I hid. Paul did not try to stop me. Then I stood up and shouted as loud as I could, "Anne, I am here. Joyce, I do not have a weapon. I am the one you want. Leave my family alone. Please! I will tell you anything you want to know."

Tom, Farber, and Mo turned and stared at me through the window. Joyce's laughter carried from the red room, and Anne and the boys came out, their hands tied to the rope. Joyce followed with her weapon pointed at Anne's head. The other three conspirators, seeing Joyce with the family and me unarmed with my hands in the air, ventured out of the conference room. Anne and the boys looked ecstatic when they first saw me. Then their expressions shifted to shock. Mangled and bloody, I must have looked like a truck had run over me. Anne finally began to cry, tears flowing down her beautiful face.

Joyce shoved her weapon against Anne's head and shouted, "Ryan, you surprise me. You have balls, but we have your family. Let me tell you how this is going down. You will hold your hands in the air. Farber, go over to him and pat him down, everywhere. He could be hiding a weapon anywhere."

With a grin, Farber thoroughly patted me down, head to toe, following Joyce's directions to the letter. He studied me for a moment. "Ryan, you should have resigned. Tom would have replaced you. You and your family would have been safe. You caused this whole damn mess by your stubborn, arrogant attitude."

Joyce shook her head and said, "Ryan, you have been hard to kill. Until now."

"What happened to Bill?" I shouted.

Joyce responded, "He was stubborn too. He refused to see how good this deal was. I told him there was enough for all of us. It would have made him very, very rich."

At that moment, I understood Jack's comments, his warning about Shakespeare's *Macbeth*—a play about brutal crimes committed to acquire power, the evil of the queen who instigates it all, and the three witches who cast a dark spell over the tragedy. They had killed and were prepared to keep on killing to get the power and wealth they lusted after. I wished I had understood that long before. Now I had to keep Joyce talking.

"Bill was my friend."

She ignored my comment. Farber continued where she had left off.

"He wouldn't listen. He gave us no choice."

Now smiling, Joyce continued, "We brought him here. Eventually, he was persuaded to write out the resignation letter I dictated. It had to be personally handwritten by him so no one could doubt it was his. Then the meat grinder did a great job. The waste empties into the bay water. Have you eaten any local fish or crabs lately?"

Joyce laughed. Mo looked at me and in a polite tone said, "Ryan, I had faith in you. Several times I pulled back the team when they wanted to have you killed. I never liked all that. I told everyone you could be very useful to us. I wanted to bring you into our team. They agreed to give you one more chance. But you screwed that up when you kept the yellow folder."

Joyce shoved my family into a line against the wall. She still held the barrel of her weapon against Anne's head. My kids were terrified. Anne was too, but she was also furious, with a defiant look despite the tears in her eyes. She looked at me and my mangled hand, the ring finger hanging loosely, and gasped.

Joyce was obviously considering what to do next. Then she looked directly into my eyes, her eyes cold and full of hate.

"Let me explain something to you. I run this team. Not Mo. Not Farber. Not Tom. I should never have listened to Mo and let you live. Big mistake. I know you, Ryan. I know what type of asshole you are. I hate men like you. If I ask you where you hid the folder, I know you will lie, trying to buy more time. But nobody knows where you or your family are. That's our little secret."

I asked, "Joyce, I'll tell you whatever you want to know. Just don't hurt my family. We won't say anything about what happened."

She barked out a short laugh. "You think you can con me? I don't want any more lies from you. Obviously, you need a strong lesson. You need to know you can't screw with me!"

"Please, Joyce, just take me. Let my family go."

"*No!* Our investors made it clear; you give us the yellow folder within forty-eight hours, or they will behead us. That is not going to happen, Ryan. You are going to tell me what I need to know. You are going to tell me now!"

Still holding my hands over my head, I swallowed hard. I knew she was capable of any evil.

Joyce smiled at me and sternly said, "You have a beautiful wife and three sons. I am going to start with the youngest." She moved quickly to put the barrel against Aaron's head. He gasped, and Anne tried to push Joyce, who hit her hard in the face.

"Anne, my dear, if you try that again, I will kill all your sons, and your husband. After you watch that, I'll kill you. Do you understand me?"

Anne sobbed and nodded. Matt pulled towards his mother, and Joyce kneed him in the groin. I watched tears fill his eyes.

"I'm glad we all understand each other."

Mo and Farber just stood there, intimidated by Joyce, who had come unglued by her anger and hatred. Tom stepped back a few feet, away from Aaron.

Joyce turned towards me; her face red and her voice filled with barely controlled rage, she slowly said, "What I was going to say is that I will ask you again, politely, where you hid the yellow folder. But this time, instead of counting to three, for each second of delay, I will kill one of your family, starting with the youngest, until you answer. When you answer, we will go get the folder. But if it is not where you say it is, I will kill the rest of your family. We will even hunt down your mother in Santa Fe and kill her. Is that clear?"

"Joyce, I gave the folder to Paul."

She studied my face for a few seconds. "Maybe. We'll see."

Mo and Farber looked relieved. Smiling, Joyce continued to hold the barrel of her gun against Aaron's head.

"Joyce, I told you where the folder is. Please take the gun away from my son."

"No, Ryan, I think I will put a bullet in your youngest's head, just to make sure you know I am not going to fool around with you anymore. I want to see you suffer when he dies in front of you and your wife."

The boom of a .45 filled the air, and a hole punched through Joyce's forehead, right between her eyes.

Her dead body flew back. She crashed against the wall and slid to the ground, dropping her weapon. Tom grabbed the AK-15. Another sharp sound, and he collapsed, dead. Mo and Farber fled into the conference room, slammed the door shut, and dove under the large conference table. Four mercenary guards raced through the door with their weapons firing towards us.

I jumped forward, pulling Anne and the boys to the ground. Looking into their terrified eyes, I whispered, "Don't move. Don't make a sound. Please play dead."

Bullets riddled the wall of the conference room, shattering the glass window. The guards were exchanging fire with Paul. They were well trained, darting from cover to cover and then firing, then moving forward. I pulled the AK-15 from Tom's lifeless hand. I quickly low crawled to my left, away from Paul and my family to a wall with stacked boxes. I made it behind the boxes without drawing fire. The guards must have thought I had been shot down by their initial blast of gunfire.

Still crawling, I worked my way slowly along the wall, behind the boxes. I wanted a better shot at the two guards closest to Paul. The other two were still working their way towards him, dashing from one cabinet to the next. It felt like a war zone.

Paul held his position at the right side of the room. Two of the guards appeared directly in my line of vision, their backs to me. Paul discarded his AK-15, out of ammo, and slammed a cartridge into his Glock. He held his fire. The guards did not see me. Slowly and carefully, I raised my weapon.

Somehow, they must have sensed me and whipped around, both spraying fire at me. I pulled the trigger. Bullets flew from my weapon, a stream of hot lead. The two guards were hit and dropped. I felt the shock of a bullet hitting my leg but felt no pain.

The other two guards rushed into the open, next to the fallen guards, and prepared to fire. My bullets blasted their bodies. I pulled the Glock from my waistband, stood up, and discharged everything in my weapon into them.

"Ryan, stop! Stop! They're dead. Your family is safe."

I dropped my weapons. With tears streaming down my face, I

fell to my knees and crawled to my terrified family, pulling Anne towards me. Taking a knife from one of the dead gunmen, I cut her and my sons free. I held Anne in my arms and kissed her again and again, neither of us caring that I was getting blood on her.

"I am so sorry. I'm so very sorry. For everything."

She touched my face, choking on her tears, and said, "I love you."

Paul crouched next to us and put his hand on my shoulder. "Ryan, my Glock was out of ammo. You saved my ass." I looked up at him and smiled. "No problem, brother. Quid pro quo."

EPILOGUE

It had been fourteen months since the slaughterhouse. On a commercial flight from New York to New Mexico, I sat at the back of coach and allowed my mind to drift and reflect on what had transpired since then. That horrific experience showed me what people would do for power and wealth. It laid open the dark side of the human soul. My physical wounds healed well, but I was not certain the emotional injuries would. Nightmares continued to rupture my sleep.

The international agencies had shut down HEF's operation, and its leadership had disappeared. The federal court blocked HEF's acquisition of the merged companies but ordered the escrow account to disburse its funds to Novation and EDGE shareholders. That placed the new company in a good financial position, issuing new stock for a company without debt.

The new board had been very supportive of me. They made me CEO and approved the synergy packages I proposed. I had been correct: most of the San Francisco headquarters folks wanted to remain in the Bay Area.

The new NYC headquarters was operating very well. People from both former headquarters had combined to form good, collegial teams. Kevin had stepped up as general counsel and was performing even better than I had hoped. Paul, as our new vice president for strategic planning, immediately hit home runs. He seemed to be truly enjoying his new responsibilities. As I expected, he continued to display endless energy. His staff thought he must be working twenty-four hours a day.

To be fully successful, a leader needed someone close by who was loyal, who could be trusted, who was discreet, and who knew how to tell the leader when he/she was making a mistake or—as Paul would say—was full of shit. At home, Anne could fulfill that need for a healthy reality check. But Paul carried that responsibility for me at work.

The company's combined international subsidiaries had totaled forty-nine in the month the merger closed. We sold seven during that first month but later acquired twelve new, good, solid foreign companies and restructured eight of our own. We also consolidated and restructured our US subsidiaries.

My new home in NYC was a luxurious four-bedroom penthouse across from Central Park, a company-owned icon that Mo had previously occupied. I often sat on the balcony and had my morning coffee overlooking Central Park West. It turned out that Mo's prior home on the Gold Coast, a 1920s mansion on twenty-six acres along the water, was also owned by Novation. I had it sold.

The company limousines chauffeured me from the apartment to my office and to a variety of high-priced, five-star restaurants, or the theater or opera or a museum or one of the constant charitable fundraisers and political events. It was also a thrill to take the company helicopter from the landing pad on our office building to the airport when I had to fly first class to some business destination. I continued to avoid the corporate jet.

Government officials, charities, and billionaires tried to get on my schedule and invite Anne and me to their dinner parties— the type of parties I had only read about in Fitzgerald novels. The media liked to run articles about me and Anne, all of which were mostly or entirely fabrications. I employed an assistant whose only jobs were to filter requests from people who wanted on my calendar to pitch something and to keep away people who wanted to use Anne or me for their own financial or political gain.

We did our best to keep our two younger sons sheltered from all this, putting them into a boys' boarding school in the city but insisting they be home with us every Friday afternoon until Monday morning when a driver would take them back to school.

A corporate CEO had not only personal money but also corporate money to donate to causes, charity affairs, and politicians or to throw business parties. I tried to stay at arm's length from the many politicians always seeking donations for their campaigns or PACs. Money was donated, but I was not tempted to confuse that with friendship. I observed that no matter how rich or powerful a person might be, it never seemed to be enough. I saw that frequently among our new society "friends." Some of my new acquaintances liked to tell me they were leaving large gifts to charity, but only when they died, and they often demanded buildings to be named after them. These were large, very expensive tombstones.

One of the things that at first was difficult for me to fully comprehend was that over 186,000 employees reported to me up the chain of command. Each of those global employees had their own family and their own network of responsibilities and obligations. Add to that the innumerable vendors and their employees. The decisions I made on a day-to-day basis could enhance or ruin the lives of thousands of people. Some decisions could impact the political stability of some fragile nations. My employees probably understood this better than I did. When I moved into my executive office, Paul gave me a lithograph of an inverted pyramid with one man at the bottom trying to hold up and balance all those above him on his back. It was a reminder. I understood that power was both seductive and dangerous. It frightened me. I also knew that leadership was service. Power and service should go hand in hand. Sadly, they rarely did.

Anne had always loved NYC and accepted a professorship at Columbia. But for security reasons, she had to be chauffeured there and back each day with a bodyguard, which she did not like. She was now with the boys in Santa Fe, visiting my mom for the summer. I was joining her.

After landing in Albuquerque, I picked up a rental car and headed to Santa Fe. When I was a boy growing up in this rugged and magical land, I found it to be desolate, dry, boring, and inhospitable. I could not wait to get to a big city. Now, looking around, I saw its peaceful beauty and the noble strength it reflected. The red and yellow rocks, the pinyon trees, the occasional roadrunner, and circling hawks brought back good memories of my youth. Apparently, until European settlers arrived in force, there were even large flocks of wild parrots there, now extinct. To me that seemed both incongruous and mystifying for such a desert landscape.

Up ahead, I beheld the yellow-and-red sandstone cliffs that parted the valley where my mother's ranch was housed. I thought about how my boys always complained that Grandma made them work too hard, tending the garden, mucking out the barn, feeding the horses, gathering chicken eggs, tending sheep, and all the other tasks of a ranch. But they loved it. I wondered how they would react if we ended up not going back to New York. Anne, unbeknownst to the boys, had been offered a professorship at the University of New Mexico in Santa Fe. It might be perfect, even though Shawn would think we were cramping his style. He was a freshman at the University of New Mexico. At any rate, the decision was on hold.

When I reached the gate to the ranch, I slowed down, not wanting to bring a dust storm in with me. I parked the truck by the horse barn next to Anne's SUV. Looking around, I noticed it was quiet, even for a Sunday afternoon. The sun was setting, showering the hills and sky with a maroon glow. A gentle breeze made the aspen trees shimmer and sing. The landscape drew me forward with gentle hands, pulling me to where I belonged.

Mom's old golden retriever and Kozlov saw me, but they did not bark. They ran over to me, shaking their hindquarters frantically as I got down on my knees and rubbed their muzzles, then put my arms around their necks to hug them.

I did not see Anne approach but felt her presence and looked up. Her beautiful face was full of joy, her lips slightly parted. "Welcome home, Ryan. I love you very much."

I stood and cupped her face in my hands, kissing her mouth firmly. Her arms grabbed me around the back and pulled me to her chest. When we parted, I said, "I am glad to be home with you. Where are the boys?"

"Your mom 'made' them exercise the horses. In other words, they went on a joyride racing down the ranch to the fishing pond. By now they're probably either skinny-dipping or fishing or both. We don't expect them home until they get hungry enough for dinner."

We held hands as we walked towards the ranch house. My mom stood on the porch, watching me limp on my bad left leg, still using my cane over a year after being shot. She wiped away tears, trying to hold it together.

"Good to see you, beautiful."

"Welcome home, son. How long can you stay?"

"We're trying to sort all that out."

"What about your big, important job? I recall seeing you on TV when they made you CEO, whatever that is. I read somewhere that top corporate people practically live at their offices."

"Mom, it's money, and often power and pride, which drives a man or woman to want those things. I plead guilty to all of that."

"All I want for you is to be a good and happy man. But never forget where you came from. No matter how grand and strong a tree may be, it cannot stand without roots."

That evening, Anne and I retired early. The boys and their grandmother were laughing, playing poker, betting pennies. It was clear they were having too much fun to miss us. We went into our bedroom and locked the door. I kissed her gently on the mouth and whispered, "I missed you so much. I hate to be away from you."

"Ryan, please take off your shirt."

I did as I was told. She looked at my scars and softly kissed each one. Then she said, "Now, Ryan, take off your pants."

I did as she wanted. She looked at the scar from the bullet hole in my leg. She touched the scar gently as tears rose in her beautiful eyes. Then she took my face in her hands. She kissed me softly, moistly on my lips. Then she pulled back and looked directly into my eyes. I caught my breath and softly said, "Anne, it's only fair that you take your clothes off too."

She slowly disrobed, keeping her eyes on mine, and gently smiled. It reminded me of our wedding night. I gazed at her beautiful body. This was the woman who had given me my three wonderful sons. She still filled me with desire. It amazed me that I was so blessed to be in love with this wonderful, brilliant, and strong woman.

"Anne, I want you." Then I pulled her close, against me, feeling the soft warmth of her body and her large breasts against my bare chest. I put my arms around her and slowly moved my hands down her back. She did the same to me. I lifted her up, carried her to our bed, and laid her down softly. That night, we did not have sex; we made love.

• • •

The next morning, Anne and I were having coffee with my mother, sitting at the same breakfast table I had used as a kid. I looked at my smiling mother and said, "Mom, Anne and I have reached a decision. Today I will send my resignation to my board of directors."

"Ryan, what are you going to do?"

"We will form a consulting company. Someday I will write a book about all this stuff. But for now, if you'll have us, we would like to stay here with you."

My mother hugged Anne, overjoyed.

A little while later, I took out my mobile phone and stepped outside to make a call.

"Hi, Ryan," Paul answered. "How is the vacation? Did you give my love to Anne and the boys?"

"Of course. But there's something I need to tell you. I am going to write a letter today to the board of directors. I am resigning."

"Shit, you cannot be serious. You're leaving?"

"Yes. My decision is final. I know you love your job, and you will be a great success without your big brother chaperoning you."

"Want to hear a hundred good reasons why you should change your mind?"

"No. The decision is final. It is something I need to do."

"Promise me one thing. Promise me that if I ever need your help, anywhere in world, for any reason, you will come and help me."

"I promise."

After hanging up, I returned to the kitchen and hugged Anne and my mom. It felt very good to have made that final decision. My mother took both my hands and said, "Son, you and Anne and the kids can absolutely stay. I can certainly use the help. Besides, you know I want you two to have the ranch. Will you take it?"

"Mom, all I can promise is we will stay at least until Anne finishes the year teaching at the University in Santa Fe."

Tears of joy floated on my mother's eyes.

"Welcome back, son."

"I am glad to be home."

• • •

As Confucius said: "We all have two lives to live; when we realize we only have one life to live, that is the beginning of our second life." Thus, it began for me.

THE END

ACKNOWLEDGMENTS

I want to give a special thanks to my wife, who has been very supportive of this effort and understanding throughout my writing. She patiently listened to me read portions of the draft and always gave me smart, good, and encouraging comments. In addition, a special thanks to Mike Bradfield, Steward Marriott III, and Lee LoBaugh for their advice and candor. I also want to express my thanks to all the people who assisted me by providing material for this book, whose contributions will be obvious to them as they read this work. In addition, many thanks to my very talented editor, Robert Astle (Highline Editorial, New York, NY), who worked so diligently and patiently to assist me with my first novel (a work of total fiction) and the sequel, which is well on the way, as well as Hannah for her wise advice. Without their help, guidance, and advice, this novel would never have been completed.

AUTHOR BIO

Leslie Lo Baugh, Jr., graduated from Georgetown law school and worked on Capitol Hill. After serving in the military, he practiced corporate law, served as general counsel in major energy companies and as partner in major law firms. He has advised business, civic, government, and Native American clients. He has lectured and written on corporate law, legal ethics, environmental matters, etc. He has received several awards and honorary positions and served as an independent observer at Camp Justice, Gitmo. He is married to Dr. Marlene LoBaugh. They have three wonderful sons, four wonderful grandchildren, and loving family and friends.

CPSIA information can be obtained
at www.ICGtesting.com
Printed in the USA
JSHW080553120523
41615JS00004B/20